THE TRACKER'S MATE

INGRID SEYMOUR

PenDreams • BIRMINGHAM

Published by PenDreams
Cover design by "Covers by Juan"

Manufactured in the United States of America Copyright © 2021 by Ingrid Seymour

ISBN-13: 9798698257042

For Billie,

You always shine and share your light.

CHAPTER 1

A fatal attraction is a curse.

No, wait a minute. Wasn't there a movie by that title? I can't call it that. Hmm…

Fierce attraction? Blind attraction? Dumb attraction?

Sure, why not? Let's go with that.

A dumb attraction is a curse.

You know the kind. Out of control, listens to no reason, makes you do stupid, stupid shit.

Yep, it's a curse, one I don't wish on anyone.

That was the kind of animal magnetism that led me to Jacob Knight.

The bastard!

He waltzed into my life the last year of high school. Before he did, I was happy, growing up with my parents and siblings: two sisters and one brother. Then *bam!* As soon as I left the safety of our little family nest, things took a turn for the worse. I thought I was ready to fly, to soar like an eagle, but it turned out I was a clumsy ostrich, destined to crash and burn. Big time.

For that, I blame Jake's silver eyes, chiseled face, mouthwatering body, and slutty reputation.

He was two years ahead of me in school. I'd always been aware of him, even in kindergarten when I should have been eating my crayons instead. In my mind, he seemed unattainable, like a supernatural celebrity in a magazine.

Except during my senior year, at a spring break party, he noticed me.

That very day, he rocked my world and my body. I should have been mortified, almost losing my virginity after he whispered a few delicious words in my ear, but I suffered no guilt. On the contrary, I felt like a woman for the first time, wild and thoroughly fulfilled.

After that, we dated for five months. Everyone was shocked.

Jacob Knight didn't date.

He seduced women, got what he wanted, and went on his merry, werewolf way. But not with me. He was in love. Or so I thought.

I'd been so sure that, after graduation, I packed my bags and moved in with him. Mom tried to tell me not to rush things, but the curse of my dumb attraction was on like blood on vampire fangs. Jake had enthralled me, and my mind and body weren't mine anymore.

He had a little apartment and big plans. We were great together, and not only as a couple. We made a brilliant tracking team and were helping people. We even solved a big missing person case for the police just in the nick of time, finding an eight-year-old girl who'd been kidnapped by a vamp who preyed on children. I was happy, even if using my tracking powers was a bitch, and I had to keep Jake in the dark about how my skills work for fear he would worry and decide we should stop being a team. We had a great thing going, and I wanted it to last forever.

Then, three months after I moved in with him, I woke up to a stack of cash on the kitchen table—enough for two-months' rent—and a note that said he was leaving me.

My life imploded, and in one fell swoop, I learned two important lessons: never fall in love and always look out for Number One.

Thank the witchlights, he's out of my life.

‮ 

છ)૭૨

I track people's mates for a living.

Humans, vampires, werewolves, Fae. You name it. I help them hook up better than Tinder can.

It's not an easy job for me, but if I'm smart, I can get far. Since I opened Sunder's Mate Tracker Agency, I can pay all my bills, and my clothes don't have holes. Better yet, they don't stink. True, my dry cleaner's monthly charges are higher than I ever imagined possible, but I slay it.

Hell, I was slaying it that night when it all began. Genuine leather pants, Louis Vuitton ankle boots, designer jacket in metallic rose gold that played beautifully against my pink-tipped hair, and a blowout that left my locks as silky as rose petals. Add to that large brown eyes, olive skin, full lips…

Hello, gorgeous!

A few of the men at the party also seemed to appreciate what they saw. Too bad I didn't appreciate them back.

Besides, I wasn't here for brawn but to snatch the next client for our agency. I had to look my best, so I had splurged on the clothes. I looked like a million bucks, *felt* like a million bucks.

"Here." Rosalina, my best friend and business partner, walked over and handed me a cosmopolitan.

I immediately took a sip. "Mmm, thank you."

She clinked her glass against mine, then savored her drink. Rosalina López was three years older than me, and whenever possible, she procured my cocktails. I was five months shy of twenty-one, and though I had a pretty good fake ID, I tried to avoid the hassle.

"When is the big reveal?" She pointed toward the suspended curtain, which concealed the scale model of "Shifting Futures," a cleverly named facility that, once built, would help wayward shifter kids straighten their ways.

We were at a charity event at an exclusive venue in downtown. The model was right in the middle, surrounded by dressed-up tables set for fine dining. A podium with an enormous screen stood at the back of the room. Flowers, vines, and water features made the space feel like the Hanging Gardens of Babylon. The witches and mages hired for the job had overdone it, though, because the flowery perfume had already overwhelmed my sensitive sniffer.

We were here to meet our future client: Celina Morelli. This hadn't been my choice for a meeting place. Not at all. The reason: the founder of Shifting Futures, Ulfen Erickson, was putting on the party, and we were not friends—not since I'd dated his son, and Ulfen took it upon himself to break us up.

But Celina had insisted, saying she was a busy woman who preferred to kill two birds with one stone whenever possible. In truth, she was probably hoping I would find her mate among St. Louis's rich and famous. If it only worked that way. I hadn't seen her yet, but we weren't supposed to meet her until after the reveal.

I shrugged in answer to Rosalina's question. "I don't know when. They should just drop the curtain already. Enough suspense. Who cares?"

4

"Plenty of people care, Toni." Rosalina waved her glass to indicate the crowd.

She tossed her long black hair over her shoulder and scanned the guests with her radiant green eyes. She looked gorgeous in her emerald sheath dress. It complemented her tawny skin to perfection and accentuated her narrow waist and child-bearing hips.

"I suppose," I admitted begrudgingly. Shifting Futures was a great charity, even if its founder was an asshat.

Shit! Talking about the head-up-his-ass founder.

I'd spotted him out of the corner of my eye. He was approaching with one of his big-money friends, both dressed in sharp tuxedos. I whirled and faced the bar behind me. I hoped he wouldn't recognize my backside. I had no interest in talking to him.

I was only here to meet my client.

Quit lying to yourself, Toni, my subconscious piped in.

To be honest, I'd gotten the peculiar idea that I might run into Ulfen's son. Stephen Erickson was the last guy I'd been able to connect with since my dumb attraction episode with Jake Knight. And it seemed I was craving a little male attention. It *had* been a while. But it didn't seem Stephen was here. Maybe it was for the best.

"Is the asshat gone?" I whispered to Rosalina out of the corner of my mouth.

She made a sound in the back of her throat to indicate the coast wasn't clear yet. I patiently sipped my cocktail. It was deliciously sweet.

"Oh, shit!" Rosalina hissed under her breath.

"What?" Panic tingled across my skin.

She turned and faced the bar, too. "He's headed straight here."

"No way."

5

"Yes way."

I was at the brink of fleeing—four-inch heels and all—when a snarly voice sounded behind me.

"Antonietta Sunder, what a pleasure to see you again." That was what Ulfen said, except it sounded more like *"Antonietta Sunder, how disgusting to see you again."*

Well, the disgust was all mine.

Cursing my recognizable backside, I turned to face my nemesis, the person I despised most in the world. Well, almost. Jake held the first prize.

"Mister Erickson." I stamped on a charming smile. "I wish I could say the same."

One of his eyebrows shot up, betraying the contempt he still felt for me. *Back at you, buddy.*

Ulfen was a man of forty-five with thick red hair and a well-kept beard. Six-foot tall and built like a bull, he was of Scandinavian descent, his werewolf line dating back centuries. He resembled his son so much that a twinge of longing stabbed my chest. Damn, even if my crush for Stephen had died of resignation a while back, I still hated this man for viciously murdering what could have been. Ulfen hadn't liked his werewolf heir messing around with a common tracker, so he put his foot down.

"What are you doing here?" he asked, abandoning all pretenses. "I don't remember inviting you."

I shrugged one shoulder and winked. "It's my thing. I enjoy crashing parties, remember?"

Right before he stuck his nose in our business, I'd interrupted a dinner party at his mansion while searching for Stephen. I'd been a bit tipsy, and Ulfen had been pissed.

He pushed air through his nose like an angry dog but said nothing.

6

And just because it would annoy him, I cast my eyes around the room. "Where is your gorgeous son, anyway? I haven't seen him."

Erickson's upper lip twitched. It was a slight movement, but I caught it. My question had bothered him, but not only in the way I had intended. I frowned. There seemed to be more to it. Were father and son at odds again? They had never seen eye to eye.

I sighed. *The world keeps turning and nothing ever changes.*

Ulfen leaned closer, his blue eyes sharp, flashing with a subtle light for an instant. "Let this be the last time I see you at one of my functions. For now, make sure you behave, Ms. Sunder. You know I have no compunctions about throwing troublemakers out."

Which was exactly what he'd done the night I crashed his dinner party. I landed on my left boob on his perfect lawn.

He turned and walked away.

"I hope his ass spontaneously combusts," I mumbled, shooting death rays at his tight, forty-five-year-old butt.

Rosalina snorted. "What a jerk." She cocked her head, also peering at his retreating behind. "Not bad for someone more than twice our age."

I hated to admit it, but she was right. I heaved a sigh. Werewolves and their genes… they were the envy of even the hottest supermodels. Women couldn't resist them, just like I couldn't resist Stephen Erickson and Jacob Knight.

What was with me and werewolves?

Stephen had been the rebound after Jake—my attempt at being normal. But it didn't work out as I hoped. If only I could track my own mate. I'd tried several times, and got nothing. It was a real bummer.

I shook my head. *Dammit!* I should have known that coming here would open the floodgates. I'd done my best not to think of hot werewolves in the past year. Rosalina had helped me, turning

7

my attention to better things. She was the only reason I was here today, the reason we had an up-and-coming tracking agency. She'd suggested tracking mates rather than tracking missing people. We had gone in together on a business loan and had big dreams for ourselves.

"Shit!" I exclaimed, gulping the rest of my cocktail. "Coming here was a terrible idea." I set the glass down on the bar and scanned the crowd.

Rosalina cringed, apologetically. It was partly her fault we were here. Everyone who was anyone in the St. Louis area was here, which was why I'd let her convince me to come. We were trying to build our agency's reputation among this type of people, hoping to gain some exclusivity. I wanted stability more than anything else. I was never sleeping under a bridge or going hungry again. I'd had enough of that thanks to Jake. I was done with being naïve. Helping others never paid off. Like my father used to say, no good deed goes unpunished. I had always thought Dad jaded, but now I understood.

Ulfen climbed on the podium and tapped the microphone. The guests' animated conversation stopped immediately. He took a paper from his jacket pocket and spread it over the lectern.

Someone walked behind the podium. I blinked. Wait, was that... Jake?

Crap!

Was he here?

I craned my neck, eyes roving around. The man came out on the other side, and it wasn't Jake, but one of Ulfen's bodyguards, tall and broad. Another werewolf of lithe movements and impeccable posture, but not him.

Man, the floodgates must've really cracked open if I was seeing things.

Ulfen Erickson cleared his throat. "I want to thank everyone for being here. Without you and your charitable contributions, this project would not be possible. This morning, we broke ground at the location where Shifting Futures will be built. Some of you were there and witnessed the natural beauty that surrounds the area. The trees, the river that runs behind the property, the hiking trails—a lovely place."

Many in the crowd nodded their assent, raising their glasses. As much as I hated the asshole, he was doing a good thing, helping young, misunderstood shifters function better in our society. I knew how hard it was to be different, to be called a weirdo because you had a supernatural talent. Though we all tried to live in harmony, regular humans simply didn't get it.

Ulfen lifted a hand, gesturing toward the center of the room where the curtain hung from a suspended metal ring, forming a giant tube around the model.

"Behind the curtain lies the architectural scale model for our new facility. The design was a generous donation from architect Amy Kahn."

Awed whispers went around the room. Ulfen brushed shoulders with some important people. Architect Amy Kahn did impressive work all over the United States, and I was sure it didn't come cheap.

"Amy couldn't be here tonight, but she sends her regards." Ulfen smiled. "Anyway, you're not here to listen to me prattle, so without further ado, I give you Shifting Futures."

There was a pause, and everyone seemed to hold their breath, then the curtain dropped and the entire room erupted in screams.

A body was hanging by its neck from a metal cable, its feet a mere inch from the scale model, dripping crimson blood onto the tiny buildings. He was naked, and a word was carved on his chest in big, jagged letters.

WAR.

CHAPTER 2

T he next morning, I was riffling through files, trying to keep last night's events out of my head, but failing.

At first, I hadn't recognized the dead man's face.

It must have been the shock of seeing him hanging, or the blood, the people screaming and running, and Ulfen's bodyguards whisking him out of the room.

But I knew the victim. His name was Blake Foster. He was Stephen's bodyguard, a strong beta wolf the family trusted. The man had been Ulfen's employee for over two decades, and Stephen had cared about him—maybe more than he cared about his father.

Who could have done such a thing? And why?

And what about the word on Foster's chest?

WAR.

Tensions in the city had been running high for many years. Organized crime factions operated by different groups—humans, vampires, werewolves, Fae, mages, and witches—all wanted more control, more power. And wasn't that always the rub?

The balance was precarious, constantly teetering at the edge of war, and someone had made a move to tip the scales. The question was… who? A name immediately came to mind: Bernadetta Fiore, the Dark Donna.

She was the most powerful vamp in the city, if not the country. She owned many legitimate businesses, and the authorities had never been able to pin any wrongdoing on her, but no doubt she and her people had their hands in every shady transaction that took place in St. Louis. Same as Ulfen Erickson. I was sure of it. The man presented a pristine front, but he was no boy scout.

Even disregarding the fact that vampires and werewolves were natural enemies, Bernadetta Fiore and Ulfen Erickson hated each other and constantly competed in their control of real estate, government, industry, and who knew what else.

Of course, the same went for all other factions. Mages or the Fae could have killed Blake, too. Maybe they'd done it to start a war between vampires and werewolves. It would be a clever move for sure.

Geez, what a clusterfuck!

I still kept wishing it had been a terrible April Fools joke. Yesterday was April 1st, after all, but that body was very real.

Gah! I shook my head. I had to stop thinking about last night. I had work to do. I checked the time on my phone. It was 8:00 AM. Rosalina would be here at any moment.

I continued riffling through files in one of her desk drawers.

Our agency was located in The Hill, a well-known Italian-American neighborhood west of downtown St. Louis. Rosalina and I grew up in the area, and we loved having our business here. Our small office was one of many on the block, a two-story narrow building with identical others on either side. On the corner, to our right, the office space stood vacant. To our left followed a dog

12

groomer, an ice cream parlor, and the dry cleaners that took half my paycheck. Across the street, there was a coffee shop and a pizzeria I loved.

Our first floor was a long rectangular room, which we had divided into three sections: the reception with Rosalina's desk and a small sitting area, my office for private customer meetings, and a compact alcove for potion-making.

One wall sported exposed brick, and the other displayed cool black-and-white photographs from local artists, all depicting couples doing romantic things like kissing, walking down the beach, getting married. You know... stuff to get people in a "mating" mood.

But la pièce de résistance hung straight ahead, an illustration of a modern cupid, a badass chick with pink hair and a crossbow, flying over clouds while aiming for the kill. I had commissioned it, and if the image showed a resemblance to me, it was merely coincidental.

Upstairs, a loft area served as my home. Nothing but a bed and a small bathroom, but much better than the homeless shelters I used to haunt.

The bell over the front door chimed. I swiveled the chair to find Rosalina holding our customary cups of coffee.

"Good morning, moonshine." She set my cup on the desk and blinked down at me, purple circles under her eyes. "I couldn't sleep one drop. I'll need about six of these today." She saluted me with her Venti cup.

"Same here." I saluted back and took a sip.

"What a clusterfuck, huh?"

"You read my thoughts!"

She shook her head. "I don't want to talk about it, though. I need to cleanse my mind, get rid of all that bad juju. Can I help you find something?" She raised an eyebrow, glancing over my shoulder at the drawer I'd been abusing.

"Yeah," I said apologetically. "I was trying to find Celina Morelli's file." In the chaos that ensued after "the reveal," we never got a chance to meet her last night.

"I moved the new clients to the other cabinet, remember?"

Rosalina set her coffee and purse down and removed her long coat. Underneath, she wore a black pencil skirt and crisp white shirt with a wide collar. She looked like a bank executive or lawyer, which was an excellent front for the kind of clients we needed to attract. She had applied her makeup to perfection. She loved watching YouTube videos on the subject, and it paid off. Though she looked just as gorgeous without makeup. Men always hit on her wherever she went, and she had no shortage of dates. I'd offered to find her a mate more than once, but she always refused, saying she wasn't ready for that kind of commitment. Whereas I wanted nothing more than to find a mate so I could feel something again, so I could convince myself that Jake had been a mistake instead of the one who got away.

I tapped a fist against my hard head. "I remember now. Sorry, it's been a hell of a week and last night laid the cherry on top."

"No worries, girl. I got ya." She sashayed toward the tall wooden cabinet and procured the file in ten seconds flat. Damn, she was efficient.

"She'll be here at 9:30," I said. "She called earlier to reschedule."

"I'll update the agenda." She batted her falsies at me, subtly asking me to vacate her space.

I stood and picked up my yummy Venti. "Thanks for the coffee."

"Mm-hmm."

I was about to enter my office when Rosalina snapped her fingers.

"Oh, I forgot to tell you. The space next door," she tipped her head towards the right wall, "someone rented it."

"Really?"

"Yep."

The place had been vacant for the last six months. When the last tenant left—a grouchy lawyer who gave us the evil eye every time he saw us—we jumped for joy. But then, we started worrying the new tenant might be worse. What if the new renter didn't approve of what we did and accused us of witchcraft? Not that witchcraft was illegal if you weren't hurting anyone. But things were going too well for any kind of monkey wrench to land in the agency's machinery.

"Well, spill! Who is it?" I demanded.

"I've no idea. Joey told me, but he had no details."

I rolled my eyes. "Great. For someone who works in a coffee shop, he certainly needs to improve his gossiping skills." Joey worked at Cup o' Java across the street.

"I told him the same thing," Rosalina quipped.

"Let's hope they're nice." I shrugged. "I'll check on the potion ingredients to make sure I have everything for Morelli. Let me know when she gets in."

"Roger that."

I walked into my office, reviewing the file. Celina Morelli was thirty-three years old, the daughter of a wealthy financier. She was a *Stale*—a regular human with no supernatural skills—as opposed to a *Skew*, which was what they called anyone else. She had been engaged twice but hadn't tied the knot on either occasion, which could only mean those men hadn't been her true mates.

A close friend sent her after we found the love of his life. Despite the reference, Celina was full of skepticism, but when I was done with her, she would be a believer. It was hard to argue with results.

I heaved a sigh. If only I could use my powers on myself.

I walked across my ten-by-ten office. My desk stood in the far corner, a large print of a cuddly puppy hanging above it. His eyes were soulful and put my customers in the right soft-hearted, love-sick mood. At the back of the room, I opened the narrow door to the potions alcove and entered.

A sturdy work table, its surface smooth from years of use, sat against the wall. An equally ancient cupboard stood to the right. It had open shelves at the top and rows of tiny drawers at the bottom. The table and cupboard had belonged to my mother, and before that to my Nonna. I had inherited more than my skills from them.

I checked the shelves. Pixie dust, seven-continent cloudmist, windblown mint leaves, volcanic ash... they were all there. Though soon I would have to replenish my stash of Pixie dust.

A series of bangs on the wall next to my cupboard startled me. Someone was hammering on the other side. I stared at the wall, hands on my hips. So the new tenant was already here and making a racket during business hours, no less.

Great!

The hammering went on for about a minute, then stopped. I waited for it to begin again, but it didn't. Good. I couldn't talk to customers like that. If it started again, I would have to go next door to shove their hammer where they couldn't find it anymore.

I went back to my desk and spent the rest of the hour reviewing Celina's file and making a few phone calls. Images of Foster's hanging body flashed before my eyes, unbidden. I couldn't get them out of my head, nor the foreboding that something bad would happen.

"Are you all right?" Rosalina asked from the door.

I glanced up, lifting my head from steepled fingers. "Oh, I'm fine, just thinking about last night."

"I've been doing the same, but it's time to look sharp. Ms. Morelli's here."

"Already?" I rose from the chair, shook myself, and straightened my knee-length dress. "Bring her in."

"You have to nail this one, Toni," she reminded me.

I nodded. "I will. I will."

If I found Celina Morelli's mate, it would open a world of possibilities for Rosalina and me. I couldn't fail.

CHAPTER
3

I smiled as Celina Morelli walked into my office. She wore a tight red dress that fit her like someone had poured it over her. Her black hair was pulled into a high ponytail, and her lips matched the shade of her outfit. She was tall and slender and wore black heels that helped accentuate shapely calves that must be the courtesy of some hot private trainer.

Oh, to have that kind of time and money. Maybe one day.

"Ms. Morelli." We shook hands over my desk.

"Please, I've already told you to call me Celina."

"Sit, Celina." I indicated the chair across from mine as I sat back.

She placed her small purse on my desk and took a seat, crossing her long legs prissy-like. Celina topped six feet with her two-inch heels and probably looked like a freaking goddess when she strutted down the sidewalk. I tried to picture her mate. I imagined him tall, dark, and handsome. But even if he resembled a bald orangutan, once I found him, she would have no choice but to fall desperately in love with him.

I got giddy just thinking about it.

God, I love my job.

Nothing like getting paid to hook up lonely people.

I laid my hand on top of the manila folder in front of me. For the sake of time and clarity, I didn't like dancing around the issue. I always spoke to my customers as candidly as possible.

"I have reviewed your file and thoroughly understand your frustration with the dating scene. You've had a certain number of relationships that must have been heartbreaking."

Celina inhaled sharply, lifting her chin to appear aloof. It was common among failed lovers to act as if they were above heartache, but I was good at recognizing the signs. This woman had been hurt. Deeply. I had inferred it from her file, and now I could see it on her face.

I'd seen the same strained look in the mirror many times. Who said young people lacked experience?

"Nothing I can't manage," she said.

"I don't doubt it. You seem like a strong woman."

This was common too, pretending one could finger-plug the heart leaks while taking on the entire world.

I'd done the same after Jake. I didn't tell Mom he'd left me, and when she found out, I pretended it was no big deal, even though, on the inside, I was wrecked. When the rent money he had left ran out, I was too proud to go back home, so I stayed on the streets, homeless, doing odd jobs that barely paid for food. That was when I met Rosalina. She helped me pull myself back together, and with her friendship, made me realize my worth. I didn't deserve what Jake did to me. But I'd learned my lesson. I would never give my heart so freely again.

So yeah, I knew all about strong façades, but Celina didn't fool me.

"I'm afraid," I said, "that even though it may be uncomfortable, you will have to open up in order to get what we need."

"Your partner warned me about this." Celina seemed on the verge of rolling her eyes, though she confined her annoyance to a slow blink. "Are tears really necessary?"

I opened my drawer, took out a vial, uncapped it, and handed it over. "I'm afraid so."

She took it with distaste. "I despise crying. It ruins my makeup"

"I can turn around if you'd like." I pushed a box of tissues in her direction and started swiveling my chair toward the back wall.

"No need. Let's get this over with."

I stopped the chair and offered her a sympathetic smile.

"My latest romantic debacle happened a year ago," she began. "I was deeply in love with him. We'd been dating for almost a year when he proposed. I was ecstatic. We set a date for a month later because we couldn't wait. We even moved in together."

Celina's voice broke, and she stopped to swallow. Tears were already pooling in her eyes, wavering in place, and though she knew we needed to fill the vial, she fought them.

"The night before the wedding," she continued, "he went to stay with a friend, so we wouldn't see each other until we got to the church." Her chin quivered. "I haven't seen him since. His friend showed up instead to let me know the groom wasn't coming. Apparently, that morning my ex ran into someone from his past, a Fae girlfriend he hadn't seen in years. It took them an hour to reconnect and discover they were still in love."

The tears finally spilled. She had forgotten about the vial, and I had to urge her to lift it to her face. She quickly placed it in the path of her tears and filled it halfway in a few seconds.

"Thank you, Celina. I can tell your tears are heartfelt. They are exactly what I need."

20

She handed the vial back, then dabbed at her eyes with a tissue. "I don't love him anymore," she said once she was tear-free.

"Of course not. He doesn't deserve it."

"It still hurts, though. The rejection."

Damn, I knew about that, too. Why hadn't I been enough? I still asked myself that question when I felt shitty.

"I can't guarantee I'll find your mate," I said, "but I assure you, if I do, you'll never feel this way again, and that hurt that still lingers will completely disappear."

She gave me a weak smile that informed me she didn't believe a word I was saying. She wanted to, but she'd come to make her friend happy more than anything else.

"How long will it take?" she asked.

I capped the vial and whirled it around, observing its contents against the light. "At least two weeks."

Celina made a face that revealed her impatience with the whole affair.

"It's not an easy process." That was an understatement, but I kept the details to myself. Few knew the toll that playing Cupid took on me. Good thing I charged for it now.

After digging into her purse, Celina came up with an envelope and slid it across the desk. "Half now, half later."

"Oh, no. We agreed. No payment until I find your mate."

It was a risk we were willing to take for the sake of increasing the agency's reputation. Running a mate tracking agency wasn't for the faint of heart or the lean of cash. With so many swindlers out there, no one paid for tracking services upfront. They wanted results first.

In the beginning, we couldn't get anyone to put down a two-dollar deposit, so we took jobs on consignment, our contracts stating that payment would come only if we found a mate.

21

Needless to say, the first couple of months in business were a bitch. We even got an eviction letter from the landlord because we couldn't make rent and paying the business loan came first. Luckily, we struck gold by finding the mate of a stubborn neighborhood bachelor. When the news got around, everyone and their toothless, troll grandma started calling, and the terms of our contract improved in our favor. There was only one problem... they still wanted our services for cheap.

In Celina Morelli's case, however, we'd decided not to charge anything upfront. We wanted her to have nothing but good things to say about us, no matter the outcome. If we succeeded, our client pool would change. Guaranteed. People like Celina Morelli would pay more for the same service, which was exactly what we needed to do more than simply stay afloat. My skills created a bottleneck. I couldn't take on many clients because the tracking trance kicked my butt every time. Also because it didn't give an exact location, which meant a little detective work was needed afterward.

"I know what we agreed," Celina said. "But please take it. It's not much more than I've paid my therapist, and I think this one session has been more productive than the many I've had with him."

"Thank you. It means a lot to Rosalina and me."

"It's only fair. Thank you for rescheduling."

"No problem." I smiled.

"It's horrible what happened last night, isn't it?"

"Yes, I still can't get the images out of my head."

"Poor Stephen. I hope they find him soon." She stood and hung the purse from her shoulder.

"Wait? What do you mean?"

"Don't you know?" she frowned. "Stephen Erickson was kidnapped a week ago. His bodyguard's murder was a threat to his father."

CHAPTER 4

After Celina Morelli left, I handed the envelope with her check to my partner.

"What is this?" Rosalina asked.

"Early Christmas," I said, though my tone sounded more like "early funeral services."

"Holy Niñito Jesus!" She stared at the check. "Fifteen thousand dollars. I thought she wasn't going to pay unless you found her a guy."

I slumped on the chair across her desk.

"Why so gloomy? This helps you complete the down payment for your new place. No more sleeping upstairs." She pointed toward the loft.

I'd been saving to buy a condo in Compton Heights. A move-in-ready two bedroom, one and a half bath unit with walnut-colored hardwoods, beamed ceilings, and a cute balcony. The payment helped fulfill that dream, but at the moment, I found it difficult to get excited.

"It's Stephen Erickson," I said.

"What about him?"

"Celina just told me he's been kidnapped, and his bodyguard's murder was some sort of threat."

She pressed a hand to her mouth, her green eyes shooting wide open. "Oh, that's awful. Are you all right?"

Nope, not by a Fae country mile. Man, the news had stirred a nasty cauldron of feelings I thought I'd sealed shut.

"That must have been why Ulfen gave me a strange look when I asked where Stephen was." I paused for a moment, thinking. "Maybe… maybe I should talk to him."

Rosalina shot to her feet. "No way! You're not doing that, Toni. You're not getting mixed up in that type of stuff again. You've come a long way, and you promised yourself."

"I know. I know." I grabbed my head with both hands. "But this is Stephen we're talking about."

"Yes, the same Stephen that left your ass because daddy didn't approve of you. And if that was the only problem, sure, I would tell you 'go ahead, track the hell out of him' but doing that type of work almost got you killed."

It was just the once. Jake and I had been tracking Emily Garner, an eight-year-old who had been snatched by a vamp that fed on children. The blood leech tried to take me out when I showed up at his lair, good thing I'd had a mean werewolf at my back, and the vamp only managed to lightly rake his claws along my stomach before Jake took him out.

"Besides," Rosalina went on, "the Ericksons are a powerful family. They can find Stephen themselves."

"I…"

"You. Promised. Your. Self," she reminded me again.

I inhaled sharply and sat up straight. "You're right. Something like this would derail us completely."

"Riiight, and if you ruin what we've got going on here," she moved her hands all about to indicate our office, "I swear I'm gonna get Abuela Esperanza to exorcise you 'cause if you go back to that shit, it would mean the spirit of stupidity possessed you."

Rosalina's Grandma Esperanza had exorcised her share of demons in her prime. Her talent had been special, but since she'd married a Stale, none had passed to Rosalina or her mother.

"Okay, okay, *sheesh*." I stood, holding my hands up to fend her off. "You're right, and that's exactly why you're here, to keep me from doing dumb shit."

"Damn right!"

I pointed toward my office. "I'll get to work on that potion for Celina. That'll keep me distracted."

"Yeah, you do that, and I'll go to the bank to deposit the check, and grab us lunch from Mama's on the way back. Sound good?"

"Perfect. Grab me some fried ravioli, will ya?"

"That's my girl." She winked and left with a skip in her step.

In the potions alcove, I gathered all the ingredients around the two-quart slow cooker and set to work. I started with four ounces of distilled water, wishing the other ingredients were as easy to get. But no. Some even came from other realms, and I could only purchase them from Fae providers at a steep price.

After the distilled water, I followed with carefully-measured Pixie dust, seven-continent cloudmist, windblown mint leaves, and volcanic ash. Earth, water, wind, and fire, respectively. The Pixie dust wasn't the make-you-fly kind, just plain dust from their tiny bedframes and armoires. What a rip off!

As I dropped in the last ingredient, I couldn't argue that potion making was witchy. Just the reason Stales called me a witch sometimes, even though the two were as different as a Chihuahua and a werewolf. Some witches could track, true, but never as well as a specialized tracker like me.

I shook the dregs of Pixie dust in its container. I would soon have to visit Yalgrun for more. Good thing Celina had been generous with her trust fund. The potion ingredients cost a fortune, so much that a spell protected the alcove—one my mother had cast. She was good at them.

Finally, Celina's tears. I used a long glass dropper to draw them out of the vial and counted. As the seventh tear splashed in, I held my breath. I'd had several brews go bad in the past. But when the potion started shimmering crimson, releasing the scent of freshly baked chocolate chip cookies into the air, I did a little dance. The smell was always something pleasant like that, either one of Celina's or her mate's favorite treats. My sense of smell was way above average, an unusual but welcomed skill. I could pinpoint scents with accuracy which helped tremendously during the tracking trance.

Still dancing, I covered the slow cooker and set it to low. It would have to simmer for at least twelve hours. With that done, I left the alcove and decided to call the realtor with my good news. I would have no trouble getting approved for a loan now. I had enough for a down payment for that cute condo. I was about to press send on my cell phone when the hammering next door started up again.

"Shit!" My jaw clenched as each blow seemed to drive a nail into my temple.

I waited for a minute. Then two. The hammering continued, and my eye began twitching. I had another customer after lunch, and I couldn't have this idiot start this up then. What if it'd happened right before Celina shed her reluctant tears?

Nope. Not doing that.

I marched out of my office and walked next door. I peered inside through the glass-paneled door, but couldn't see anyone. Pulling on the handle, I found the door open. I let myself in.

"Hello," I called over the incessant hammering.

No one responded.

"Of course," I mumbled under my breath.

I pushed past the reception area, which looked a lot like ours, walked through the door at the back, and halted.

A man wearing a tight white T-shirt and tighter blue jeans stood with his back to me, attacking the posterior sheetrock wall as if he meant to kill it, which I guessed he did since part of it already lay dead on the dusty hardwood floor. Dust clogged the air. I waved it away for a better look.

The man was tall, about 6'2", with broad shoulders and a narrow waist. Sweat covered his neck, which trickled downward causing the shirt to stick to his muscular back. And his butt was... well, I didn't think there were words to describe it. Perfect, maybe? My mouth watered as I admired it.

Then, his scent registered in my hypersensitive nose, stirring an avalanche of memories, and a thrill ran up my spine. Panic burst inside my chest. That heady scent and my mouth... it had never watered at the sight of any man, no matter how hot, except...

I have to get out of here!

I took a step back to flee, but too late.

The hammering had stopped, and he was turning to face me.

Jacob Knight was back.

28

CHAPTER 5

We stared at each other for a long minute without saying a word.

His gaze held mine with such intensity that I couldn't have glanced away even if I'd tried. Almost eighteen months ago, Jake had walked out of my life without leaving the smallest trace behind, and now without a warning, he was back.

He was more handsome than ever, broader, more rugged, his muscles honed to perfection. His light brown hair sported a different style, short on the sides, and messy on top. Perfectly-trimmed stubble edged his jaw, and a new crease sat between his thick eyebrows as if he'd spent a lot of time worrying about something. And his eyes—those eyes that still haunted my dreams—they shone silver with the light of an exposed light bulb above him, drawing me in, pulling me into the darkness of his bottomless pupils.

Something else that didn't escape me was his intoxicating scent, a combination of his musk, pine, and rain. God, it was heavenly.

Shit! From the way my heart was pounding, it seemed his presence still had the same messed up effect it always had.

"Hello, Toni," he said, at last, his voice the same deep baritone that could melt me into a puddle when he whispered in my ear.

A million possible responses went through my head. I had imagined a ton of them, played them out like rom-coms where he fell at my feet asking for forgiveness, or like heart-wrenching dramas where I gave him the finger and left him as messed-up as he left me.

The silence stretched. The going-mute scenario never played in all my imaginings. I always thought I would have something smart or biting to say to him, but all my words had died and gone to hell.

He set the hammer down on the worktable and took a step closer. "It's great to see you again." He captured his lower lip between his teeth as if he could bite the words back.

"What are you doing here?" Those were the words that finally made it out of my mouth. At least I managed cold and unwelcoming.

"I'm back in St. Louis. For good."

For good.

The words unleashed a storm in my gut, and I was glad Rosalina hadn't returned with the fried ravioli. Though maybe, vomiting on his work boots would have been a well-deserved welcome.

For good. I fought to ignore that bit.

"I don't mean here in St. Louis," I said. "I mean here in this particular building. Tell me you're just the handyman."

He smiled crookedly and hooked a finger in the work belt that hung around his waist. "That and also the new tenant."

"NO!" I stomped my foot like a cross three-year-old.

Jake blinked in surprise. "Actually, I'm pretty sure it's a *yes.*"

"You can't. You can't rent this place. You have to find another one. Preferably across town, across the world. Or maybe in hell."

He furrowed his brow. "And why is that?"

I opened and closed my mouth, but no words came out.

"I like it here. It's nice."

"My agency is next-door, Jake. You cannot… do whatever it is you're doing here." I couldn't fathom why he needed office space. Jake had never held a job in his life, that I knew of. His mother had left him a sizable inheritance when she passed away.

"It's a free country, Toni. I can open my PI firm wherever I want to."

"What?!"

PI firm? That distracted me for a moment. He was a private investigator? Since when? I shook my head and tried to ignore this curveball. The first pitch he'd thrown was the only thing I needed to focus on.

"My PI firm—" he began.

"Scratch that. I don't care about it." I held both my index fingers up and pointed them at him. "You can go privately investigate a troll's behind for all I care, but you cannot open your office here."

"Why?"

"Because." Really? I knew him to be smart, so he was being dense on purpose.

He pursed his lips—those full, chiseled lips that drove me to distraction—and thought for a moment. "Okay."

"Okay?"

"Give me a good reason, and I'll find another place." He raised his eyebrows and waited for my answer.

Again my mouth did that thing where it opened and closed but no words came out. What the hell?

Jake continued to wait, his crooked smile growing slowly as he watched me struggle with what to say. He knew perfectly well why I didn't want him here, but I was damned if I'd give him the satisfaction.

"I'll give you one good reason," I said. "Because if you don't leave, I'll fucking kill you."

I whirled and left with the firm intention of finding a silver bullet or wolfsbane. When I stomped back into our office, Rosalina was back at her desk.

"Where were you?" she asked, turning away from the computer. "I thought—" she stopped and inspected me up and down. "What happened? You look like you've seen a ghost."

"No, I saw a damn werewolf. That's what." I clenched my fists and growled.

Rosalina did a double-take. "Did you only see this werewolf? Or did he bite you too?"

I held both my index fingers and pointed them at her, something I seemed to be doing a lot of today. It seemed it was my way of saying I was on the verge of going on a murdering spree, and they needed to get out of my way unless they had a death wish.

"Werewolf bites don't turn you. That's a myth." I knew Rosalina was only joking, but I was losing it.

Perfectly aware that I was in no shape to talk to anyone, I marched up the steps to the loft. There, I kicked off my heels and started pacing. A double bed, a nightstand, a chair, and an armoire comprised the bulk of my furniture.

"What the hell is going on?" I mumbled at the floor.

In the span of two hours both Stephen and Jake had reared their heads from my past. I hadn't uttered their names in months, and now they were back… in one form or another.

"This isn't good."

Okay, if Jake didn't want to move, Rosalina and I would find a new place and—

"Toni," Rosalina poked her head from the steps and peered up at me.

I ignored her and kept pacing.

"Toni, there's this really hot guy downstairs asking to see you."

"Oh, no!" I whirled and headed toward the steps.

Rosalina pressed herself to the wall and let me pass. I stormed into the reception area to find Jake waiting there. He had put on a button-up shirt and tucked it into his jeans.

"Get the hell out, Jake. You have no right."

"I didn't mean to upset you," he said as calm and collected as I'd ever seen him.

He had disappeared for a year and a half, then materialized out of thin air, and he was acting as if nothing had happened? Did he have amnesia?

I took a deep breath, using all my strength and will to reign in my emotions. They were wild, like a category-five hurricane bent on destruction, so it wasn't easy.

Don't give him the satisfaction, Toni. He has no hold over you.

Maybe it was too late. He'd already seen what his mere presence could do to me. Still, I'd learned a thing or two since he'd left. I had changed. I took a deep breath, and as I let it out, I neatly folded my emotions like a piece of paper and tucked them away in a private corner of my heart.

"I'm not upset," I said, my voice as calm as Jake's.

He frowned, his silver eyes scrutinizing me, searching for the turmoil I'd locked away. But it was gone, and I'd thrown away the key.

"Look," he started, "I'm back because—"

"I don't care why you're back. Like you said, it's a free country. You can move in next door if you want. And I can move out if I want."

"Wait, what?!" Rosalina asked from behind me. "Move out? But we love it here."

I glanced back over my shoulder. "We'll talk about it later."

"Okaaaay," she said.

"You don't have to do that," Jake said. "I will terminate my contract if that's what you want. It doesn't matter. That's not why I'm here. I'm here because I need your help, because you're the only one who can find Stephen Erickson."

CHAPTER
6

My mind stuttered, slowly trying to process what Jake was saying.

I'm here because I need your help, because you're the only one who can find Stephen Erickson.

The cogwheels inside my brain had suddenly gone rusty, screeching to a halt.

Jake and Stephen. Stephen and Jake.

It didn't compute. As I tried to say something and only puffs of air came out of my mouth, I began to think I was permanently broken.

As usual, Rosalina came to my rescue. "So... you're Jake Knight?"

He glanced at my friend, reluctantly tearing his eyes away from me. "I am."

"And you're trying to find Stephen Erickson?"

"Yes."

Rosalina shook herself and blinked. "How the hell do you know Stephen?"

Here was the question I'd been wanting to ask. It snapped me back to my senses. "Yeah, how the hell?" I demanded.

"That doesn't matter right now," Jake said. "His life is in danger. We have to find him before it's too late. You saw what they did to his bodyguard."

"Wait, how do you know that?" Then I remembered. "You *were* there. I saw you"

He nodded.

"And I thought I was going crazy."

"Look," Rosalina took a step forward and stood next to me, "it's very *nice* of you to be so determined to find Erickson. I commend you for it, but Toni isn't going to get involved in this."

Jake frowned. "I'm sorry. I don't know who you are, and why you're trying to speak for Toni." His piercing eyes shifted to me. "The woman I know speaks for herself."

"Yes, she does," I said. "And she *isn't* going to get involved in *any* of this."

That new crease between his eyebrows grew deeper. "I don't understand."

"I don't do that kind of work anymore. If you haven't noticed," I gestured around the office, "I run a mate tracking agency."

Now, it was Jake's turn to act as if the cogwheels in his brain needed grease. He narrowed his eyes, frowned deeper, cocked his head to one side, opened and closed his mouth... And after all of that, he said absolutely nothing, which gave me an odd sort of satisfaction.

"Things are finally looking up for me, Jake," I continued, "and I don't intend to ruin what I've accomplished."

"It's Stephen we're talking about." He sounded truly confused.

"I've no clue how you know Stephen but don't try to act as if we're all long-lost friends because we're not. I went on a few dates with him, and then he broke up with me because Daddy Ulfen didn't approve. That was all. If he told you more than that about our relationship, it doesn't give you the right to come here acting like this."

"Toni, I don't… understand. You like to help people."

"And you know where that got me?" I paused, feeling a lump of familiar anger build in the pit of my stomach. "Nowhere."

When I should have been working and saving money, I had selflessly tracked people who'd gone missing, expecting nothing in return. Yeah, saving that eight-year-old from that blood leech before he managed to hurt her and returning her to her parents had felt awesome. I would never regret saving little Emily Garner. But in the end, all I had left were two-months' rent, an empty bank account, and deep depression.

"But this is someone you know. Someone you shared something with. How can you turn your back on him when it's in your power to help?" Incredulity contorted his face.

"Just the way you *and* he turned your backs on me," I said. "That's how."

Jake flinched but recovered quickly. "I don't recognize you."

The words hurt. I couldn't deny it. Maybe because that innocent girl who once used her talents for good was dead. Or because my half-frozen heart couldn't warm up toward Stephen, a person I'd known and liked. Or because the man I'd loved most in the world seemed so disenchanted of what I'd become.

"What did you expect?" I asked, my voice quiet. "That I would be the same naïve, pliable girl you left behind?"

He lowered his head as if searching for an answer in the floorboards. He found none.

"Pain takes its toll, Jake. It shapes you, and it rids you of your soft edges. I've been honed, and there's nothing soft about me anymore."

He met my gaze, and what I saw in his eyes made the half of my heart that wasn't frozen twinge. I knew him well, all the creases in his face, and the way they arranged themselves to convey emotion, even against his will. Pain shaped his expression. But that wasn't all, regret and longing were also there.

At last, he spoke, his deep voice raw. "I understand. I'm sorry to have bothered you."

He turned and walked to the door. There, he took a deep breath as he stared at the glowing "open" sign affixed to the window. Deciding on the spot, he glanced over his shoulder.

"I think I'll keep the office. But don't worry, I won't bother you anymore."

He left, and as the bell above him chimed, my knees unhinged and I collapsed in Rosalina's chair.

CHAPTER
7

U p in my loft after work, I picked up the container of fish food and dropped five pellets into the bowl.

"Eat, boy." I tapped the glass.

Cupid, my red and purple betta, floated at the bottom, oblivious to his dinner. Maybe he was mad because I'd forgotten to feed him last night.

"He's not eating," I complained, glancing back at Rosalina who was sitting on my fuzzy Papasan chair, massaging her feet.

"Stop projecting all your troubles on that fish." She set down one foot and started on the other. "Gah, I hate breaking in new shoes. They're cute, but they're killing me."

"I'm not projecting. You know I need to do a good job with Cupid. I mean, to move up to a cat, I have to keep this fish alive."

Rosalina rolled her eyes. "Cats take care of themselves. They can probably even take care of you."

"I seriously doubt that." I stared at Cupid, leaning over his bowl. Finally, he floated over and gulped one of the pellets. "Good boy!"

Feeling as if I'd ran three marathons and then had been hit by a train, I kicked off my shoes and collapsed on the bed.

"What a day." I sighed.

"Are you all right?" Her voice took on a serious tone.

I pulled the pillow over and squeezed it tight. "I don't know. I feel a mess."

"I don't blame you. A lot just hit you. How do you feel about Jake being back?"

I pressed a finger to my lips, then cupped both my ears and moved my hands around like radars. Werewolves could hear through walls if they tried.

Rosalina frowned. "Wanna get out of here? Go get some dinner? You never ate your fried ravioli. You must be hungry."

It was early for dinner, but I was starving. Stress always had that effect on me. "I'll have to eat something light, though." I wrinkled my nose. "I have kick-boxing class later."

"Why don't you skip?"

I made a face. I didn't like to skip. The exercise helped with the aforementioned stress.

"You deserve a break, especially with Morelli's tracking coming up."

She wasn't wrong about that. Tracking always left me exhausted and banking my energy before the trance really helped. I'd never been as careful about using my powers as I was now, and I owed my prudence to Rosalina, who always had my best interest at heart.

"All right, let's do it," I said. "I honestly think I can devour a large pizza all on my own."

After I changed into jeans, we locked the office and walked arm-in-arm down the street, our heels clicking against the sidewalk. I even managed not to glance in the direction of Jake's office. I would have to decide what to do, whether to leave the building or stay. But I'd gotten there first, dammit. He should be the one to leave.

Maybe I could sabotage him. Hmm, that was a worthy thought.

We chose Giovanni's Pizzeria across the street. It was a cozy place with a brick magical oven that infused their pizzas with unique secret flavors. The owner was an Italian mage with a specialty in culinary potions. The place packed a good crowd all the time.

We got our favorite table. I inhaled the delicious smells, pinpointing known ingredients and wondering about some I'd never come across. When the food arrived, we ate like lions at the zoo. As we fought over the cheese sticks and marinara dipping sauce, we talked about inconsequential stuff like whether Italian sausage or pepperoni pizza ranked first and the cute outfit she wanted to buy for her Abuela's birthday party in a couple of weeks.

"That's my Toni," Rosalina said as I threw back my head laughing when I learned that Abuela Esperanza planned to rap during the party.

The comment sobered me up a bit. I wanted to keep talking nonsense, but we needed to discuss what had happened. It always helped me to talk to Rosalina. She was the voice of reason when my emotions got messy—not to mention I'd tasked her with keeping me on the right path. Without supervision, I tended to do some dumb shit.

Seeing that I was ready to talk, she gave me a sweet smile and said, "So, what are we gonna do? Stay? Leave? Give it some time to see what Jake does?"

"That last one seems the most reasonable," I said. "His PI business might tank."

"PI business? I thought you said he was a professional bum."

"I never said that."

41

"You said he never had a job, that he was independently wealthy." She waved her hand in the air as if it was all the same.

"He is. That's why the PI business seems unnecessary. Although…" I paused. With my stomach full, and my temper simmering at a low burn, I started thinking more carefully about Jake's career choice.

"Although what?" Rosalina picked a pepperoni piece off our pizza and popped it in her mouth.

My thoughts got ahead of myself as understanding dawned on me. "It's because of his brother," I blurted out.

"Huh?"

"I've never told you, but Jake had a brother who went missing. They never found him."

She leaned closer. "Really?"

I nodded. "He disappeared when Jake was thirteen. He was two years older. Neil, that was his name. It pretty much destroyed Jake's family. His father lost his mind searching for him. A few years later, he drank himself to death. Then I swear Jake's mother died of a broken heart."

"That's terrible"

I should have known about it since Jake and I grew up in the same circles, but it wasn't something anyone liked to talk about, so Jake had told me. I still remembered that night. He had nearly cried, and all I could do was hold him, words sticking to my throat. I'd known even then that words meant nothing against something of that magnitude.

I sighed. "Jake always wanted to find him, at least know what happened to him. I think not knowing was the worst."

"Gah, I would die if something happened to Vannia."

Vannia was Rosalina's sister. She was a senior in high school just like Lucia, my youngest sister.

"Anyway," I said, sadness heavy in my heart. "I guess that explains his PI calling."

"And what about him and Stephen? How do you think they met?"

I glanced around the pizzeria as if the answer could be found in the pictures hanging on the wall.

"They're both werewolves," I said lamely as if that could guarantee a friendship when it was the complete opposite. Werewolves stuck to their own and tended to hate members of other packs.

"I thought you said Jake was a lone wolf? Don't some people call him Jake Lone?"

"Yes, after his parents died, he lost all connection to his pack. He retreated."

Rosalina frowned. "And Ulfen Erickson's pack is pretty tight, so why would those two suddenly start hanging out? You don't think it was because of you? Maybe they like exchanging make-out stories."

I made a strangling motion toward her neck. "Not funny."

She snickered, then sobered. "Whatever the case, it's weird."

Talking things out with Rosalina and filling my stomach with greasy dough set me at ease. In the end, we decided not to do anything rash. Our lease wasn't up for another couple of months, anyway.

"We're almost out of Pixie dust," I said. "I think I'll go by Yalgrun's tonight. Want anything?"

"Oh, yes! Get me some of that Puck stool."

"Ew, how you put that stuff on your face, I just can't even…"

She thrust her chin in my direction. "Look at this skin. Flawless. The stuff works."

I shrugged. I couldn't argue with that. Her skin *was* flawless. Still, I wouldn't put Puck poop or anyone's poop on my face—no way. I wondered if she would continue this particular beauty routine if she laid eyes on a Puck while lifting his stubby tail to do his business. I snickered at the image.

"What?" she asked.

"Nothing. I'd better get going." I checked the time on my phone. "Yalgrun closes in an hour."

"I'll give you a ride."

"Nah, I'll walk. I need the exercise since I missed class."

We said goodbye in front of the restaurant, then walked our separate ways. It was close to seven, which shocked me since that meant Rosalina and I had talked for nearly two hours. I smiled to myself. Whenever I was with her, time just seemed to fly.

CHAPTER
8

There were many gates to Elf-hame, the Fae realm. Some were well known, but the majority weren't. Most people knew those intended for tourism and light shopping. But others, like me, had access to select entry points through which a less *sanitized* version of Elf-hame could be observed.

To gain access, I had applied for a business license. It took over four weeks to secure it, and it gave me access to a nearby gate located in Tower Grove Park, only a fifteen-minute walk from the agency. The name of the trading post was Pharowyn.

Walking briskly to get my heart going, I reached the park's west gatehouse, then headed for the Turkish Pavilion, a large gazebo with a cupola roof painted in red and white stripes. When I arrived, I sat at one of its tables. The place was empty but for a jogger who stood at one corner, stretching, headphones stuffed into his ears.

I traced an elf rune on the table's surface with my index finger, a symbol assigned just to me, and waited as my surroundings gradually changed, a new reality bubbling into existence. The jogger disappeared, as did the pavilion, and was replaced by an outdoor tavern, located in a busy cobblestone market street.

As soon as I materialized, a young, slight Fae rushed to my side, inclined his horned head, and spoke in his tilting accent. "May I serve you something, respectable lady?" He wore a rough tunic with wooden buttons and cropped brown pants with leather shoes no more substantial than ballet flats.

"No, thank you, *Abin Cenael*," I answered, using the phrase "respectable sir" in turn.

His cheeks colored at the term, and his eyes flashed disappointment at my refusal.

"I'll get something on my way back," I said. "I need to catch Yalgrun before he closes."

He beamed, his beautiful turquoise eyes sparkling, surely looking forward to a tip in human money. It was widely accepted in Elf-hame's trading posts.

I abandoned the tavern's table and headed down the stall-lined alley. Here, most of the available goods consisted of food. Exotic fruits and vegetables, grilled meats, honey cakes, candy. My mouth watered as the different delicious scents fought for my attention. Generally, eating Fae food was a terrible idea. It could enthrall you and ruin you for any other type of food, but not here. Trading posts had laws against enchanted food. I ate the hazelnut and rhubarb tarts all the time. They were to die for.

The people behind the stalls were all Fae of different kinds. Gnomes, dryads, knockers, pucks, you name it. They sported horns, hooves, tails, wings. Some were beautiful and others not so much. The customers, on the other hand, were more of a human persuasion. At least in aspect, since they included vampires, shifters, and the like. They were all Skews like me, though. No Stales got access to Fae posts like this one.

Ignoring the food, I took a right into the next alley and entered an area with stone and mortar shops, places more permanent compared to the transient, removable stalls. One of those places was Yalgrun's Wares.

I bounded up the steps that led to his heavy front door and pushed it open. A wooden chime clattered above me, and Yalgrun looked up from his spot behind the counter.

He came from an Elf-hame town called Bladuh and was one of the most intimidating-looking creatures I'd ever seen. At seven-foot tall, he had a body made out of tree branches and vines. They twisted into each other, forming a massive torso, neck, arms, and legs. The same continued over his face and formed two horns that stuck straight out of his head. He had entirely black eyes, two holes for a nose, and a mouth that sometimes clanked if he spoke without care.

But however intimidating he might appear, once he opened his mouth, you couldn't help but love him.

"Toni Sunder," Yalgrun said in his melodic baritone voice. "Your presence graces my humble shop."

"Hello, *Abin Cenael*, how do you fare?"

"I fare splendidly. I hope you do as well."

I shrugged. "I've been better but can't complain."

Yalgrun's thick, ropy fingers lay interlaced on the wooden counter, which seemed to grow from the floor planks. He had four fingers on each hand, and I couldn't help but count them each time I saw them. "Trouble brews in your realm, I hear."

I frowned up at him. "Oh?"

"News reached us of the werewolf heir taken into captivity."

Wow, news had traveled fast indeed. I wondered if that meant the Fae had something to do with the kidnapping.

I nodded. "Yeah, it's unfortunate. I actually know him."

47

Yalgrun scratched his head, making a sound like two pencils tapping together. "Truly?"

"Truly."

His face creaked as he grimaced with regret. "I am so sorry to hear this."

"Well, we hadn't talked in a while, so…"

I let that hang, feeling awkward until I pulled a shopping list from my pocket and set it on the counter. "I'm running out of a few items, including Pixie dust."

He took the note with incredible gentleness, which seemed at odds with his large fingers. "I got a new batch just yesterday."

"Awesome." Just the reason I loved shopping here. Always the freshest ingredients.

He set about gathering my items, humming and lumbering around his high shelves. He pushed around jars, wooden boxes, dissected branches, rocks, and corked bottles full of strange liquids. I wiggled my nose as if that would get rid of the million scents that filled the shop.

The chime clanked as another customer entered the shop. I glanced back and had to do a double-take. Fae individuals always left me in awe, but this time I was dumbstruck. I snapped my mouth shut, my teeth clicking, and forced myself to breathe before I passed out at the sight of the male who strolled in.

He was magnificent. A walking dream imagined by a skillful artist. He had a warrior's body, broad, tall, and muscled in all the right places. Long, blue-black hair fell chest-high around him, graced with narrow braids kept in place by silver beads. A pattern of intricate tattoos ran down the right side of his face from his temple down to his neck, where it disappeared under a black, embroidered tunic. Pointed ears decorated with silver cuffs stuck out through his luscious locks.

48

And his face… oh, my God, his face. Everything about it was chiseled perfection. His straight nose, strong jaw, high cheekbones, and devastating lips. Thin eyebrows that rose at an impish angle framed a pair of serious, cobalt-blue eyes.

He bowed as he noticed me watching and waited by the door, large hands clasped in front of him. I had never wanted to be anything but human, but at that moment I would have sold my unborn children to be the kind of Fae this male could fall for.

Geez, grow up, Toni.

I shook myself and turned to Yalgrun, who still perused the shelves and, at last, came up with Rosalina's puck stool, which I recognized by its black jar covered with a green cloth secured with twine.

Yalgrun lumbered back in my direction and noticed the newcomer. His large, black eyes widened to the size of apples, and he clumsily set his load on the polished counter, jars clinking precariously against each other.

"Prince Kalyll," he said with a bow.

Prince? Kalyll?

If I had my facts straight, this was the Prince of the Seelie Fae. The eldest son of King Beathan Adanorin and Queen Eithne Adanorin.

Holy shit!

Did princes do their own shopping in Elf-hame? Judging by Yalgrun's reaction, I didn't think so.

"And you must be Yalgrun of Bladuh," the Prince said with a quick smile and a beautiful deep voice.

"I am honored," the shop owner bowed, his back creaking like an old door as his horns almost touched the counter. His head shifted from the Prince to me then back again. He didn't seem to know what to do: finish filling the order of a lowly human or tend to his future king, even if he'd just shown up.

I decided to make things easier for him. "I can pack all of this while you see to your new customer."

Yalgrun seemed relieved and moved down the counter to take Prince Kalyll's order. While I wrapped my jars in brown paper and stuffed them in a cloth sack, I stole a few glances at the Prince's profile. He murmured to Yalgrun, who quickly filled Kalyll's order and got paid with several gold coins.

Before I even finished packing my items, the Prince walked out the door with a quick farewell. As I paid a stunned Yalgrun in my lame American dollars, he took the money absentmindedly.

"Prince Kalyll is a hottie, huh?" I said.

Yalgrun's brow knitted together. "Hottie?"

"Um, never mind. Thanks for this." I gestured toward the sack that now hung from my shoulder. "I'll see you next month."

"Well met."

"Well met." I gave him a small wave and left the shop.

I was walking back toward the exit point, thinking about Rosalina's reaction when I told her I'd seen Prince Kalyll Adanorin when someone rushed me from the side, forcing me inside a narrow alleyway and sending me crashing against a stack of wooden crates. Empty boxes rained all around me as I fell. A sharp corner dug into my back. I cried out in pain and tried to hold to the cloth sack, but it slipped from my hand.

Heart thumping, I pushed a crate off my chest and blinked up to find a man looming over me. He was dressed all in black, wore a leather cloak, and had spiky, bright red hair—not natural but from cheap dye or a spell gone wrong. His eyes shone the color of a pale sky, which let me know he was an Azure Mage. A crackling spell erupted in his hand, and he pointed it straight at my face. My lungs froze, and a second cry got caught in my throat.

"You're coming with me, little tracker," the mage said as he pulled his hand back.

The hell I am.

Acting on pure instinct, I lunged forward, wrapped my arms around his ankles, and took him down. He fell on his ass, his spell shooting up into the sky. Cursing, he reloaded his hand with more magic and prepared to shoot.

This time I went for his balls and drove my fist right between his legs. He howled in pain, and his spell fizzled down to nothing, sputtering to tiny sparks as he cradled his package. I scrambled away from him, picked up my bag, and jumped to my feet. I started to run out of the alley, but Prince Kalyll appeared out of nowhere and blocked my path. I shrieked and froze.

The Prince stood staring down at my attacker as he twisted like a wilted earthworm. With one powerful arm, he grabbed the mage by the scruff of the neck, lifted him to a kneeling position, and pressed a dagger to his throat. The mage mewled and went still. Tears rolled down his cheeks, probably in honor of his lost progeny since his balls were now stuck in his kidneys.

The Prince sneered as the mage whimpered, then, without warning, whacked him in the back of the head. The man's joints unhinged, and he went as floppy as a marionette, the light disappearing from his eyes.

Prince Kalyll eased him to the ground and carelessly sheathed the dagger at his waist.

"Are you hurt?" he asked.

"Is he… is he dead?" I asked, hiccupping.

"No. Do you know him?"

I shook my head, surprised by Kalyll's cool and calculated demeanor.

"Spells are forbidden here," the Prince spat. "I have no tolerance for rule breakers. Are you hurt?" he asked again.

I shook my head, staring at the designs in Kalyll's tunic, avoiding his intense cobalt eyes at all costs.

The Prince poked the mage with one boot. "Why would this man want to hurt you?"

"I... I don't know."

"Do you come here often?" Kalyll's voice rang with suspicion.

Oh, crap! Would he blame me for bringing trouble into his realm?

"About once a month," I answered, then hurried to add, "Maybe he was a mugger." Though he'd said "you're coming with me, little tracker," which meant he'd known who I was. But why would anyone want to kidnap me?

The Prince inclined his head, his midnight-blue hair swinging to one side. "Mugger?"

"A thief."

He took my sack, quickly peered inside, then offered it back. "I doubt it. Unless you have gold or lots of your paper money."

I took my humble purchases and hung the bag over my shoulder. They seemed to be intact. "I don't have either."

Kalyll made a sound in the back of his throat. "Then you should take account of your enemies."

I didn't have any enemies—at least that was what I'd believed just moments ago. God, I needed to get out of here, go home. My nerves were wrecked. But would Kalyll let me leave? The Fae resolutely dispensed punishment to any visitor who broke their rules. Exhibit A: the unconscious mage.

"What is your name, human?" he asked.

I winced, imagining myself trapped in a Fae prison for the rest of my days. "Toni... Toni Sunder."

"I will escort you to the exit point to make sure you get back safely, Toni Sunder."

I heaved a sigh of relief.

As we exited the alley, I glanced back at the mage, wondering what would happen to him. Would they send him back to our realm? Or keep him here? If so, would anyone outside of Elf-hame be notified?

"My men will take care of him," Kalyll said as if reading my mind.

He gestured toward a couple of Fae guards, who wore leggings stuffed into boots and black tunics with an embroidered shield in the middle. They'd been standing at either side of the alley and quickly rushed in and picked the mage up by the arms.

"We follow procedure when these things happen," Kalyll continued. "They are part of our agreement with your kind. It will all be done according to our shared laws, I assure you. You can check with your authorities in a few days to report the attack and learn the man's identity."

I'd never been in a situation like this before, so I hadn't known of these procedures. But knowing the incident would be reported put my mind at ease somewhat.

When we made it to the exit point, Kalyll inclined his head and left me without a word. I thought of ordering something at the tavern to help calm my nerves, but I was too worried to linger in Elf-hame, so I sat at an empty table, traced my rune on its surface, and materialized back in my realm.

CHAPTER 9

Darkness had descended in my realm.

I had been so bent on leaving Elf-hame that I didn't think what would be waiting for me back here: a large park in the middle of the night. Clutching my sack, I left the pavilion and rushed back home. I walked at a clipped pace, glancing left and right, searching for would-be attackers, almost giving myself whiplash.

I made it back to my street in record time, sweating like a racehorse and fresh out of breath. Relief washed over me when I spotted the sign above our door. I couldn't wait to get inside, lock the door, and hide behind the protection of Mom's spells.

Before going in, I peered all around to make sure the coast was clear. The coffee shop across the street had already closed, and only the pizzeria remained open, so no people roamed the street anymore.

Hands shaking, I keyed the lock, put the sack on the floor, and stepped inside. Just as I started to close the door, a man appeared out of thin air and shoved the door open again. It hit my forehead, causing me to drop the keys and lose my balance.

Shit! Not again!

I staggered backward, arms windmilling. Darkness enveloped me, and as the bell chimed above, he rushed me, knocking me to the floor and forcing a piece of cloth against my mouth. A sharp scent invaded my nostrils, sending lances of pain into my sinuses.

Bleakkiss! I'd smelled it before, and I knew exactly what it would do to me.

Pressing my lips together, I held my breath and tried to fight the panic raging through my veins.

You know what to do. You know what to do.

In kick-boxing class, the teacher shared self-defense techniques all the time.

Shit, which one applies now? Think. Think.

My thoughts were a jumble. Nothing came to me. My lungs burned from the lack of oxygen, and my mind went blank. That was when my instincts took over.

Reflexively, I curled up on my side, bringing my thighs to my stomach. Then, sneaking a knee against the man's hips, I uncurled, pushing with all my strength. The move worked as intended, extending and weakening my assailant's hold. As he struggled to get a better grip, I swung my leg, threw it over his neck, and flipped him over, ending on top. The bleakkiss-soaked cloth fell from his hand as he fought back. I bared my teeth and jammed the palm of my hand against his nose.

It broke with a crunch.

The man cried out, gurgling as blood filled his mouth. I jumped to my feet, rushed to Rosalina's desk, and pulled out the 9mm snub-nosed revolver I kept stashed in a drawer. I knew how to use it, and I would if it came to it.

"Don't move or I'll redecorate the place with your brains."

Just as I reached for my cell to dial 911, the door to the office burst open and a tall, black figure rushed in. I aimed the gun at the broad chest and nearly pulled the trigger, but stopped when I noticed the glow of silver eyes.

Jake.

"Toni, are you all right?" he growled, his voice a rumble of anger and wildness.

"I'm fine." I re-aimed the gun at my fallen attacker and pulled the phone out of my pocket.

Without warning, Jake grabbed the man by the collar, hauled him upright, and slammed him against the wall.

"Who the hell are you?" he demanded.

The man groaned and turned away from Jake. Blood oozed from his nose, sliding down to his mouth and chin. I'd done a number on him. Just what he deserved, *the asshole*. I hoped he would have a crooked nose for the rest of his life.

"911, what's your emergency?" the responder asked on the other side of the line.

"Someone attacked me and tried to…"

What exactly? Rendered me unconscious, for sure. But why? To rape me? I doubted it, considering this was the second incident tonight. There was more to this.

I began again. "Someone broke into my office and attacked me. He's restrained now."

The responder rambled something I didn't fully grasp since I'd become distracted by Jake slamming the guy against the wall, rattling his brains.

"What did you want with her?" he snarled.

The man shook his head and said nothing.

I couldn't fully see Jake's face, but in his profile, I noticed his ears growing pointed, and fur sprouting down the back of his neck and arms. Large claws and fangs slid into place. He roared in the man's face, a savage sound that turned my insides to runny gelatin.

A stain spread down the man's jeans and the sharp scent of urine filled the air.

"Ma'am? Ma'am? What's going on there?" The responder's voice broke through the receiver. "Units are on their way. Hold tight and remain on the line."

Jake wrapped his clawed hands around my attacker's throat. "I'll ask you one more time, and if you don't tell me what I want to know, I'll rip your throat out."

Mr. Wetpants whimpered, his knees buckling from fear as Jake crushed him against the brick wall.

"What did you want with Toni Sunder?"

"T-they sent me to kidnap her," he said in a nasally tone.

Kidnap? Again? What the hell was going on?!

"Who?" Jake roared.

The man whined in the back of his throat, looking as if he would wet his pants again. Jake tightened the hold, his claws drawing blood.

"Jake, please," I pleaded.

If he killed the man, it would be a mess, bigger than it already was, and I didn't have the guts to see someone's life cut short. Besides, a murder in our office would not be good for business. The police would be here at any moment, anyway. They could deal with him. But Jake ignored me and leaned more heavily into the smaller man.

"Last chance... answer or I swear you'll wish you'd never been born. Who sent you?"

Mr. Wetpants sighed in resignation. He knew Jake meant every word. "It was—" the man's voice cut off.

Jake slackened his hold on Mr. Wetpants' throat.

The man tried again. "It was—" his voice cut off again.

"Dammit." Jake shook him.

The man tried for the third time. He opened his mouth, shaping a name, but it never came out because he gagged as if to throw up. Jake let him go and took a step back, wiping bloody hands on his jeans. Mr. Wetpants grabbed at his throat and fell to his knees, an awful crackling sound coming from his mouth.

"What the hell?" Jake glanced at me then back at the man.

I was still frozen, the phone in one hand and the gun in the other. "What's happening to him?"

Jake shook his head as a swarm of black beetles crawled out of the man's mouth. In seconds, they covered his face, then went back in through his ears, nostrils, and eyes. I turned away in horror.

The scuttling sound of the bugs went on for a moment longer, then there was a thud, followed by silence.

I glanced back. The man laid on his side, black, empty sockets where his eyes had been.

Jake and I were still staring dumbfounded at the ruined shape when patrol cars screeched to a stop outside, sirens wailing and flashing in the night.

CHAPTER 10

An hour after the attack, Jake and I entered the police department escorted by the two officers who drove us there.

At the counter stood a dark-skinned man in shirtsleeves, and loose tie, a hand smoothing his graying goatee. His sharp brown eyes traveled over a piece of paper, moving quickly. Noticing our approach, he set the page down and walked in our direction.

"You all right, kid?" He held me at arms' length, scrutinizing me from head to toe. "I just heard or I would have come myself."

Detective Tom Freeman became part of my life the night Jake and I rescued the Garner girl. He had been the detective leading the case and grilled us for hours until he was satisfied with every detail. Through the ordeal, he met my dad, and they struck up a friendship. When Dad passed away of pancreatic cancer a year ago, he asked Tom to take care of me, an assignment he took seriously. We had coffee at least once a week. He was the one who insisted I keep a gun in the office, and the one who took me to the shooting range to practice. He had also suggested kick-boxing.

He had kids of his own, but one lived in Los Angeles and the other in Denver. His wife had passed away from a heart attack before she turned fifty, and it seemed I'd become his family's poor substitute. I loved the man to pieces.

"I'm fine," I said.

Satisfied, he took a step back, his gaze drifting to Jake, who stood behind me.

Tom's expression tightened. "And look who the cat dragged in."

The words crackled with hostility. Tom's capacity to switch from nice to mean and back again always surprised me. He could play good cop, bad cop all on his own. But even though he saw his share of bad shit and knew how to handle it, he didn't let it darken his soul.

"Detective," Jake greeted.

Tom turned. "Follow me."

We went into his office and sat across from him, while he glared at us from behind his desk.

Yes, Jake and I had helped solve the Emily Garner case, but other times, we'd also stuck our noses where they didn't belong, pissing people off. Tom had gotten us out of a few binds with his superiors. Like the time I called his boss a racist twatwaffle because he hadn't bothered to look for a missing Leprechaun that left Elf-hame by accident and got lost in the St. Louis Galleria Mall. *Excuse me, but that's a bigass place for such a little guy.* Good thing I'd found him and returned him home safely before he got too comfortable and started jumping out of toilets in the lady's bathroom. The gates to Elf-hame were highly monitored for a reason.

"The pair of you again," Tom said. "As if we don't have enough problems already."

"There's no *pair of us.*" I scooted my chair away from Jake's. "It's just Jake over there, and me over here."

"It's good to see you too, detective," Jake said, always the smart ass.

Tom rubbed his stubble making a *sandpapery* sound. Dark circles surrounded his eyes, which suggested things around The Hill had him burning the midnight oil.

He made a tired, come-here motion with his large hand.

"All right, tell me what happened?"

Jake opened his mouth to speak, but Tom halted him with a raised index finger. "Not you, Knight. Toni."

I gave Jake a satisfied grin. As teenagers, Jake and I had spent many hours in this very office, mostly talking ourselves out of trouble, and Tom had always picked me first to explain things. He said I made more sense and gave him fewer urges to break someone's neck.

Jake huffed and murmured under his breath. "Typical."

Without embellishments, I explained everything that happened from the moment I left Rosalina outside the pizzeria to the moment the cops showed up.

"Shit," Tom said when I was done. "Not more of this supernatural crap! Beetles? The Seelie Prince? Really? And they never said who sent them." Tom was a Stale and hated dealing with Skew cases because they messed up his closing rate. Vanilla, human crimes were much easier to solve and kinder on his record.

I shook my head. "The first guy never had a chance and the second... I think someone put a spell on him to make sure he didn't rat them out."

"I'm sure that's what they did." Tom rubbed the back of his neck. "We've seen it a lot lately. It happened to a couple of eyewitnesses."

"Eyewitnesses?" Jake asked.

Tom's attention shifted to Jake. "It's none of your concern."

"It is if it has anything to do with Stephen Erickson's kidnapping."

Tom cocked his head to one side and steepled his fingers. "And what does that have to do with you?"

Jake reached for his wallet, pulled out a business card, and slid it across the desk. "Everything. His father hired me to find him, but more than that, Stephen's my friend."

He'd been hired by Ulfen? He never mentioned that tidbit.

The detective glanced down at the card. "A PI? God protect us!" He considered for a moment. "Look, I don't need you causing trouble for us, Knight. Let us do our job."

"I don't want to cause trouble for anyone. All I want is to find Stephen before it's too late."

Tom smiled stiffly. "Then we have the same goal. I hope I don't need to remind you that if you find out anything important, you should communicate it to the department immediately."

"That's right, you don't have to remind me."

The detective shook his head. "I see you haven't changed one bit, which I'm afraid doesn't bode well for either of us."

Jake didn't bother to contradict him. Instead, he gave him one of his crooked, signature smiles—the ones that melted hearts and scorched lingerie.

Tom turned fatherly eyes in my direction. "Sorry, this happened, kid. We'll see what we can find out about that mage and Beetlejuice. I'll keep you posted."

I nodded. "Thank you."

"Bernadetta Fiore sent them," Jake said.

Tom's eyes narrowed. "It's not wise to throw accusations without proof."

Jake huffed.

Tom turned to me. "I would assign you a police escort, but we're short-staffed. Why don't you stay with me tonight?"

"It's fine, Tom. I'll be all right."

Jake watched with interest, one eyebrow raised.

Tom rubbed his forehead, preoccupied. "You shouldn't be alone."

"If you want, I can—" Jake began.

"No." I glared at him, cutting short whatever he'd been about to suggest.

"I can take care of myself. I'd already subdued the intruder when you showed up, remember?" I turned to Tom. "And thanks to you, I know how to use a gun, so I'm fine." I paused, then almost asked if they had any leads on Stephen's case but thought better of it. "Is that all?"

Tom nodded. "For now."

"Wait," Jake said as I stood, "you're not going to ask her to help us find Stephen?"

Tom's deep brown eyes went from Jake to me, then back. "No, I am not. Ms. Sunder has declined to aid our department in missing person cases even in a salaried capacity."

Yep, Tom had offered me a job. I would've helped his closing rate in Skew cases, but I picked the cheerier path of mate tracking. I didn't have his strength of character and probably would turn into a psycho bitch if I saw the same thing every day.

Jake pushed air through his nose. "Yeah, I heard she turned selfish."

"She has her reasons, and I respect them," Tom said the last few words with emphasis, hinting that Jake should respect them, too. Opening a folder, Tom started perusing it, a clear indicator that he was done with us.

"Thank you, Tom," I said. "Good luck with your case. And get some sleep."

"I'll sleep when I'm dead," he said, without looking up.

Pulling my phone out of my back pocket, I walked out of Tom's office and started dialing Rosalina's number. Jake's hand on my shoulder stopped me in my tracks.

"So now you call him *Tom*?" he asked.

"You've been gone for a while. A lot has changed around here."

I stared pointedly at his fingers on my shoulder. He let go and held up his hand, apologetically. His silver gaze intent on mine, he leaned closer. I immediately pulled back, my eyes falling to his mouth of their own accord.

He pinched his eyebrows and scoffed. "Don't flatter yourself, sweetheart."

Anger twisted in the pit of my stomach like a writhing snake. *The bastard!* I wanted to slap him right then and there, but I controlled myself. As ideas went, starting a brawl around all these uniformed cops didn't exactly get the prize.

"I see you're still the same narcissistic jackass you've always been," I shot back. Still as hot as hell and able to set my panties on fire with one smoldering look, too. *Damn him!*

God, I hated him.

"I only want to warn you." He leaned closer again, his deep voice a mere whisper that made the tiny hairs on the back of my arms stand on end. "You have to be careful. This wasn't a random attack. I think it's related to Stephen's disappearance."

"Stop trying to make everything about Stephen." I held his gaze, resolutely. Even if my panties had turned to ash, I still had my pants on and could hold my own. "The Hill has never been a safe place. Things like this happen."

"Kidnapping, Toni?"

He had a point. Hit-and-runs, burglary, armed robbery, spell robbery... they topped the list of what we normally dealt with, but kidnapping? That belonged in an entirely different category. Still, he wouldn't drag me into anything I didn't want to be part of. It'd taken a lot of work to build my life back up, and I wasn't going to throw it all away for a pair of smoldering clear eyes and a hot body. Not to mention *other* hot things...

I squared my shoulders. "Like I said, I know how to take care of myself, and even if I didn't, it's not your job to worry about me, is it? You quit that job a long time ago, so you need to stop pretending you care when what you're really worried about is a fat paycheck from Ulfen Erickson."

His expression tightened. A muscle jumped in his jaw and his eyes smoldered in an entirely different way. *Uh-oh, I'd pissed him off. Good!* To my surprise, when he spoke, his tone sounded noncommittal.

"I don't want anything bad to happen to you, Toni."

"Isn't that charitable of you? But I'll be fine. Don't worry your werewolf head about it." I turned and walked away.

I thought I'd gotten rid of him, but he caught up to me outside.

"I hope you're not going back to your office," he said, trying to sound casual.

I ignored him as I stood at the edge of the sidewalk and thumbed through my contacts. It was past midnight, and a blanket of dark gray clouds covered the sky. I hoped it wouldn't rain. At least not until I got to Rosalina's.

"Do you have somewhere to stay besides the loft?" he asked.

How the hell did he know I lived in the loft?! I raised my eyebrows at him. "You've been spying on me, I see."

"It's my job to know things," he offered.

"If that's the case, then you should know where I'm headed. Now, if you'll excuse me, I have to make a phone call."

I walked away and dialed Rosalina's number.

"Is everything all right?" was the first thing she said, her voice in a panic.

"Not exactly, but I'm fine," I reassured her. "I need to crash with you for a few days if that's okay?"

"Of course! What happened?"

"I'll tell you later. Right now, I need to get out of here. I'll be there in twenty."

I disconnected the call, then got an Uber. I couldn't get away from Jake fast enough, and I didn't like the way he stared at my driver one bit. He certainly looked like someone who thought it was his job to worry about me.

CHAPTER 11

The next day, I woke up with a terrible headache. My head pounded, and no amount of Rosalina's strong Columbian coffee did the trick. She stood by the stove, scrambling eggs, and frying bacon, while I sat at her kitchen table, holding my head. She lived in a small, two-bedroom, one-bath condo in Soulard. She'd moved in only six months ago and loved it.

In part, our partnership had made it possible. She'd had savings from before, but the agency kept us solvent. We made enough to pay our loan, rent, cover our bills, and still have enough money to do fun stuff, which was more than most people our age could do for themselves.

From what I'd learned about Rosalina during the short sixteen months since I'd met her, she'd always had a good head on her shoulders. She got good grades in college while studying Business Administration, even as she worked odd jobs in her free time and saved as much as possible. I met her at one of those jobs. Starbucks, evening shift after classes, I'd ordered an espresso, and when the change in my pocket came short, she waved it off and said it was on the house. Not only that, but she also noticed my gaunt face and the slobbery way I ogled the pastries behind the glass display.

I'd been on the streets for a month by then, but I hadn't stopped being embarrassed by charity or hunger. I bit my tongue and took the cup because of the hollow in my belly. Grateful for something warm—it was freezing outside—I sat in a corner, nursing my coffee, and listening to Christmas carols from the overhead speakers.

At closing time, I walked out and glanced around, trying to decide which way to go. My hands itched to call Mom or Daniella, my older sister, but I hated the thought of going back with my tail between my legs, and I didn't want to hear the inevitable "I told you so." Stubbornness and pride ranked high on my list of personality traits. So instead, I set my jaw and walked toward Tower Grove Park. I'd slept there before anyway.

"Hey," Rosalina called, rushing out of the coffee shop, a paper bag in hand.

I turned to face her.

"I thought you might be hungry." She offered me the bag.

I stared at it with a frown.

"It's just an egg muffin. They're pretty good," she said with a gentle smile that, for some reason, made my heart tighten weirdly.

I was broke and on the streets, and that espresso had been more than I'd expected. And now, here was food. My stomach gave a painful pang, and I couldn't refuse it, not even after hefting the bulk of my pride on top of my shoulders.

Slowly, my hand reached for the paper bag. Rosalina waited, wearing the same comforting smile. Something about her sincere expression touched me in a way nothing had. Maybe because, at that moment, I'd become as vulnerable as an abandoned kitten. Either way, I immediately wanted to know her, to be her friend.

"Thank you," I said, my voice breaking.

"No worries. Are you all right?" she asked, her expression full of genuine concern.

I nodded, a lie. I was scared, worried I'd end up in a ditch with my throat cut, another victim of the high crime rate in St. Louis.

Rosalina's lips had tightened. I could tell she hadn't believed me. "Um, I live nearby. Would you like to hang out for a bit? We could watch some Netflix or something."

The rest was history.

Now, I smiled fondly at my friend as she walked up to the table, carrying two plates. She handed me one and sat across from me. "Eat up! You're gonna need your strength for the trance."

I dug into the eggs and bacon. She cooked them just the way I liked them, the eggs underdone and the bacon crispy.

"Thank you," I said through a mouthful. Normally, I didn't eat a hot breakfast. The loft didn't have a kitchen, so my first meal of the day came out of a mini-fridge. A yogurt or cheese stick that never did the trick.

Rosalina picked up her coffee cup and held it thoughtfully. "The news are disturbing this morning. Some battle between vampires and werewolves broke out in The Scourge."

The Scourge was a commercial district reserved for supernatural beings. Regular laws didn't apply there, and Stales and vulnerable Skews entered at their discretion.

She continued. "A band of werewolves immolated a couple of young vamps. They held them in the open 'til the sun came out."

I grimaced. "What a horrible death."

"The article suggested the vamps belonged to Bernadetta Fiore's faction and that the attack might have been in retaliation for Stephen Erickson's kidnapping."

"Things are getting uglier by the minute."

"Yes, they are."

We sat in silence for a moment, then Rosalina got to business.

"Okay," she held a piece of bacon between her thumb and forefinger as she spoke, "we need to go to the office to pick up the potion. Hopefully, the trance won't take a huge toll on you this time, and we can go back later to straighten things out."

"Sounds good." I really needed this trance to be easy. I had to be at my best to deal with the current shit storm.

"God, I swear, if I could get my hands on that bastard who attacked you, I would kill him all over again," Rosalina said. "And instead of beetles, he would have fat, juicy cockroaches coming out of his asshole and going back into his mouth."

I burst out laughing. "Maybe there's a reason you're not a witch."

"Who says I'm not a witch? Check out my wand." She waved her piece of bacon in front of my face.

Slowly, and in her company, my headache dissipated. She could always distract me, even from attempted kidnapping. I still hadn't told her about what had happened in Elf-hame, but why worry her more?

An hour later, we got to the agency. She parked her car by the front door, a red Scion, or the "box with wheels" as I liked to call it. She had bought it about three months ago. It wasn't new, but it was in great shape. Only twenty thousand miles on the odometer, not a scratch, no collision reports, and no stench of cigarettes inside. She fell in love with it immediately, even if it looked like a cube and had the aerodynamics of an armoire.

Today, Rosalina's black hair tumbled in curls onto her shoulders. Her eye makeup sparkled flawlessly and matched the subtle blue of her blouse.

We walked toward the door. Yellow tape stretched across its width. I tore it off and crumpled it into a tight ball, a surge of last night's panic filling my chest.

"This can't be good for business," I said, as my eyes drifted next door without my permission.

Rosalina placed a finger on my chin and redirected my attention to the door. "Eyes on the prize, remember?"

I nodded and took a deep breath. Before we left her place, I'd reminded her to remind me to forget about Jake.

"God, you didn't say it was this bad." Rosalina's face fell as she peered through the glass-paneled door.

"I don't think it—" I stopped when I pushed the door open and saw the mess: file cabinets open, trampled papers on the floor, Rosalina's desk ransacked and her laptop gone. I walked in, rendered speechless by the disaster.

"It wasn't this bad when I left with the police," I heard myself say.

"Then what happened?"

"I don't know." I pressed a hand to my forehead, trying to wrap my head around what this could mean for the agency. Would this give us a bad name? Would we lose potential clients? At the thought, my head snapped toward my office.

"The potion!" I exclaimed.

I clutched my purse tightly since I'd stashed the revolver inside. With two attempts on my person, I felt safer carrying it around. I stepped gingerly around the files on the floor and went into my office. A similar disaster welcomed me there. They'd ransacked my desk and taken my laptop, too.

"Shit," Rosalina mumbled as she walked in behind me.

Hand trembling, I opened the door to the alcove. Had they been able to break Mom's protective spell?

Please don't. Please don't.

But they had. My heart sank. Everything inside was a wreck. The shelves and tiny drawers I kept clean and organized were empty, their contents strewn on the floor, all my ingredients ruined. Their distinctive scents wafted in the air, creating a messed-up potpourri that made me wince. A familiar scent rode the air, but I couldn't put my finger on it.

Dammit, I would have to go back to Elf-hame and spend a boatload of money to replace everything.

And Celina's potion? I didn't want to glance up to find it broken and spilled over my worktable.

"At least, the potion's okay," Rosalina said before I could look.

I let out a pent-up breath of relief. With the potion intact, I could still work today and keep one of our clients happy. We would have to cancel a couple of appointments until we restocked, a luxury we couldn't afford since we could only take so many customers a month. What a mess!

Rosalina placed a warm hand on my shoulder. "It's fine, Toni. Don't worry. The insurance will pay for the laptops and anything else that's broken. I'll get to work on submitting a claim, and I'll call the police, try to find out what happened. The rest should be easy. I'll pick up all the files and make sure everything is there."

I nodded. "You're a saint, Rosalina. Thank you."

"No need to thank me. We're a team."

I glanced down toward the floor at the broken bottles and ruined ingredients. "Damn! All this is expensive."

"We'll claim it all as a loss," Rosalina said with confidence. "Who could have done this? And why?"

"I have no idea. Maybe a competitor? A maniac? I don't even want to go upstairs," I said, picturing everything wrecked on the floor, my underwear, and maybe even poor Cupid, which I hadn't fed. Again.

"I'll check." Rosalina ran upstairs. A short minute later, she returned. "It's undisturbed," she said with a frown.

"That's odd. Not that I'm complaining. Is Cupid all right?"

"Yeah, he's fine."

It seemed unlikely that whoever had torn up the office looking for who knew what would leave without searching the loft.

"Maybe we'll need to splurge and get that alarm system we've been talking about. Just another layer of protection besides the spells," Rosalina said.

"Yep, well…" I rolled my shoulders, forcing myself to relax. "Let's make a list, so we can divide and conquer."

"On it. Let me find a notebook and pen."

She went back to look at her desk. That was when my subconscious, which had been busy coping with the loss, came up with a name for the familiar scent I'd detected among my ruined ingredients.

Jake!

He had been the one in my potions alcove. But why? Was he trying to sabotage me? Ruin my tracking business so I would help him? God, I was going to kill him.

Fury lighting my fuse, I whirled and headed out.

CHAPTER 12

I burst into Jake's place with my ass on fire, though this time from rage. He'd left the door unlocked again, though no one was here, at least not in the front room.

"Jake!" I hollered as the front door swung closed behind me. "Jacob Knight!" I called again.

He appeared through the back door, wearing nothing but a pair of jeans and biker boots. He was cleaning his fingers with a rag. They had something white on them that looked like caulking. A light sheen of sweat covered his broad muscles. And I swear if I hadn't been so pissed, I would've babbled like a fish. Instead, my anger redoubled. No one had a right to be this damn hot, sexy, and infuriating.

"You're here," he said, relief in his voice. "Something happened—"

"It was you, wasn't it? Your twisted way of dragging me into this Erickson mess."

He frowned and discarded the rag on the floor. "What are you talking about?"

"Our office, all our stuff... *you* did that?" I wanted it to sound like an accusation, but it came out as a question instead.

"Wait, you think I trashed your office? You really think me capable of that?"

"You've done worse," I shot back. "Your scent is all over the place."

A muscle jumped in Jake's stubbled jaw. After a tense moment, he scoffed, shaking his head. "Look, this is what happened. Early this morning, before dawn, I heard noise next-door. Thought you might be back, so I got dressed and went to check. By the time I got there, whoever trashed the place had left. I called the police. They came and checked it out, but..." He lifted his hand and shrugged. "So no, *I* didn't do it."

I raked stiff fingers into my hair, a jumble of emotions crashing inside my chest like wrecking balls. Okay, maybe he hadn't trashed my office, but only one day had passed since Jacob Knight came back into my life, and everything was upside down.

"You know," I said. "Both Mom and Daniella told me many times that you were no good for me, but I never listened."

Jake's silver eyes darkened, and his shoulders tensed as he held my gaze.

"It wasn't until the day you left that I saw the truth, and now it's like I'm seeing it all over again, like a freaking déjà vu. You just got here yesterday and look at how *peachy* things are going."

"That's not fair," he said in a low whisper, scarier than any outburst he might have had.

He walked closer, his body lithe, his muscles flexing under golden skin. I took a step closer, too. I wasn't going to let this thing between us control me. To my satisfaction, he shuddered and stopped. His gaze slid down the length of my body. He licked his lips, then clenched his jaw.

A thrill of smug pride went through me. It seemed the fierce attraction he'd felt for me before lived on. The knowledge made me feel great and awful at the same time. Great because it seemed he hadn't left the past behind either. And awful because it confused me, because it gave me new questions about his reasons for leaving me.

Of course, I had to quickly remind myself that attraction and love belonged on entirely different planes.

"Just stay out of my way," I said. "Then I won't have to blame you if anything else goes wrong."

I took a step back, ready to leave.

"You're in danger, Toni, and it has nothing to do with me."

"That's not what it looks like from my end."

"What happened between us is clouding your judgment and putting your life in danger," he said. "If you ask me, this is what's happening... whoever took Stephen doesn't want him found, for obvious reasons. They know you used to have a relationship with him and might decide to track him, so they are trying to make sure that doesn't happen. You're an amazing tracker, and they know it."

"You're the only one trying to pull me into this. *I* don't want to get involved, so stop giving those criminals any ideas."

He ran a hand through his soft hair.

Soft? What the hell, Toni? Stop thinking like this.

But how could anyone blame me? I knew exactly how amazing his hair felt between my fingers. I'd touched it many times, raking my hands through it as we made love. I shuddered. *Gah!* This was deteriorating quickly. I had to get out of here. Turning on my heel, I headed for the door and opened it.

"You're already involved, whether you want to be or not." Of course, he always had to have the last word.

I stomped back to my office with his voice ringing in my ears.

"He's infuriating," I growled as I stormed in and collapsed on a chair.

Rosalina was bending down, gathering papers, and pulling them into a pile. She rose to her full height of 5'5". She had on flats.

"I could have told you that going over there would be unproductive, but…" She shrugged.

"The most infuriating part is," I hated to admit it, "that he's right."

Her perfectly plucked eyebrows went up. She abandoned the papers, sat down, and gave me her full attention. "This must be good if you're agreeing with him." She wiggled her fingers in a "come here" motion. "Spill, girl."

I repeated what Jake had said almost word by word. As I went, Rosalina's expression changed, gradually growing concerned. "We should have realized the kidnappers would come after you," she said when I finished.

"I know, but I was so busy being mad at Jake that… Oh, never mind, what do you think we should do?"

"Move to China?" she suggested. "This isn't good. Bernadetta Fiore and her people are ruthless, and open war between her and Ulfen Erickson doesn't bode well for anyone."

"If it was the Dark Donna who kidnapped Stephen."

"Who else? I think the constant feud between vampires and werewolves has finally reached a boiling point." Rosalina rose from the chair and began pacing the office. "Toni, this is bad."

She was telling *me*? I'd nearly been taken last night. Twice. Had Bernadetta sent Beetlejuice and mage? I didn't know her, so she had no reason to want to hurt me. But who was I kidding? Vampires, especially powerful ones like her, had no respect for life and took whatever they wanted without asking for permission.

"Well, I'm not moving to China or anywhere else," I said, resolutely. "I can't let Jake and his world ruin my life again."

"As much as you hate it, you're also part of that world, Toni," she reminded me.

For over a year, I'd had a glimpse at a normal life. Yes, I'd been using my Skew powers to make a living, but we only accepted Stale customers, with few exceptions. Their lives were easier, simple even, and I liked pretending I was one of them. Was my time of peaceful existence over?

"Thanks for reminding me," I huffed.

"So, what then? Do I buy those plane tickets to China? Or we could go to Spain, my Spanish would come in handy."

"Not a bad idea," I pretended to consider it, but who was I kidding? I couldn't leave St. Louis. My family and everything we'd worked so hard for was here.

"Maybe we just lay low until this resolves itself," she suggested, knowing full well we weren't going anywhere. "We can work from my place and set up meetings with prospective customers at coffee houses or restaurants. That would also help you stay away from…" She hooked her thumb toward Jake's office.

"Sounds like a plan. I'll get some stuff from upstairs."

"And I'll gather a few files, also I already called my sister and asked if I could borrow her spare laptop. She said no problem."

"Awesome! We're in business again. Let's take butts and kick names." I stood and we high-fived each other. We had both laughed at that line from one of The Avengers movies and liked to use it pretty regularly.

CHAPTER 13

B y that afternoon, I'd made Rosalina's guest bedroom mine. The clothes that I'd stuffed in a carry-on bag already hung in the closet and Cupid's fishbowl sat on the dresser. But more importantly, Celina's crimson potion sat on the night table, waiting in a shallow bowl. I'd closed the shades, and even though the sun had reached its peak, almost no light seeped into the small, carpeted room. I'd changed into comfortable clothes: my favorite pair of pajamas, a flannel number with a heart pattern.

Chewing on my bottom lip, I worried that more kidnappers might come after me, but this place was armed to the teeth with protection spells. Mom had gone to town with her best work and, on top of that, the complex boasted Stale and Skew security—one of the reasons Rosalina had bought the condo.

She appeared at the door, still wearing her office clothes, though barefoot rather than in her flats.

"Ready?" she asked.

I gave her a decisive nod and sat at the edge of the double bed. The potion shimmered in the bowl, looking as if a constellation of stars was trapped in it. I dreaded this part, not so much because of the trance, but because of what would happen afterward.

Magic always came with a price, and the price I paid turned out to be a real pain in the ass.

Rosalina gave me a reassuring smile. "I'm right here. I'll take care of you."

And she certainly did. Best of all, she made sure I had company on the other end of the trance. I'd done it alone before, and a few times it had been nothing short of terrifying.

Inhaling deeply, I stood and faced the bowl. Maybe this time, it wouldn't be so bad. I could only hope. Slowly, I dipped my hands into the potion, up to my wrists. When I took them out, it looked as if I'd donned a pair of shiny, sequined gloves. What had been a liquid now clung to me like a second skin. Holding my hands up like a freshly scrubbed-in surgeon, I climbed into bed and made myself comfortable.

Rosalina walked over, and being careful not to touch my outstretched hands, pulled the covers up to my chest. She knew I liked to be warm. Plus, the covers made me feel safe, contained somehow.

"Toodles." I wiggled my fingers.

She smiled, a bit sadly but reassuringly.

Slowly, I lowered my hands, and lightly pressed stiff fingertips to my closed eyes. My lids tingled. Next, I tilted my head back and ran my fingers downward until I reached my nostrils. The scent of chocolate chip cookies assaulted me. My tongue flicked out, tasting the potion. It reminded me of the same sweet treat. Lastly, I touched my ears, involving all my senses.

After a long minute, the potion disappeared, leaving my hands and face clean as if it'd never been there. I blinked my eyes open and lowered my hands to my sides. As I peered up at Rosalina, she appeared like an angel from heaven, glowing warmly while tiny stars flickered all around her... just what I liked to see before the spell took me.

Of their own accord, my eyes closed, and I found myself in what looked like a kindergartner's Saint Valentine's Day goodie bag. Shiny glitter floated all around me against a deep blackness. Individual pieces twinkled while silence reigned, an indication the potion had taken hold.

It was so peaceful, I could drift there forever, but I had to get to work.

Tracking someone with my skills required the use of my senses. I could use four of them, but I only ever wanted to use one. That would have been too easy, though.

I always started with my strongest, yet most-disposable sense: smell.

Gradually, I activated it, and my iridescent limbo filled with a host of scents that sent my memory banks into hyper-drive. The sense of smell is the best at retrieving memories and bringing back moments and places that seemed forgotten. Like how a whiff of cannoli or homemade marinara reminds me of Nonna, cooking in her large kitchen, slapping my fingers out of bowls unless I meant to help.

Faster than my little sister, Lucia, can go through boyfriends, I examined the scents waltzing into my sparkling universe. I detected many distinct ones—car exhaust, cigarette smoke, cologne, mulch, B.O., grilled meat, and more—all from places one of Celina's potential mates was currently roaming.

Most people believed that only one mate existed for them, and I didn't like to contradict them. It kept confusion to a minimum and stopped skeptical clients from asking questions that would be too hard to explain. More than seven billion people live on earth. Thinking that only one other person can be someone's perfect match is ludicrous. True, some of them might not speak the same language, but still. They make translation apps for a reason.

As quickly as possible—the longer I stayed under the trance the longer my recovery would be—I cataloged each scent, trying to find it in my Rolodex of memories, hoping it came from a location familiar to me, hopefully somewhere in St. Louis or at least a city I had visited. I made it a point to travel to different places to fill my catalog and increase my success rate.

One smell, in particular, I pinpointed without trouble. It came from a hamburger joint that I liked. The problem: it was a chain. There might be thousands of them all over the country, and maybe even the world, but since I recognized it, I latched on to it. Still, this clue was too broad. I had to narrow things down.

Dammit! Like I'd said, getting away with using only one of my senses would be too good to be true.

It was time for the next most-disposable sense: hearing. But before I moved on, I focused on a strong male scent that was unique. It was the most prevalent scent from one of Celina's mates.

When I felt certain I'd committed it to memory, I let my ears come out to play. Immediately, my shimmering surroundings filled with a cacophony of sounds. Horns blowing, a sledgehammer, the din of voices in a crowded place, someone coughing, a lawnmower, the low bass of a rap song, a loud fart. Most of them were useless, sounds one could hear almost anywhere. I riffled through them in frustration, discarding them, shutting them down one at a time, gradually bringing down the cacophony to a bearable level.

Shit! This was taking too long already. I knew I had to hurry, but the stress of it made me clumsy. I stumbled over the sounds, hesitating to send them away even when they were irrelevant.

Finally, over the racket of all the remaining sounds, one caught my attention. It repeated itself over and over, which meant the potential mate, my mark, heard it often, maybe even every day.

Better yet, I recognized it!

It came from the bells at the Cathedral Basilica, announcing the top of the hour.

Bingo!

Maybe St. Louis didn't have seven billion inhabitants, but with nearly three million in the metro area, the probabilities of finding mates right here didn't suck. Besides, who could be more compatible than someone living in your own backyard?

Wasting no time, I snapped out of the trance and breathed a sigh of relief when I came to.

Rosalina always said that watching me during a trance scared her, that my eyelashes didn't flutter and my chest barely rose and fell. From the sound of it, I appeared dead or comatose, but I never had trouble breaking out of a trance, though sometimes I wondered… what if I got stuck in one of them?

My eyes sprang open. Exhaustion weighed my every limb, making me feel as if I'd partied hard and been put away soaking wet.

Rosalina sat next to me, holding my hand. She smiled when I met her gaze and seemed relieved to find that I'd only used two senses. She could tell because I hadn't lost my sight and I could still see her.

Besides feeling like a wet rag, the price I paid for tracking amounted to losing the senses I used during the trance. Of course, the loss of my senses kicked my butt the worst. For every minute I stayed under, my senses went dormant for an hour. In the past, I'd been deaf, blind, anosmic (unable to smell) and hypoesthetic (numb to the touch). I'd yet to lose my sense of taste. I'd never used it during my trance. Learning what my mark ate every morning for breakfast didn't seem useful.

Right away, the lack of smells hit me like it always did. Losing my most powerful sense was awful, worse than dumpster diving and inhaling the rotten juices like crack cocaine would be. I was sure of it. The way the air just went blank, dead, deeply unnerved me and left me feeling unmoored. The silence, I could handle. The peace, the solitude in the absence of all sound wasn't bad. But the lack of scents... too weird.

Rosalina signed, her hands moving as she formed the word "read." She held up her e-reader.

I said "yes" but didn't hear myself.

She and I were studying sign language so we could communicate. It had been her idea. She also tried hard to make the periods when I was deaf as comfortable, stress-free, and restful as possible. Reading did the trick.

Her head snapped up, her brows drawing together as she listened for something.

"What is it?" I asked.

She beat her fist on her open palm to indicate someone was knocking at the door. In one fluid motion, she jumped to her feet, her back turned and stiff.

Shit! Something told me the knocking wasn't friendly.

I scrambled out of bed woozily, imagining another Beetlejuice trying to tear the door down. My weak legs protested as I stood.

God, they've found us!

I glanced around, searching for something to use as a weapon. The bedside lamp screamed, "pick me!" I clumsily threw its shade on the bed, unplugged it, and held the base like a bat, ready to hit whoever walked through the door right in the gonads, because I was certain the intruder had a pair of them. My arms trembled like ramen noodles.

Rosalina's shoulders relaxed.

Huh? No Beetlejuice?

She turned and glanced at the lamp and my threatening stance. She laughed and shrugged, seeming to say, *"Yeah, sure, go ahead and leave him gonadless."*

I was confused, to say the least.

Rosalina signed for me to put the lamp down, then painstakingly formed four letters with her fingers.

J-A-K-E.

I rolled my eyes. "Ugh, I'm going to kill him."

Why in the hell couldn't he leave us alone?

CHAPTER 14

"Tell him I'm not here," I told Rosalina.

She nodded, walked out of the bedroom, and closed the door. I sat at the edge of the bed, biting my thumbnail and bouncing my knee.

How in the name of a million witchlights had he found us?

It's my job to know things, I heard his obnoxiously sexy voice inside my head.

This was the worst possible time for Jake to show up. I had purposely kept the side effects of my powers secret from him. At the time, I'd been afraid he would refuse to let me use them. Losing my senses was traumatic, but that wasn't the only problem. When I tracked people in trouble, I got a full blast of what they felt. Fear, desperation, despair, pain.

Mate tracking was a walk in the park compared to that.

Now, it didn't matter if Jake found out, but my burden felt private, and I didn't think he deserved to know.

My heart pounded in my chest as I tried to imagine why he'd come. What was he telling Rosalina out there? Had something—

The door to the bedroom slammed open, and Jake stormed in, Rosalina hot on his heels, pulling on his massive biceps with no effect. His mouth was moving at a thousand miles per hour, and I had no godly or ungodly idea what he was saying.

My gaze darted from him to Rosalina, my eyes practically screaming for help. She took a step back out of Jake's line of vision and began signing. She tripped over the words in the worst possible way. And I didn't blame her because I doubted even one of those professional TV interpreters used during press conferences would've been able to keep up with Jake's twaddle. Honestly, it had to be twaddle. No one could move their mouth that fast and make any sense.

Rosalina signed something that read like "Pink puppies have taken over the White House."

I stared at her, open-mouthed. "What?"

She tried again. "Finger, fucking finger."

What was she going on about? Whatever it was it sounded dirty. Or did she want me to give Jake the finger? I'd gladly do it, but I didn't want to be out of context. It would let him know I had no clue what was going on.

Jake glared at me, his frown causing that little groove between his eyebrows to appear. He seemed expectant, probably waiting for me to say something. Rosalina signed some more, but I couldn't make heads or tails out of any of it. Jake's attention snapped to Rosalina.

Her hands froze in midair. She smiled awkwardly and smoothed her dress, trying to act nonchalant. Holy goblins, she would starve in Hollywood.

Jake made a "what's wrong with you?" face, then he grabbed her by the arm, led her out of the room, and clicked the lock behind her.

"Hey, this is her place. You can't do that," I said, furious at his nerve.

He whirled, his lips already moving faster than Mom's when she found out I'd been out past curfew. I backed away as if his silent words were lashes. He pressed forward, driving me against the bed, and kept ranting.

I'm freaking deaf, right now. I've no idea what you're saying, I wanted to yell in his face, but I couldn't. I didn't want him to know anything else about me. Once, I'd given him everything. I'd opened up about my feelings, my teenage secrets, and fears. And how had he treated me?

Nope. Not doing that again.

"Stop!" I pushed him out of the way.

As Jake staggered backward, I rounded the bed and walked to the window, my back to him.

The thing about not being able to hear… it allowed me to shut the world away. I squeezed my eyes shut, picturing Jake behind me, still ranting about helping him find Stephen. I couldn't imagine anything else bringing him here. He'd come back from the past with a one-track mind and a bone to pick.

After a long moment, a hand settled on my shoulder. I glanced at it, hoping to find delicate, manicured fingers. But instead, I found Jake's large and strong ones. He made me turn, gently, which surprised me. However, the fury absent in his touch was evident in his stormy, silver eyes. His lips had stopped moving, and instead, formed a thin, unforgiving line.

Slowly, his hand slid from my shoulder down the length of my arm, unleashing a violent shiver across my body. Then, he pressed something into my hand and squeezed my fingers around it, until I crumpled what felt like a thick piece of paper.

He let go and took a step back. His head shook from side to side as disappointment and incredulity washed over him. Without another word, he walked away. As the door swung open in his wake, Rosalina appeared at the threshold.

Her expression told me everything I needed to know. Whatever had brought Jake here was bad. Really bad.

Afraid to look, I brought my hand up and unclenched my fist, releasing what turned out to be a Polaroid picture. Carefully, I smoothed it open and stared at the image in horror.

My stomach convulsed, and I dropped the gruesome photograph and ran to the bathroom.

With the image of a swollen, severed finger flashing before my eyes, I retched until my ribs ached.

There had been a caption under the photo that read: Stephen Erickson's Ring Finger.

CHAPTER 15

"Jake said a note arrived with the actual finger," Rosalina explained once my hearing had returned five hours later. "It also said that if Ulfen doesn't comply with their demands, they'll deliver Stephen's head next."

My stomach did a flip, then filled with about two tons of guilt.

We sat in her living room, several boxes of Chinese take-out strewn about the coffee table. Rosalina was on the sofa, and I was cross-legged on the rug, a greasy plate in front of me. After puking violently, no one should eat. At least that was what seemed reasonable, though I seemed to challenge that theory every time I threw up. I'd demolished an entire order of shrimp lo-mein all by myself.

"What are their demands?" I asked, patting my belly.

"I didn't exactly have a chance to ask. Jake is... something when he's mad."

I considered for a moment, avoiding Rosalina's gaze, fearing her reaction at the direction of my thoughts. She had kept me on a straight path for over a year. Without her, I wouldn't have gathered the pieces of my life back together. Hell, I would be addicted to drugs or scattered in pieces all over the city.

"Um," I started, my voice breaking, "please, don't be mad at me but—"

She shook her hands. "I already know what you're going to say."

"I *have* to help. If I don't, Stephen…"

"Stop! Do you really think you have to convince me? I thought it would be easy to coach you from the sidelines and tell you to stay out of it, but man, it's hard."

We both smiled sadly.

Her change of heart didn't surprise me. This was Rosalina, the woman who picked up stray teens off the streets and invited them to watch Netflix.

"Yes, it's really hard." I patted her hand.

She stood and started pacing along the coffee table. "I'm not even the one with the skills to help, and I can see why you got involved in this kind of stuff before, how Jake dragged you into it."

"And now, it's happening again." My voice sounded so resigned it scared me.

"It feels like giving up, doesn't it?"

I nodded. "Like Jake's winning."

"That's infuriating," Rosalina growled, picked up an egg roll, and bit its tip off.

Yep, totally infuriating. And yet, here I was, trapped by my damn morals and facing one single way out: tracking Stephen, even if it killed me.

Why, oh why did I have a Mother Theresa complex? A baby one, but still.

Rosalina gave me a sad smile. She knew me well enough to figure out what I'd decided.

"Early tomorrow," I said, "can you drop me off by Mom's. I think I need my car."

℘℧

At 7 AM the next day, Rosalina dropped me off in front of Mom's house, the place where I'd grown up.

The two-story cape cod had light gray siding and teal shutters. A white railing surrounded the teal-painted porch. The front door sat off to the side, flanked by hanging plants, matching teal porch steps leading straight to it.

I stood on the sidewalk for a long moment, a familiar heaviness weighing my heart down. I hadn't felt this way in a while, and I hadn't missed it. Mom wouldn't like this, not at all. I stretched my back, feeling stiff. I'd missed kickboxing class again last night, and it showed—not that I was in any shape to work out after a trance.

A car came driving up the street behind me. I felt it slow down, and out of nowhere, panic hit me. I hurried away from the curb, glancing over my shoulder as a sporty convertible came to a stop. A handsome teenage boy sat at the wheel of a black BMW. He angled his shoulders in my direction, resting his tan forearm casually on the steering wheel. He smiled, checking me out without shame.

"Good morning," he purred.

Damn, where did these kids get their confidence? It had to be the cars they drove, had to be.

He was handsome. I had to give him that. Large brown eyes, trendy brown hair, strong jaw, and GQ features the envy of the Sexiest Man Alive, whoever they'd picked this year.

"Good morning," I replied with a raised eyebrow.

"You must be Lucia's sister."

92

"And you are… ?"

"Connor, her boyfriend."

"I see. I'll tell her you're here." I turned and walked toward the door, sure the kid was checking out my ass. I resisted the urge to glance back and give him the finger. Funny how I kept calling him a kid, but I wasn't that much older. Three years at most.

The moment I stepped onto the stoop, I breathed a sigh of relief. Home was safe. It had always been. Mom kept protection spells around the entire property capable of stopping intruders, magical attacks, and horny boyfriends. I glanced back at Connor and found that, indeed, he was admiring my posterior. I sighed.

I placed a hand on the door handle, and it unlocked for me. This was also part of Mom's spell. No one who'd ever lived in the house would be kept out. Protection spells were her specialty. She could have probably made a lot of money casting them over businesses and homes, but she never cared about money, only about protecting her own.

Closing the door behind me, I walked in. The smell of breakfast sausage wafted through the air. I placed my purse on the console table and took a moment to peer at the portrait that hung above it. Six people peered down at me. My parents, brother, two sisters, and a younger version of me. It had been taken when I was fifteen, the last year we would all be together, before Leo moved out to travel the world. I'd only seen him twice since then: the first Christmas after he moved out, and during Dad's funeral. Now, only Lucia still lived at home, and even she would be graduating soon.

Dad was a Stale, but all his children were Skews because of Mom. She came from a long line of witches, mages, trackers, healers, you name it. Leo, her eldest, was a skillful mage. Daniella, her second was a witch with great healing abilities. I was a tracker, and Lucia, the youngest, also a witch with strong telekinetic powers. We all had a variety of skills that seemed to keep changing and growing with time.

Nonna had been a tracker, too, which allowed Mom to pinpoint what I was early on. When Snitch, our dog, went missing, and I found him twenty blocks away from home, his chew rope in my tiny five-year-old hand, Mom knew. After that, she let me spend summers with Nonna in upstate New York, and I trained with her. She called me her little hound and said I had more talent in my pinky than she ever did in her whole body. She taught me everything she knew and suggested I trained with others to explore the depths of my powers, which she insisted hadn't peaked yet. But that sort of training was expensive, and I was happy with what Nonna had taught me.

I crossed the foyer into the living room. The decor hadn't changed in years, same tan sofa, same walnut TV cabinet, same scratched end tables, same lamps with tasseled shades, same faux Persian rug.

Wishing to catch Mom and Lucia in their natural habitat, I peeked around the corner. My sister sat at the kitchen table, while mom stood in front of the stove, her back turned. Lucia was wiggling her fingers, her eyebrows furrowed in concentration. I followed her gaze and realized she was using her magic to nick a twenty-dollar bill out of Mom's pocketbook, which rested on the island.

My mouth dropped open as I watched the bill float in Lucia's direction. *Really?!* I tried to decide what to do. Should I stop her? I never stole from Mom or Dad—no matter how desperate I got. This was wrong.

But if I said something, Lucia would get mad at me, which might be counterproductive at the moment, considering the hot boyfriend outside and her need to steal money—a sign that she might be in some kind of trouble and in need of a conversation with her Big Sis. I decided *mum* was the word.

Just as Lucia was about to snatch the bill from the air, Mom suddenly whirled and pointed a spatula straight at my sister.

"Gotcha!" she exclaimed, a gleeful look in her eyes.

"Oh, c'mon," Lucia whined. "I almost had it."

Mom noticed me then. "Antonietta!"

She set down her spatula, turned off the stove, and ambled over to wrap me in her arms.

Mom was a petite fifty-one-year-old woman with a few extra pounds "stocked-piled for the apocalypse," her words not mine. In her youth, she'd been 125 pounds of pure curves and sex appeal, also her words. Now, she was critical of herself, though she had no reason to be. She speed-walked circles around the neighborhood and, in my opinion, and probably the opinion of half the middle-aged men in The Hill, she looked fine in her yoga pants.

"How long have you been standing there?" Mom asked with a huge smile. She looked very pretty with her hair and makeup already done, and her colorful apron that read "I don't need a recipe... I'm Italian." We'd all inherited her golden tone and brown eyes as opposed to Dad's paleness and blue eyes.

"Long enough to witness Lucia's attempt at thievery." I gave my sister a raised eyebrow.

"What's up, Toni?"

"Hey, Luz."

She nodded and walked toward the island. She was wearing skinny jeans with holes, black Converse, and a red hoodie. Her long, brown hair was loosely curled and flowing down her back, and she had those perfect, symmetrical eyebrows that made me suspect she watched the same YouTube videos Rosalina did.

"I'll get it next time, Mom." She stuffed the twenty in the pocketbook. "You'll see."

"You're welcome to try," Mom said in a singsong voice.

I walked to the stove, snatched a piece of sausage from the skillet, and popped it in my mouth. "What's this all about?" I mumbled.

"Just a bet she and I have," Mom said. "If she can take the money without me noticing, she can keep it."

"How's that an appropriate game? And how come you never played it with me?"

Mom put her hands on her hips. "Hey, with only the two of us 'round here, we have to keep things interesting."

Lucia glanced past the threshold, toward the living room, frowning. "Connor is late."

"Oops," I *thunked* my head with the heel of my hand. "I was supposed to tell you he's out there."

"Gotta go." She popped a forkful of eggs into her mouth, picked up her backpack, and pointed an adamant finger in my direction. "You need to come back at a better time so we can talk."

"I will," I promised and returned her hug as she leaned over and squeezed me.

With a smile, Lucia turned on her heel and rushed out of the house.

"Do you know this Connor guy?" I asked Mom when I heard the front door close.

"He's Lia Baresi's kid. He gets good grades, brings her home before curfew, and brings me chocolate. I think that's all I need to know."

God, how things had changed! The list of things she used to require from Daniella's boyfriends as well as mine was way longer and meaner than that.

Mom served two plates and set them on the table. She also poured me a cup of black tea, her favorite thing to drink in the morning.

"How are you, honey?" Mom scanned me carefully. "Are you feeling well?"

"I guess."

"Any headaches?"

"Just one the other day." Mom worried too much. Since I was little, headaches bothered me every once in a while, and she pestered me about them all the time.

Mom pursed her lips, looking worried. I sipped my tea and glanced around the kitchen, noting she'd gotten a new copper adornment to go on her knickknack shelf. She had a farm theme going, and she'd added a rooster.

"So what brings you here this early?" Mom asked with a slight frown that let me know she already suspected something was up.

"Um, I came to get the car. I'll need it for a few days."

The car was a convertible 1970 Camaro Z28 in light blue with two black stripes running down the hood. It had belonged to Dad and was now mine. I kept it here, stored in Mom's garage since I didn't need to drive anywhere most of the time. I lived, ate, satisfied my salted-caramel ice cream cravings, and got my clothes dry cleaned all on the same street. In the end, it was cheaper to Uber when I needed a ride.

"How come?" Mom narrowed her mascaraed eyes.

I shrugged one shoulder and shoveled sausage into my mouth until I felt like a squirrel getting ready for winter. I had never been able to lie to Mom. I thought getting older would help, but the woman's eyes were like squishy lie detectors.

She waved her fork around. "Are you done?"

I swallowed thickly and plastered on a smile. "Good sausage, Mom."

"Same sausage you've been eating for twenty years. From DiGregorio's. Now, spit it out."

I wrinkled my nose. "That would just be gross."

Mom gave a tired sigh and patiently waited for me to break down and spill every single bean. I pondered how to start: the piecemeal method or the ripped-off-the-Band-Aid one. After a moment's thought, I decided the former had no real benefits, the chew-out would be the same either way. Besides, she would eventually find out. She always did. Gossip spread through The Hill like a tsunami.

"I need the car because I'm staying with Rosalina, and I gotta go to the police station to talk to Tom to tell him I'm gonna help him track Stephen Erickson." No doubt she'd read the papers and knew of the kidnapping and the brewing war, so I didn't elaborate. And cleverly, I left out all mention of Jake.

Mom did a slow blink as she processed what I'd just said. As the full meaning of my words hit, her face went red. I winced, waiting for it: a rant, a scolding, an are-you-out-of-your-mind? But all I got was a "hmm" before she resumed pushing pieces of egg around the plate.

Odd.

I sipped my tea and watched her over the rim of the cup. I waited. Still nothing. I should've considered myself lucky and left it at that, but I was a glutton for punishment.

"No... disapproving words?"

"Oh, there are plenty of them spinning 'round in my head," she admitted.

"But...?"

She picked up both our plates and took them to the sink. "But I think you know what they are." She scraped the leftovers into the garbage disposal, then pulled the Camaro's keys out of the junk drawer.

"Here you go." She deposited them in my hand.

I frowned at The Gateway Arch keychain. Dad had gotten it during our first and only visit to the monument. He had let me pick it and said, "For *our* car." I was the only one ever interested in helping him work on it after he got it. Leo had already left home, and Daniella and Lucia didn't care about getting their hands greasy or spending hours polishing metal to a perfect shine. More than anything, I'd loved spending time with Dad.

Mom laid a hand on my shoulder.

I glanced up.

"In the past year," she said, "you've surprised me with your decisions and everything you've done to pull yourself out of a dark place. You're a big girl now, Antonietta. And big girls make their own decisions."

Aw, that was nice. It sounded like Mom finally trusted me.

Should I tell her about Jacob Knight's involvement?

Nah, that would just undo a very nice moment.

Mom smiled. "I'd like you to come for lunch one day this week. I'll cook you creamy tortellini."

Yum, my favorite!

"Just take care," Mom added, "and don't get tangled up with Jake Knight again, m-kay?"

₮℞

I drove the Camaro with the top down, enjoying the way the engine roared and the wind blew in my hair. When I approached the police department, I prolonged the inevitable and took a few laps around the block, enjoying myself a little more.

Finally, I parked in a spill-over lot and crossed the street, almost turning tail a couple of times, though the image of that severed finger quickly set me back on track. I was glad I could work on this with Tom. He would have my back and wouldn't try to take advantage of me. I wouldn't want to work with anyone else in the police department. Too many crooked cops.

A small white van sat in front of the door, a logo that read "Vinnie's Donuts" stamped on the side.

A woman was digging in the back, stacking several boxes on top of each other. Despite my nice breakfast at Mom's, a donut sounded pretty good, preferably a chocolate sprinkle one. Maybe Tom would give me one.

To my dismay, when I walked in, the first person I saw was Jake Knight. He was talking to a uniformed police woman and noticed me before I had a chance to scurry back outside. Immediately, he apologized to the officer and marched in my direction.

Dammit! I wished I knew what he drove, so I could avoid him. The woman with the donuts walked past me headed for the front desk. She deposited her load on a far corner of the counter and walked back out at a clipped pace. She gave me a dirty look when she noticed me watching her.

Disgruntled much?! She probably hated donuts and any *donut-vores* that gave her dreamy eyes as if she were some sort of candy fairy.

"What are you doing here?" Jake asked sarcastically. "Come to ask about your *break-in?*"

"None of your business," I answered like a twelve-year-old, but hey, he'd started it.

He was wearing an aviator jacket with a plain white T-shirt inside. His jeans were well-worn and molded to his muscular thighs like soft butter molds to toast. *Hot damn!*

A couple of female officers walked by and blatantly checked out his derrière, reminding me of high school all over again.

"Yeah, guess it isn't any of my business," he said.

Just as he started to leave, Detective Tom Freeman walked out of his office and waved. I gave him a smile. Jake glanced back over his shoulder and glared at the detective.

Then, the donuts exploded.

CHAPTER 16

The world rumbled, and I flew off my feet and slammed against the wall behind me. The back of my head hit with a *thunk*, and stars exploded in my vision. I collapsed to the floor like a puppet. Something heavy fell on top of me. Heat enveloped me, making me feel as if my skin would peel off and melt away into a puddle. My ears rang.

Cries of pain filled the air. I shifted, sending a stab of agony down my spine. I pushed at whatever was on top of me. A person. Jake. I could tell by his unmistakable scent.

I touched something wet and thick. I struggled to open my eyes against the heat. I barely managed. Jake was unconscious.

Everything around us was destruction. A twisted chair lay on top of Jake. I pushed it off with some effort. It rolled out of the way with a clank. Above us, ceiling tiles hung loose, exposing thick pipes and short-circuiting cables torn by the explosion. Light flickered.

Someone lay on their stomach a few feet away, the police woman who'd been talking to Jake. Her clothes were scorched, and a ragged hole oozed blood on her side. I clenched my eyes shut and pushed Jake off me, halfway wiggling from under his heavy frame.

The back of my head and spine screamed in pain, but as I assessed myself, I found no other injuries. Jake, on the other hand. My stomach did a flip at the sight of his back. I pressed a hand to my mouth. His aviator jacket and T-shirt were riddled with holes, and so was his back. He looked as if he'd been hit with a shotgun. There was a bigger wound in his right hamstring. Blood dribbled from it, rapidly staining his jeans crimson. God, he had taken the brunt of the explosion, which had saved my life.

With his werewolf powers, he would heal but not if he didn't get medical attention. Now!

I glanced around at all the chaos, the bodies. A numb stupor threatened to take hold of me. I tore my eyes away from the destruction and forced myself to focus on Jake.

"Hey." I caressed the side of his face. "Jake, wake up."

My throat felt raw. I winced as the heat that blazed by the front desk flared up, igniting the ceiling.

"Jake!" I shook him.

He moaned and blinked his eyes open.

Oh, thank God. "We have to get out of here. C'mon, help me."

I rolled him over onto his back. He gritted his teeth in pain and growled.

"I'm sorry. I'm sorry. I'm sorry," I repeated nonsensically.

Hooking my hands under his armpits, I tried pulling him to a sitting position, but he was too heavy. His boots slipped on a fallen ceiling tile as he attempted to help me. I tried harder, leaning into him, my cheek pressed to his.

"C'mon, you can get up," I whispered in his ear. "You can do it."

He bent his knees and pushed up. I pushed, too, helping him get close to the wall for support.

"Freeman," Jake rasped.

"I know." My heart twisted, hoping against all hope that Tom was all right. "First, let's get *you* out of here."

I coughed and closed my eyes against the acrid smoke. We started walking, Jake's arm across my shoulders. My back throbbed with the added weight. The fire behind us flared higher. I felt it on my back, like a giant rake trying to strip me down to the bone. The smell of burning hair pierced through my senses.

The exit sign glowed on the wall along with a flashing emergency light. Charred furniture blocked the door, which seemed miles away. We would never make it. Jake lost his footing, and we staggered forward and fell.

"Crawl," I said, but I knew it was useless. He could barely move.

He gave me a push. "Get out of here, Toni."

"No, I won't leave you."

The ceiling tiles above us crackled as they burned. My eyelids fluttered, then closed. My chest moved shallowly. I rested my head on the floor and coughed weakly. This was it.

Crap, I hadn't even started helping, and it had all gone to shit already. No good deed goes unpunished—not even ones that hadn't begun yet.

The front door burst open. Flames whooshed towards it. Jake and I huddled close together as they licked the air above us. I covered my face with both hands. My exposed skin sizzled, and I moaned in pain.

Firefighters rushed in, pulling at a hose and spraying water. Two men wearing masks rushed in and pulled us out, our feet dragging behind us. I was out first, then Jake. Others came to help. They grabbed our feet, lifted us off the ground, and deposited us across the street on a patch of grass.

Paramedics rushed to us, pressed oxygen masks to our faces. Healers moved their hands over our bodies, and the pain subsided a little.

I lifted a hand towards the burning building. "The others," I mumbled behind the mask.

"We'll help them, honey," the paramedic said. "You did good. You did good. Now just breathe."

As if I'd just woken up from a tracking trance, everything before me turned dark, and I couldn't hear or see anything anymore.

CHAPTER 17

I wanted to know who the hell had taken my clothes off and left me in a hospital gown with a huge slit down my ass. Really? Wasn't it enough to have burned half to death but they also had to strip me of my dignity and undies in the process? At least my phone and car keys had survived and sat on the night table.

Standing next to a tall bed with railings, I fumbled with the strings behind my back, trying to tie them in a way that would cover both butt cheeks. I needed to get out of this sterile room and find Jake and Tom and... all those officers who had been busy at work, the woman Jake had been talking to.

My hands trembled. I couldn't tie a simple knot. I growled in frustration and stared at my fingers. They looked different, covered in newly healed skin. I'd been lucky, the healer doctor had said. She'd had to give me morphine for the pain while she worked on me for over an hour, restoring the skin on my forearms and hands, but the injuries had been superficial enough to only need an outpatient procedure. My back felt strange too, same as my fingers, but the pain was gone. I could still smell burning hair all around me. I would need a haircut, for sure.

Lucky, she'd said, which made me wonder... what did that mean for the others?

Determined to get some questions answered, I reached toward my back again, fumbling for the strings. I'd finally grabbed hold of them when the door to my room swung open. Jake stood at the threshold. His silver eyes held mine for a long moment, then he let out a pent-up breath and walked in.

He wore a gown just like mine and stood barefoot. He had been worse off than me, but he seemed fully healed, too. Oh, the benefits of being a werewolf. I envied him that.

He closed the door behind him and approached. Without a word, he came around and tied the strings at my back. He was probably getting a full view of my backside, but I didn't care. Not at the moment.

When he finished and walked back around, I said, "You all right?"

He made a sound in the back of his throat and nodded once.

"Freeman?"

He shook his head. "I don't know. I came to check on you first. Let's go find out."

Jake and I walked out of my room and headed toward the nurses' station, our bare feet slapping on the linoleum floor.

One of the nurses glanced up from her computer and frowned at us. "What are you doing out of bed?"

"Werewolf." Jake pointed at his chest as a way of explanation.

The nurse raised her eyebrows and nodded as if saying "okay, fine," then glanced at me. "And what about you?"

"We need to know where Tom Freeman is. Is he on this floor?" I glanced down the long corridor as if I expected an arrow to appear in midair, pointing us toward the detective's room.

The nurse frowned at us. "Is he a relative of yours?"

"Listen," Jake said, leaning over the counter and staring her down, "we were in that explosion with him. I think that gives us the right to ask how he is."

It really didn't, but it kinda made sense. The nurse thought so too because she sighed and tapped a few keys into her computer.

"Tom Freeman," she read. "He's in the intensive care unit on the second floor. Doctors and healers are working on him. He's scheduled for a second surgery tomorrow." She glanced up. "His injuries must have been substantial."

"Will he recover?" My voice quivered.

"You'll have to talk directly to his doctors and healers to find out more."

"What about the other people in the station?" Jake asked.

The nurse sighed. "Names?"

Jake shrugged.

She gave us an unapologetic head-shake. "I'm sorry. I wouldn't know."

We thanked her and walked back to my room. I sat on the bed, feeling confused and unsure of what to do next.

Jake remained by the door, a hand on the handle. I blinked at him, vaguely wondering why he was just standing there, looking uncomfortable, and I didn't think it was just the unflattering gown.

At last, he blurted out, "Thank you."

I cocked my head, frowning and, of all things, wondering if he was wearing anything under the gown.

"You know… for helping me… back at the station."

I shook my head and struggled to focus on what he'd just said. Then the penny dropped. "You don't have to thank me."

"I think I do."

"No, you don't. I would have done that for anyone, even a stranger."

"Oh." He lowered his gaze and started backing out of the room.

"Jake, I... I didn't mean it like that."

"It's fine. It doesn't matter. Look, I hope you feel better soon. I can tell you're still..." he waved a hand around his head as if suggesting I wasn't all there at the moment. "Anyway, I'll see you around."

"Are you leaving?"

He nodded. "There isn't much time left for Stephen. That explosion... I'm sure it was Fiore and her people. They want to delay the police effort, throw them for a loop. The detectives were closing in on them. Now, they'll be occupied with this mess. I have to find him before it's too late." He turned to go, the gown fluttering around his muscular calves.

"Wait!"

He glanced over his shoulder, a muscle jumping in his jaw, his eyes all pupil, dark like onyx.

"Um, I didn't go to the station to... ask about the break-in." I paused to let that sink in.

When it did, one of his thick eyebrows rose. "I see."

His mouth stretched in a smile that made me feel tingly all over. His demeanor, which had been stiff and guarded, relaxed a bit, giving me a flashback to the tenderness I knew him capable of. He extended a hand in my direction, palm up.

"Come with me?" he said, his timbre soft and hopeful.

"Like this?" I gestured towards my hospital gown, then his.

He shrugged as if he didn't have a care in the world, and why should he? The moment he got outside, he could shift and thick, beautiful gray fur would cover him. Though not if I went with him, I supposed.

I returned his shrug, grabbed my phone and keys, and took his hand. His fingers tightened around mine. They were warm in my freezing hand and felt delicious. His temperature ran a little high all the time, a werewolf thing. It immediately reminded me of the many nights I'd spent in the heat of his arms.

God, was this a mistake? Would he ruin my life again?

For an instant, the urge to pull back came over me. I could wait to talk to Tom. He would get better soon, wouldn't he? Or maybe I could talk to someone else at the police department who would hire me for the job, and provide the protection I needed. But who could I trust? Tom was the only one I knew. Besides, the time wasted trying to find someone else could make the difference between getting Stephen back in one piece and never seeing him again.

There was no time.

So when Jake gently tugged on my hand, I went with him, and we padded down the hall, our asses hanging out in the air.

CHAPTER 18

From the hospital, Jake and I *Ubered* to the police station. Yellow tape surrounded the entire building, and there were no signs of activity.

Only a handful of hours ago, it must have been a madhouse of firefighters, detectives, bomb squad personnel, reporters, and gawkers. Now, with twilight falling quickly, the place felt like a spook house.

A few cars remained in the spill-over parking lot, including my Camaro. I breathed a sigh of relief at the sight of it.

"Where's your ride?" I asked Jake, glancing around.

"Around the corner, but I have to get a spare key. I don't know what happened to mine. I'll get it later."

From there, I drove to Jake's office, where he changed into jeans, a Y-neck shirt, a black moto jacket, and biker boots with buckles on the sides and a heel that added an inch to his height—not that he needed it. He also picked up a duffel bag with a change of clothes and some necessities. Apparently, like me, he'd made the place his home, and we were neighbors in more ways than one.

Afterward, we drove to Rosalina's. I called her on the way there to tell her to expect visitors and quickly explained what had happened.

Twenty minutes later, we sat in her living room. I'd changed into comfortable jeans and tank top, glad to be rid of the stupid buttless gown. I sat cross-legged on the love seat, and Jake occupied the large sofa across from me, while Rosalina sat to the side in an armchair, her large green eyes going back and forth between us.

She still seemed in shock at the events and at the fact that Jacob Knight was in her condo and not even yelling at anyone—not something either one of us could have foreseen.

After rescuing me from the streets, Rosalina also rescued me from the hole Jake left in my life. I'd lost count of how many nights I'd spent sobbing and cursing Jake's name while she comforted me and came up with creative insults to make me laugh. Cunning canine, bloody bitch, lousy lycanthrope. She loved alliteration.

"Toni, I understand you're in pain," she'd said once. "You love him, and there's nothing wrong with that. All our lives they teach us to give, to nurture, to put ourselves last, but I'm telling you that this notion is all wrong. I'm not saying you shouldn't love, just that you should love yourself a little bit more. Men can be real assholes."

"Jake isn't like that," I blubbered.

"Still, he left you without an explanation, and now look at you. You're falling apart, but you still have a life to live. For yourself, whether or not he's here. And you have to choose to live better than this because you'd better believe he's out there having fun and not bawling his eyes out to a friend."

At the time, I had wanted to believe that he missed me as much as I did, but why would he inflict that kind of pain on himself when he could've come back and told me he loved me, and I would've welcomed him with open arms as if he'd never left.

It took a couple of weeks, but Rosalina's advice finally started to make sense. I'd felt less than whole without Jake, but I finally learned that I wasn't. I was still one-hundred percent Antonietta Luna Sunder. With or without Jake, I had a life to live, and it could be a good one. Then time showed me that, indeed, it was. I still had a heck-of-a-lot to live for, even if I didn't think another man could ever measure up to Jake, even if I suspected he'd broken my heart for good, and it would never function properly again. Hell, it hadn't functioned properly with Stephen. I had liked him, but without passion.

And now, here he was, sitting in front of me, looking hotter than he ever had, and resurrecting all kinds of memories from the mental attic where I'd stuffed them.

God, this is *a terrible idea.*

Maybe if I didn't look at him. My eyes flicked to Rosalina as I figuratively strapped on my big girl panties and reminded myself that, for a year, I'd been happy because I'd taken care of the person who mattered most in the world…

Toni.

Rosalina smiled at me. All in all, she was handling this well, though the slight pinch of her eyebrows didn't escape my notice. Behind her nonchalant exterior, she was judging. Hard.

I cleared my throat and met Jake's gaze. "Okay, so… I will help you, but first, I want to understand why Ulfen won't give the kidnappers what they want. If he can bring his son home, and he's just being an ass about it, I'm not going to risk my life."

"Ulfen can't give them what they want because their demands are ridiculous. They aren't made in good faith."

"Why not?"

"They want his pack to leave St. Louis."

"What?! That *is* ridiculous."

Werewolves and their packs were territorial as hell. If Erickson and his people left their homes—which was as likely as the Fae leaving Elf-hame—they would find conflict everywhere they went. Other packs would chase them away the moment they tried to settle in their territory. Not to mention that, as an alpha, Ulfen's job was to protect his pack, above everything else, even his family. Besides, who gave Bernadetta the right to try to kick anyone out of their homes? *The nerve!*

"Okay, I'll play," I said, "but you have to promise that, after this, you'll leave me alone."

Jake's eyes narrowed. He wasn't a promise kind of guy. In fact, he hated promises. He'd told me so repeatedly in the past, and I'd never been able to extract a vow from him, no matter how small.

He hesitated for a long moment, but at last, he inclined his head, solemnly. "I promise."

"Good." I swallowed thickly, a funny feeling in the pit of my stomach. Was this promise what I really wanted from him? God, I'd thought I'd gotten over this man, but maybe I was just full of crap. I pushed those thoughts aside and got to business.

"Now, first things first," I said. "I'll need something of Stephen's. You know how it works." When I needed to find a known mark and had an item that belonged to them, I didn't need to brew a potion, which would save time. An excellent prospect since the sooner I could finish this, the sooner I could get back to normal.

Jake sighed in frustration. "I've been trying to get my hands on such an item since I got back into town, but I haven't been able to."

I frowned. "Wait, I thought you two were close friends."

"Yes, but his place burned to the ground, and his office was ransacked like yours. They took every personal item that could be used for tracking, so I got nothing."

"Then we need to talk to his father," I said. "Ulfen must have something of his son. Or a girlfriend… How about a girlfriend?"

"Stephen wasn't seeing anyone and Ulfen… um… he's not cooperating."

"What do you mean? I thought he hired you."

"I lied. Actually, he blames me for some of Stephen's behavior. He's warned me not to bother him again unless I want his pack to tear me to pieces."

Rosalina left her chair and slowly walked backward into the kitchen. Every few seconds, she stuck her head out to listen, then finally came back out with a bag of microwave popcorn. She retook her seat, opened the popcorn, and started eating as if she were at the movie theater.

Jake and I gave her a sideways glance, then refocused.

"What behavior?" I asked, then shook my hands in front of me. "Never mind, I don't need to know about that. All I need is for you to bring me something that belongs to Stephen, so I can get to work."

"Haven't you been listening? I told you I don't have anything."

I flipped my hands, palms up, and gave him an annoyed glare. "Then how the hell do you expect me to track him?"

"*You* can talk to Ulfen, tell him you're willing to help."

I sputtered a laugh. "That's your plan?"

He nodded, giving me a look that seemed to say "there's nothing wrong with my plan."

"If you truly were close friends with Stephen, he would have told you that his father hates me."

Rosalina made a sound of agreement in the back of her throat. She was too busy stuffing popcorn into her mouth and licking her fingers to do much else.

"Stephen did tell me what happened. I know Ulfen hates you for the same reasons he hates me. He thinks you were pulling Stephen away from his duties. But when you offer to track Stephen, he'll put all that aside."

Rosalina raised her hand as if she were in school. We glanced in her direction.

"You don't have to raise your hand," I said. "What is it?"

"This is something I've been wondering. Ulfen Erickson is loaded, hasn't he already paid someone to track his son?"

Jake nodded. "In fact, he has. Several trackers, but they've all failed. Ulfen's people have been all over the city chasing their useless leads. Fiore is good. She must have someone running interference, botching the tracking spells. I don't know."

"So what makes you think *I'll* succeed?" I asked, confused.

He huffed. "You're a much better tracker than any of those bozos. Besides, you know Stephen. You had a close relationship with him. You know that can play a role."

It was true. Once you connected with someone at a certain level, it was easier to find them. That was why I had never tried to track Jake, even though he'd left one lonely T-shirt behind. I found it under the bed when I vacated the apartment. It was the only thing he didn't pack, and it had been an oversight. Clearly, he hadn't wanted me to find him, and I'd, at least, had enough pride not to go chasing after him—even if I did sob my eyeballs out.

I stood and began pacing in front of the love seat, a hand pressed to my forehead. "I don't know, Jake. Ulfen will probably kick me out, too."

"You have to give it a try. I feel that you're Stephen's last hope."

"*Sheesh!*" Rosalina exclaimed. "Don't tell her that. It's already bad enough."

Jake's jaw tensed, and he gave my friend one of those intense looks that could make guys twice his size cower under a table. Rosalina pushed to the edge of her chair and met his mean glare with one of her own. She wasn't easily intimidated—even by a werewolf.

"Jake," I warned. "This is *her* place, and you need to respect that."

I almost felt Jake reeling his anger in as if it were a huge, thrashing shark that had smelled blood. He didn't like anyone telling him what to do and what *not* to do. It was the alpha in him. It had always been a problem. He inhaled sharply and gave Rosalina an apologetic nod.

I brought us back to the matter at hand. "So we go see Ulfen tomorrow and—"

"Tomorrow?" Jake rose to his feet, gaping at me as if I'd lost my mind. "We can't wait. We only have four more days to find Stephen."

"What?! Why didn't you mention this before."

"I did." Jake regarded me with a deep frown, looking confused.

Oh, shit! He must have said it when I was deaf. I glared at Rosalina. Why didn't *she* mention this before? She gave me a forced grin and a tiny shrug.

I pretended to smooth one of my eyebrows while I hid my face behind my hand. "Um, yes, you did. I just... I don't know... the explosion and everything… it's all moving so fast." I glanced at Jake through a gap between my fingers.

He was still frowning, and I could tell he didn't quite buy what I was saying.

"So we go now?" I said, half statement, half question.

He nodded.

"Where do we go? Ulfen's house?"

"No. His house is a fortress. We wouldn't get past the front gate. But I know where to find him."

As we prepared to leave, Rosalina held my hands tightly. "Be careful,"

I gave her a reassuring squeeze. "I'll do it just this once, then we get back on track."

"I know."

I left with Jake, fighting the conflicting emotions that crowded my chest and reminding myself that this was all about saving a life, and *that* couldn't be a mistake.

CHAPTER 19

J ake sat in the passenger seat of my Camaro, which he'd pushed back to accommodate his long legs.

"I always loved this car," he said, petting the dashboard as if the car were a dog.

I started the engine, frowning. "Where to?"

His comment had sounded as if he was reminiscing about the good ol' times, and I didn't like it. That past hurt. I wanted to look forward, get this over with, and escort Jake and all this nonsense back out of my life.

He sat back and buckled up. "Get on I-44. I'll tell you where to get off."

We drove in silence for several minutes. The air felt thick, and I couldn't stop my hands from twisting over the wheel, making the leather squeak.

"That's starting to drive me crazy," he said as we got close to the Botanical Gardens exit.

"Sorry." I popped a piece of gum into my mouth and started chewing, focusing on keeping my hands still.

Jake tapped his fingers on his thigh, bouncing his knee nervously. I got fixated on the movement, and *it* started to drive *me* crazy.

"Can you stop?" I glanced at his nervous leg.

"Oh, sorry." He stopped and placed his hands flat on his thighs. He stared at them as if it were taking all his concentration to keep them still.

"This is awkward," I finally said, feeling stupid. I hadn't felt this inadequate in a very long time, and I didn't like it.

"It is," he admitted. I expected him to say more, but he just stared straight ahead. "Get off here."

I exited the interstate and took a right on South Vanderventer Ave. As I drove, trying not to think of the huge elephant inside the Camaro, one of Dad's pearls of wisdom came to me from the recesses of my memory.

"Always speak your mind, honey. I can't read your thoughts, and if you let me guess what you're thinking, I'll probably guess wrong. So just tell me, what the hell is on your mind?"

I smiled to myself.

"Something funny?" Jake asked.

I shook my head. "Just remembering Dad and something he used to tell me all the time."

He grew quiet again. A question buzzed inside my head, something I had asked the universe a thousand times after Jake left, except the universe had never answered. And now, the one person who could solve the puzzle was here, and I couldn't bring myself to ask. The worst part was… I was afraid of what he might say, of how his explanation might undo me once more—even if I'd learned to love myself properly, and I thought I understood my worth.

But who was I kidding? I *had* to know.

"Why did you leave?" I blurted out.

"I wish I could—" he said at the same time but stopped abruptly. He let out a sad chuckle that was deep and throaty.

"It's not funny." I pressed on the brake and stopped at a red light.

"No, it isn't. It's anything but."

He instructed me to take a right on Kentucky Ave and to park the car. We sat quietly for a moment after I shut off the engine.

I took a deep breath and let go of all the advice swimming in my head. It seemed like there were twenty people in there trying to tell me what to do. Dad, Mom, Daniella, Lucia, Rosalina, Tom. They'd all told me to forget Jake and not spend more time worrying about him. For better or worse, I stifled their murmurs and decided to just be me.

"I think we should talk," I said, without glancing in his direction. "I'd like to talk, to understand."

I waited for Jake's answer, watching him out of the corner of my eye. His fingers were digging into his thighs, and the hints of claws flashed for an instant. *That bad, huh?*

"Never mind," I said. "Just don't get blood in Dad's car, okay?"

Realizing what he was doing, he relaxed his hands. "I think talking will make things worse."

"Excuse me?" Anger flared inside of me, and words crowded inside my mouth.

Of course, you think talking is going to make things worse and prefer disappearing off the face of the earth. And why not? It's a hell of a lot easier.

That was what I wanted to say but anger didn't let me articulate it. Clearly, here lay the proof that all the advice swimming in my head was there for a good reason. People much smarter than me had been kind enough to provide it because they knew the stuff I came up with on my own sucked.

"Just forget it," I said. "It was just a brief moment of insanity that prompted me to ask."

He ran a hand through his hair, and I could feel the frustration leaving his body in waves, like ripples in the water after a rock breaks its surface. His energy felt like a rocket ready to blast off into space, and with no way out, it seemed a distinct possibility he might blow up inside my car.

Just when I thought he might go all supernova on me, he let out a pent-up breath, and as if making a decision that had cost him dearly, he angled his body in my direction and looked me in the eye.

"I never meant to hurt you," he said in a quiet tone that sent a shiver up my neck.

Something about his expression made my stomach shrink to the size of a pea. I could tell from the sadness in his eyes that he really believed that talking would be something we might regret.

But how could that be? Dad always said that talking was good, that letting your feelings stew was like building a bomb, that things left to interpretation would get twisted into lies and mistakes. Did his advice not apply in this case? Should I leave good enough alone like everyone had advised?

Yet, how could I live without knowing? How could I live believing something that might be a lie? And maybe Jake was mistaken, and once we talked, this hollow in my heart would go away, and I would be able to forgive him and live the rest of my life without shadows that belonged in the past.

I sighed. "Whether or not you meant to hurt me, you did."

"I'm sorry." His apology sounded sincere, and even though he'd broken my heart in two, I had no reason to doubt he truly felt sorry.

I wished he would say more, but he didn't, and that made me wonder if his silence was meant to spare me additional pain.

You don't need to know, Toni. You don't need to know.

After a long silence, he took a deep breath and glanced out the window. "Ready to face Ulfen?"

"As ready as I'm ever going to be."

CHAPTER 20

J ake took me to a club on The Grove, a bustling commercial district that extended for about a mile down Manchester Ave. The name of the club was The Chained Wolf, a place I'd seen before—Rosalina and I loved partying at The Grove—but had avoided it like mange because… well… werewolves and I just didn't mix.

I hadn't even known the club belonged to Ulfen Erickson, so now I had another reason to avoid it.

"Ulfen spends a lot of time here," Jake said, scowling at the sign, a neon design in purple, depicting a howling wolf with a ball and chain attached to one of its hind legs. Music blasted from within, and about ten people were waiting in line to get in.

This wasn't the type of place I would have guessed Ulfen Erickson would frequent, much less own. A club where yuppies met for Tinder hookups wasn't exactly a proper married-man hangout zone. Not that I ever got the impression he loved his wife. Stephen had always complained about the way Ulfen treated her. Apparently, infidelity had become one of his favorite pastimes. I would guess the club gave him ample opportunity to find young women to seduce.

"He thinks because he's an alpha he can do whatever he wants," Stephen had told me more than once, which made me wonder about the alpha *I* was currently tangled with. Jake certainly looked like the kind of man who could get away with doing whatever he wanted, including breaking a nineteen-year-old's heart. He was strong, attractive as hell, and—

Gah! I really needed to chuck these stupid thoughts in the garbage. Finding Stephen should be my whole focus. I would put *all* my senses into finding him and then get back to solving the love life problems of the rich and famous of St. Louis.

"Let's go through the back." Jake headed toward a side, dark alley.

"Why?"

"The bouncers have instructions to kick me to the curb on sight."

"Lovely."

At the back of the building, we waited behind a dumpster. The smell of dead rats wafted in the air. I held my breath while Jake kept an eye on the back entrance. Two bulbs on either side of the metal door provided the only illumination.

I'd just been about to ask how long he planned to wait when the door opened. Jake put an arm out in front of me, pressing my back against the wall, and squishing my boobs. *Really? Way to cop a feel, dude.* I held my breath as the sound of steps echoed in the alley. Something heavy crashed inside the dumpster. I spooked, and my heart skipped a beat, but I managed to bite my tongue and not make a sound.

The steps retreated after a couple of beats. Jake grabbed my hand and pulled me out of our hiding place. We dashed toward the door, which was slowly closing. He caught it just in time. His gaze locked on mine reassuringly. A little grin tipped his mouth as if we were playing some sort of hide and seek game. He had no qualms about this in the least.

Me, on the other hand, my heart was thumping out of control.

After a short moment, he nodded, pulled the door open, and we slipped inside. A long hall stretched in front of us, lined with boxes. I read some of the labels: Patron, Koval, Grey Goose. From the looks of it, they had enough booze to keep the young masses of St. Louis drunk for months on end. I could smell alcohol in the air.

"C'mon." Still holding my hand, Jake guided me down the hall.

At a fork ahead, he stopped and cautiously glanced in both directions, then we kept going. The sound of music grew louder as we approached a swinging door with an eye-level window. The bottles inside the boxes rattled with the beat of the music's low bass. Jake peered through the window, then pushed the door open, and we were in.

"See," he said, whispering into my ear so I could hear him over the loud music. "Piece of cake."

It didn't feel like a piece of cake at all. It felt like spicy jalapenos burning my throat and giving me heartburn. Ulfen was a dangerous werewolf. More dangerous than most, anyway.

The club was crowded, hopping with young couples out for a good time. A techno beat rattled all my internal organs, and strobe lights primed me for a category-four seizure. Most of the patrons appeared to be Stales, but my sharp nose told me otherwise. Plenty of supernaturals mingled in the crowd, shifter werewolves, most likely.

We walked further in, approaching a line of tall tables. People stood around them, chatting and drinking. Beyond the first row, another one followed, then came a crowded dance floor with fog twirling around the ravers' legs. A DJ and a group of dancers stood at the back on a raised platform, the centerpiece of the entire place.

On pedestals above the crowd, both men and women gyrated provocatively, wearing a variety of leather bottoms and tops that left little to the imagination. A blonde wrapped her legs around a pole, defying gravity, and a man mock whipped a were-cowboy with a crop. Many openly displayed their shifter traits, glowing eyes, furry ears, and claws, and playfully growled and howled as they danced.

I tore my eyes from the interesting scene, reminding myself that I hadn't come to check out the merchandise, no matter how hot.

To the left of the dance floor, a fully-stocked, busy bar glowed with neon strips, the bartenders dressed no different than the dancers on stage. They skillfully juggled liquor bottles and handed out drinks left and right.

"This way," Jake said, leading me forward.

Tucked in a corner, round tables and comfortable red-leather booths lined the wall. At the far end, Ulfen sat with a group of people: two men and four women.

"You go first," Jake said. "I'll be right behind you. He'll get pissed faster if he sees me first."

Which meant that, either way, the alpha was going to be pissed. Lucky me.

I swallowed thickly and took a deep breath, preparing for Ulfen's intimidating glares. Like Fiore, he had the reputation of being ruthless. Not that I needed to go by hearsay, I'd experienced his tough nature firsthand. He had always scared me. And the fact that Jake followed a step behind me did little to reassure me. This was Ulfen's place, which was packed with *his* people.

But we were here to offer our help. Even if he hated us, he had to listen.

Squaring my shoulders, I walked in his direction, radiating a confidence I didn't feel.

Fake it 'til you make it, baby!

Ulfen's nose twitched, and his eyes snapped in my direction, pinpointing me with the accuracy of a sniper. His upper lip rose, revealing his upper teeth. I pressed forward, my confidence growing as anger flared in my chest.

He pushed one of the women from his lap and shooed everyone away. His guests scurried quickly, scooting sideways out of the circular booth and disappearing into the crowd. I would never understand people who let others treat them that way.

I stopped in front of the table, holding his gaze. "Hello, Ulfen."

"What are *you* doing here? I thought I made it clear I didn't want to see you again."

Even though I stood above him, he made me feel small with his don't-fuck-with-me presence and rumbling voice. Still, when I spoke, my own voice came out steady.

"I'm here to offer my skills to help you find your son," I said.

His blue eyes narrowed. "Is that so?"

I nodded.

"Stephen has been missing for over a week, why the sudden interest? I thought you only tracked people's mates these days."

At that moment, Jake stepped forward, peeling away from the crowd, and joined my side. Ulfen's blue gaze flashed threateningly, grabbing the edge of the table with white-knuckle strength as if he meant to fling it at Jake.

"I convinced her to help," Jake said.

A low growl sounded deep in Ulfen's chest. The table groaned under his grip. My bones turned to Jell-O, and before I realized what I was doing, I reached over and interlaced my fingers with Jake's.

For a beat, Ulfen looked like he might blow his top and spew lava like a volcano. It would be Pompey all over again. Would a virgin sacrifice calm him down? I doubted we could find one in here, though. Time to run.

To my surprise, the werewolf got his rage under control and let go of the poor table. He smoothed his dark gray jacket and loosened his tie. "Sit down."

Jake and I exchanged a glance. With an awkward grin, I quickly let go of his hand and slid around one side of the booth. Jake went in through the other, leaving Ulfen in the middle, a fair distance away from both of us.

"Thank you for doing that," Ulfen told Jake between clenched teeth. "The trackers I've hired have had no luck." He turned to me. "I hear you're good."

"I am."

I was young, and I couldn't boast about having the years of experience other trackers had, but I had found little Emily Garner when everyone else had failed. That had given me a certain reputation. Yet, I had to assume the people Ulfen had hired were halfway decent. He had the money to pay for the best.

"What do you need?" Ulfen asked.

Every tracker is different. Some needed specific items like a comb with hair or something the missing person wore around their neck or wrist, and for these trackers, nothing else would do. In my case, I can use anything that belongs to the mark, anything they'd ever laid a claim to… from a toothbrush to a house.

"Anything that belongs to Stephen will do," I said.

Ulfen nodded, reached in his jacket pocket, and pulled something out. He slid it across the table in my direction. It was a silver cufflink in the shape of a crescent moon. I blinked up and scrutinized Ulfen's face. His blue eyes rested on the cufflink, appearing heavy and regretful as if he didn't want to part with it.

"We found this in his car the day they took him," Ulfen said. "It was attached to a torn sleeve. He fought them. There was blood. I've been carrying it with me since that day. Will it do?"

I swallowed a lump in my throat. I would've never taken Ulfen for a sentimental man, but at the moment, he didn't resemble the person I thought I knew. Right now, he was no more than a concerned father holding on to a bit of hope.

Hesitantly, I lifted a hand and picked up the cufflink. It felt wrong to take it, and I almost suggested he should keep it and give me something else, but we had no time for that. "It'll do."

Ulfen's eyes flicked toward Jake, then he cracked his neck and sniffed, his face returning to the impenetrable mask he always wore. "How long will it take you to track him?"

"A few hours, at most."

He frowned, looking worried or skeptical, I couldn't decide which.

"That fast?" he asked.

I nodded. "When I have an item from my mark, I can find them quickly, if there are no… aggravating circumstances that is."

"Aggravating circumstances," he repeated. "I can assure you, with Bernadetta Fiore at the bottom of this, aggravating circumstances are guaranteed."

"Are you sure it's her?" I asked without thinking.

"Of course it's her." Ulfen pounded a closed fist on the table.

I flinched.

"Who else would dare mess with me?"

I had no answer for his question and instead held up the cufflink. "I'll get this back to you along with Stephen's location, I hope."

130

"How much?" Ulfen asked.

I shook my head. "It's not about money."

He huffed but didn't press the issue. "If you want, you can do your… thing in my house. We could leave now and—"

"No, thank you," I said emphatically. "I have to do this in my own space or it won't work."

This was a lie, of course, but since every tracker works differently, he had no choice but to believe me. Very few knew how my skills worked, and I liked to keep it that way.

Ulfen pulled out a business card from his breast pocket and flicked it across the table. It slid over the smooth surface, and Jake caught it before it fell to the floor.

"Call me as soon as you know. That's my private cell phone number." Ulfen gestured toward the card.

I stood, the cufflink held tightly in my fist. "We'll find him."

"Don't make promises you can't keep." He seemed vulnerable as he said this, as if he were afraid of hope.

"I'll do my best. That, I can promise."

CHAPTER 21

"I thought he didn't give a shit," Jake said as we drove back to the police station to pick up his ride.

"Me, too."

I never thought Ulfen capable of feeling anything but contempt and greed, but it seemed his old rock of a heart had a tender spot. I huffed at the thought.

"What?" Jake asked.

"I guess Stephen was wrong. He said his father hated him."

"I honestly thought he did. The things Stephen told me about him…"

"Maybe he only cares about the family's future. Stephen is his heir, after all."

Jake stared at his hands pensively. Maybe, like me, he had started reevaluating what he knew. Maybe Stephen was nothing more than a rebellious son going against his father. God knew Stephen wasn't a humble man. He had grown up spoiled and rich. He'd been a total wild pup in high school and early years of college. A balls-to-the-wall rager with a couple of DWIs and arrests due to drugs. The man I'd met later on had been nothing like that, though. He still loved to party, but responsibly. His friends said he'd finally turned the corner onto the good path. I hadn't dated him long, but I had to agree. But perhaps, family disagreements still lingered despite Stephen's improvements. Or maybe the change hadn't been enough for Ulfen.

Who knew?

In the end, the specifics didn't matter. Blood is thicker than water. Family always comes first, especially among werewolves. They stick together, protect each other, and are loyal to their pack mates.

I glanced over at Jake. He chose to be a lone wolf, which had always puzzled me. He'd left his pack after his parents died, and it was hard for me to understand why he would isolate himself when he could have that kind of loyalty.

We passed in front of the police station. It was eerily quiet, no lights inside the building. Both Jake and I stared at the torn door, blasted windows, and sooty walls. Three police cars sat in the front, keeping guard of the exposed building.

Echoes of the explosion and people's screams rang in my ears. I tightened my hands around the wheel and kept driving, wondering how Tom and the others were doing.

I went around the corner and shifted the car to neutral. Jake didn't get out. He just sat there, staring straight ahead, his chest rising and falling with each deep breath he took.

"Are you sure I can't come with you?" he asked after a long quiet moment.

"You know how it works."

"Do I?" He glanced at me, his eyes dark and serious.

"Yes, it won't work if you're there. Your aura will interfere." This was the lie I'd told him before, and the lie I would stand by, now.

His mouth twisted to one side. "And your coworker's aura doesn't?"

"Rosalina? No, not really. But she's not a Skew so… not much of a supernatural aura."

Something told me he didn't believe me. In the past, he had, but something was different now. He didn't trust me, just like *I* didn't trust *him*. But whatever, he could take a major hike up Screw-You Mountain, for all I cared.

Moving slowly, not a word of thanks or anything, reluctance dripping off him, he got out of the car and walked toward a badass Harley, a softail with a low seat and leather studded saddlebag. So now he drove a motorcycle instead of a beat-up truck. Good to know what to look for, so I could run the other way.

Jake threw a leg over the bike. He had no helmet, but it didn't matter. If he splatted and cracked his head in half, it would heal quickly. He could afford to be irresponsible.

I shifted to first and headed to Rosalina's, watching him get smaller in the rearview mirror.

When I got there, I found her awake, curled up on the sofa with a blanket, and watching *Supernatural* reruns on Netflix. As I closed the door behind me, she glanced up and gave me a bleary-eyed stare.

"Thank God you're home." She pressed the off button on the remote control and rose to her feet, the blanket Abuela Esperanza had crocheted for her dropping to the floor. "How did it go?"

"Fine. We were able to talk to Ulfen." I walked into the kitchen and poured myself a glass of water.

She followed me into the kitchen and pretended to check my head from different angles. "Well, if he tried to bite your head off, at least he didn't succeed."

"He was pretty pissed at first, but in the end, he gave me this." I pulled the cufflink out of my jeans pocket.

"You're in for it, then."

I sighed and nodded.

"When do you want to do it?" She hoisted herself on top of the counter and sat with her legs dangling. She wore a pajama set with a red tank top and white shorts with the imprint of kisses.

"I'm too tired now. Tomorrow. First thing."

"What you mean is later today."

Shit! It was already tomorrow.

After a quick shower, I crawled into bed, wearing a loose T-shirt over a pair of comfortable cotton underwear. The sheets felt cool and wonderful against my legs as I tried to push away the memories of the blazing heat that had lapped at my skin, burning, making me feel like a rotisserie chicken.

When I closed my eyes, I saw the hanging ceiling tiles, the sparking wires, and Jake's bleeding back. It seemed impossible that the explosion had happened only this morning. I was grateful for the healers at the hospital and was reminded of Daniella, my older sister. She worked at St. Louis Children's Hospital, doing just that type of work. She had saved countless lives in the two years she'd been working there. I hadn't seen her or talked to her in almost a month. I made a mental note to call her once this was over.

I could have died today, and the last thing I'd told my sister was "keep your nose out of my business." She had been trying to advise me not to buy my own place yet. She said I should save a little more, make sure my business got a good foothold before I jumped into such a big responsibility. Daniella, as the oldest, had always been the most sensible. She'd only been trying to help.

And what about Leo? I didn't even remember the last thing I'd told him, but I doubted either Daniella, Lucia, or Mom could remember either. We hadn't seen him in over a year, and we only knew he was all right because, every once in a while, he sent Mom a postcard from whatever city he was visiting. The last one we'd received had come from Peru. Machu Picchu, that was where he'd been. We all wished we could write him back or at least that he would send pictures of himself, but he seemed to be doing some soul-searching and needed this time to himself.

I would write him a letter the first chance I got. I did that whenever I missed him extra hard. Normally, I would tell him about my day and that I loved him and missed him, then I would fold the letter, put it in an envelope, and stuff it in a drawer with all the others. When he got back, I would give them all to him and demand that he told me everything he'd done and seen.

With a sigh, I rolled onto my back, stared at the ceiling, and prayed I would be able to track Stephen. Even if I wasn't looking forward to the task, I would do my damn best to find him to get Jake off my back for once and for all.

CHAPTER 22

I woke up at 9:30 the next morning, assaulted by the deep hunger that sometimes attacked me and nothing seemed to satiate. I sighed and sat up, thinking it might be a ten-blueberry-pancake kind of day. On top of that, the skin on my forearms itched as if I'd gotten into poison ivy, which probably meant I was allergic to the new detergent. *Great!* Scratching and yawning, I got out of bed and slipped on a pair of sweats and slippers and went to the kitchen. Rosalina wasn't up yet, so I decided it was my turn to be extra nice to her.

The kitchen was familiar. I knew where everything was, and it took me no time to get a pot of coffee going along with blueberry pancake batter. When I heard Rosalina moving around in her bedroom, I heated the skillet and started cooking. By the time she came out, I had a stack of golden flapjacks ready to eat along with butter, honey, and marmalade.

"It smells delicious." She sat at the kitchen table with her eyes closed and her nose up in the air as she enjoyed the smell of a hot brew and griddled pancakes.

We dug in and didn't exchange a word until we'd eaten at least two pancakes each. I snatched two more, drizzled honey on top, and let Rosalina start the conversation.

"I'm glad you used the blueberries," she said, sipping her coffee. "I was afraid they might start mutating."

"They were frozen blueberries. They don't mutate. They just shrivel away, but they looked fine."

"I bought them during my smoothie craze. I'm surprised."

"One of them did jump off the counter calling out Geronimo," I joked.

Rosalina laughed her goofy laugh that must have some sort of magical qualities because it always cheered me up no matter what was going on in my life.

Together we washed the dishes and put everything back in place. After that, she gave my hair a quick trim to get rid of the damage the explosion had caused.

We each had two cups of coffee before we started talking about work and customers. Yesterday evening, she'd gotten messages out to two clients and canceled our appointments. She'd also cleared my schedule for tomorrow since we didn't know what effect today's tracking might have on me.

When I finally gathered the courage to get started, I went into the bedroom. Three more days. That was all Stephen had. I'd gotten all the rest I needed. Now, it was time to act.

"Should I expect Jake bursting through the door?" Rosalina asked as I made myself comfortable in the middle of the bed.

I shook my head. "He'll stay away. I told him I would call him." I glanced at my phone on the night table. "He might get impatient and call before I'm done, though. If he shows up, please make sure he stays away while I'm recovering."

Rosalina gave me a raised eyebrow and placed her hands on her hips. "I can't stop that man if he decides to come in here. I tried before. He was like a freaking tornado tearing through the apartment."

I laughed. "I'm sorry. I told him he was out of place, but he should be better now that he's getting what he wants." That made him sound selfish, so I added. "He's not a bad guy."

I don't know what made me say that. For the past year and a half, I'd thought of him as nothing but selfish and low. Why did I feel the need to defend him now?

"Girl, don't let his *hotness* get in the way of your judgment."

"Do you think I'm doing that?"

It was an honest question. I felt I couldn't trust myself around Jake. When he looked at me, it was as if he'd cast out a net, and I, like a stupid fish, got caught in it every single time. His spellbinding eyes seemed to pull me to him and turned me into a little moon that revolved around his entire world. It was pathetic.

"Honestly?" Rosalina's face pinched tightly as if she didn't want to answer.

"Honestly."

She put a hand out and tipped it from side to side. "Kind of."

I deflated. "I swear I'm trying my best, but I don't know what it is about him. It's been like that ever since I've known him, which is pretty much my entire lifetime. I would see him walking down the halls in school, and I would forget whatever I was doing. Like he was a damn, mental eraser. *Whoosh*, everything gone."

"Was there drool?"

"Definitely."

We both laughed.

Rosalina sat at the edge of the bed, growing serious. "Is it because he's a werewolf? I've heard shifters can be... I don't know... entrancing to certain women."

"Maybe, but why me?" I whined, punching the mattress with closed fists. "Hand me that cufflink. It'll take me out of this misery."

It would send me into a different type of misery, but at this point, I honestly didn't know which was worse. Rosalina pressed the cufflink into my palm, closed my fingers around it, and patted my hand. "Try not to go too deep, okay? Pull out if it's taking too long."

I nodded and watched her leave and close the door behind her. Nerves stirred in my stomach, making me feel nauseous. Maybe eating all those pancakes had been a bad idea.

The cufflink poked my palm as I tightened my hold on it. I closed my eyes, trying to focus, but the ball of dread that had made itself comfortable in my chest since I decided to get involved grew to epic proportions as I tried to push myself into the trance.

I opened my eyes, confused. I never looked forward to this, but this dread was unlike anything I'd ever felt. Was I afraid of the aftermath? Or of what I would find out?

What if Stephen was dead?

I had tried to track a dead person once before, and I never could forget how it felt to go in and find nothing. Nothing at all. The vast, unending blankness had stripped me of all my emotions until I felt raw with the knowledge of only one thing...

Cold, unforgiving emptiness.

I didn't want to feel that again. It was one of the reasons I preferred to be a mate tracker. There was always someone out there who could make another one happy, so I never had to face that emptiness.

I shook my head.

He's not dead.

If he was dead, they wouldn't be threatening to cut his head off, would they? They wouldn't be making demands that Ulfen couldn't meet. There seemed to be a hole in that logic, but I had to believe he was still alive.

I sighed. No use in postponing the inevitable. I had already agreed to this, and I wouldn't back out. I clasped my hands together around the cufflink and let my power flow. Green magic sprang from my fingers and whirled around my hands. This was different from mate tracking, easier because I had something of Stephen's.

I closed my eyes. This time there was no glittery world, just blackness. No potion, no sparkles. Gradually, I released my senses... Scent first, as always.

Immediately, a pleasantly sweet, warm scent surrounded me. The smell was familiar in a way, yet I couldn't quite put my finger on it, which bothered me the more I tried to pick up its subtleties. Underneath this scent, I tried to find others, but this one was overpowering and made it hard to identify anything else. I struggled for several long moments, knowing that the longer I went, the longer my food would taste like cardboard—smell made such a huge difference when trying to enjoy your grub.

At last, the hint of a few other scents took shape: vanilla and cinnamon and maybe also lavender. Those were the scents I could put a name to, and they could be anything: someone's perfume, a cinnamon roll, a vanilla latte. They didn't help.

Frustrated, I released my sense of hearing next, and the usual cacophony of sounds assaulted me. I listened for several beats, waiting for the racket to die down as I sifted through the different sounds. The noise barely subsided. Some sounds fell away, but most stayed, mainly the constant, unrelenting hum of an engine. In the background, I perceived the drum of traffic, tires against asphalt and gravel, the occasional blare of a horn, the squeal of brakes, the rattle of loose chassis—all diminished by the tireless hum.

Oddly, just like with the scents, one thing overpowered all others, obscuring what should be the main clues.

I tried harder to pinpoint unique sounds, like a bell tower, the horn of a basketball game, a certain tune, a voice I might recognize. Nothing like that came to the surface, only that hum. Useless.

Fear gripped me, knowing what came next. It had been some time since I'd engaged my sight, and I hated to do it. It terrified me. Being deaf was difficult enough, but losing my vision left me feeling as vulnerable as a newborn kitten. I didn't know how to navigate life without my senses. I was trying to get better at it, but the process was slow. Logically, I knew other people led perfectly capable, self-sufficient lives without them, but there was nothing rational about my fear. It was born of a raw and unadulterated self-preservation instinct.

Hunkering down, I forced the uneasiness away, knowing this trial would only make me stronger. Gathering all my courage, I released my sense of sight.

My eyes opened to utter darkness.

Panic seized me at the complete absence of light.

I glanced all around, searching for the smallest pinprick of illumination. I found nothing, just absolutely blackness.

Where are they keeping you, Stephen?

A room without lights would still have windows, a door. Slivers of light, no matter how thin, would get through, but not here. Wherever Stephen was, his kidnappers had purposely sealed every source of light.

Frantically, I peered around in every direction, pausing to make sure I didn't miss something. My heart hammered while the sweet smell, the unrelenting hum of an engine, and the darkness combined to a crescendo of unbearable stimuli. I whirled and whirled, panic mounting, and a sense of dread and disappointment settling on my shoulders.

For the first time, I had failed to find a known mark, and because of it, Stephen would die.

CHAPTER 23

When I broke out of the trance, utter darkness still surrounded me. For a panicked moment, I feared I'd gotten trapped in that limbo, unable to escape, but it was just the blindness. I sat up with a jerk, my shaking hands flat on the bed in an effort to feel grounded. My breaths came in fast, but I couldn't hear them. The world was silent, dark, and void of all smells.

Where am I? Where am I?! The question was irrational, but the panic was real.

I felt three taps on top of my hand, then the bed dipped. Relieved, I clenched Rosalina's hand and pressed it to my chest. My heart pounded like the drums of the salsa music she liked to dance to. Sensing my distress, she moved closer and wrapped me in a tight hug, hands smoothing my hair, warm breath brushing my ear in words of comfort that I couldn't hear.

"I couldn't find him," I sobbed, fighting the knot in my throat, my exhausted body collapsing against her.

She pulled away, took my hand, and traced several circles in my palm.

The letter "O".

She was trying to tell me it was okay. We had come up with several hand gestures to help us communicate. Nothing fancy, but we could understand each other. She pressed a cool glass to my hand and wrapped my fingers around it. I drank the water greedily until I finished it.

After she took the glass away, I held both palms up in question. She tapped my left hand five times. I collapsed back on the bed. Five minutes, I'd been under for five minutes, which meant it would take five hours to regain my senses. This was the longest I'd ever been under and for nothing.

I felt Rosalina's fingers slide down my chest bone. Sign language for "*Hungry?*"

I shook my head.

Her fingertips alighted on my forehead next, then slid downward gently, gathering at my chin. *Sleep.*

"I can't. I'm too restless. My heart is dancing to some of your salsa music." She had Cuban roots and grew up speaking Spanish. Odd for someone raised in The Hill with all the Italians around, but her family remained faithful to their origin, which was so cool.

She repeated the sign. *Sleep.*

I sighed. "I'll try."

Rosalina signed on my hand that she was leaving. The bed shifted as she stood, and I imagined her walking out of the room and shutting the door behind her.

I knew that time would pass faster if I just slept, but I didn't think I would be able to—even despite my deep fatigue. I closed my eyes, and even here, on the bed, my mind stirred with the memory of that sweet smell and the unrelenting hum of an engine, and since darkness still surrounded me, I felt as if I were still in the trance.

You're not. You're not. You're free.

I touched the bed, my pillow, my face to convince myself. I tossed and turned, willing sleep to come.

Only five hours. You can sleep for five hours.

I lay on my back, on my belly, on my side.

How long has it been? How much longer?

In this state, I always found it impossible to calculate time. I didn't know how long had passed when Rosalina came back into the room. She snatched my hand and scribbled something in it, too fast for me to understand.

"Slow down," I said.

She traced a single character on my palm. The letter "J".

"Jake?" I said.

She tapped my palm once for *yes*.

"He's here?"

Another single tap.

"Can you keep him out of the room?"

I waited for another tap, but instead, two came. She released my hand, abruptly, which let me know that Jake was trespassing again.

Shit.

I rolled over, turning my back on the door and lay as still as a log. I imagined him standing behind me, screaming, demanding why I was in bed while Stephen was out there, his life on the balance. What did he think of my silence?

A heavy hand landed on me. It wrapped entirely around my shoulder.

Jake.

The bed dipped, then he pulled me, forcing me to face him. I kept my eyes squeezed shut, the shame of my failure mixing with the shame of my vulnerable state. Tears filled my eyes, and the next thing I knew, his arms slid around me, pulling me into a tight embrace.

I fit into his arms in a familiar, practiced way, and suddenly it was just Jake and me. I lay my head on his muscular chest as he stroked my hair, his warmth and strength feeling like a force field around me. I instinctively took a deep breath, hoping to find comfort in his scent, which was imprinted in my mind like a seal. It was unlike anything else I'd ever sensed: strong, masculine, maddening, and known to turn me on faster than flipping on a light switch. But despite a hefty lungful of air, I smelled nothing.

My heart ached, and the tears that had gathered in my eyes spilled onto my cheeks. For a moment, I feared I might start sobbing like a baby right in his arms, but no more tears came. Somehow—since the last time I'd cried, which had been for him—I'd become stronger. It still hurt, the broken heart, and unanswered questions, but I no longer needed to melt into a puddle of tears because of him.

Instead, I simply accepted the comfort of his touch and found that forgiveness was a possibility. Jake wasn't a monster. Like I'd told Rosalina, he wasn't a bad guy. He had been good before, and I could see that he hadn't changed. He had his reasons for leaving me, and though he'd hurt me deeply, he'd taught me a valuable lesson.

Strength and self-love are just as important, or perhaps more, than the love we feel for others. If you can't take care of yourself first, how in the hell can you take care of others?

Jake held me for a long time, his fingers tracing circles on my back. My hands remained at my sides. I was afraid of touching him, to feel the peaks and valleys of his torso, the latent strength in his muscles. Maybe it was a good thing I couldn't smell him, hear him, see him.

This was nothing but a moment of weakness that I could later forgive myself.

ഹൗ

Sometime later, small sounds popped around me, and a faded light glowed against my eyelids. The weak smell of roses tickled my nose as I swam in a state between sleep and wakefulness.

A cold hand pressed to my forehead.

"Hey, Toni the Tiger, how are you feeling?" Rosalina's voice entered my consciousness, faint as if she stood far away.

I opened my eyes. She sat next to me, blurry around the edges. My senses had started to come back, but just barely.

A candle burned on the night table, the source of the light and pleasant scent. Rosalina always made sure to welcome me back in the best way possible. She was the best friend anyone could ever ask for. I was so lucky to have her.

"I'm okay," I said, then I remembered that Jake had been here. I scrambled to a sitting position. "Jake… he knows… he—"

"Shh, it's all right." Rosalina patted my hand. "He doesn't suspect," she said in a whisper, close to my ear. "He just thinks you were distraught."

"Are you sure?"

"Yes, lay back down and rest. It's late."

I lay back down, relieved. I didn't want to have to explain myself to Jake or anyone else. The way my skill worked felt more personal than ever, something I was willing to share only with those I trusted most.

I took a deep breath and relaxed into my pillow. Given my state, sleeping was the most sensible thing I could do, so I let myself doze off again.

CHAPTER 24

The next time I opened my eyes, my senses had fully returned. I was alone in the room, and it was dark outside. Everything looked sharper around the edges, brighter in color, real. I squinted at the alarm clock on the night table. It read 11:17 PM. I had been asleep for way more than five hours.

My stomach rumbled. I had missed lunch and dinner, and I was a wimp when it came to missing mere snacks, especially when that intense hunger hit me. I got out of bed, scratching my itchy arm, and quietly patted out of the room. I headed straight for the kitchen. Rosalina had left the range light on, and I had to smile when I saw a plate on the table. It held a sandwich, covered in plastic wrap, a banana, and a bag of chips. I went to the refrigerator, poured a glass of milk, and returned to the table, ready to eat. I was ravenous.

I was about to sit when I noticed movement out of the corner of my eye. I started and raised the glass of milk as if it were a weapon. What did I think that would do? Give the intruder calcium poisoning? Death by milk wasn't a thing, or was it? A pair of eyes flashed in the darkness from the living room. My heart went into insane mode, pounding against my rib cage like a giant's fist.

"It's just me," Jake's deep voice came from the darkness.

He approached slowly, the light from the kitchen gradually revealing his tall frame.

"You scared the shit out of me. What are you doing here?"

As he came fully into the light, I took him in. He was wearing unbuttoned jeans and a wife-beater that clung tightly to his muscular torso and left his rounded shoulders and perfectly shaped biceps out for inspection. He was barefoot and his light brown hair stood on end.

"Rosalina let me stay on the couch," he said.

"She did?"

That little traitor. She and I would have to talk. How dare she allow a hot-blooded male to sleep mere feet away from me when I hadn't had sex in over a year and a half, and when said male was the last one *and* only I'd ever had sex with? What the hell was she thinking?

Clearly, she was getting her some. Otherwise, she wouldn't be this inconsiderate.

"For protection," he said. "I insisted."

"My mom cast protection spells on the condo when Rosalina bought it, and the complex has its own security, so you don't need to worry about it." I sat in front of my sandwich and started peeling off the plastic wrap, but my stomach flipped in weird ways, chasing the hunger away.

Jake sat across from me, resting his interlaced fingers in front of him. He had a new tattoo around his left biceps, an arrow that wrapped around, its tip and fletching almost meeting in the front. His other biceps sported a bursting sun, its rays spilling around his shoulder. I knew it well, had traced it with my finger many times as I drifted to sleep by his side.

He was very familiar with my first tattoo as well, a small nautical compass under my right breast. I'd gotten two new ones since he'd been gone, though. The word "tracking" with a lifeline at both ends, and the newest: an ornate heart with a crescent moon in the middle and an arrow going across both. The first was on my left forearm and the other under my collar bone.

"Protection charms are good," he said, "but you can never be too careful. Bernadetta has all manner of witches and mages at her disposal. Some of the best, and after what happened at your office… well, I've been worried ever since."

I opened the bag of chips and dumped them on the plate. I picked one and popped it in my mouth. It was salty and greasy and made me want another one. Those tricky bastards had it right, you couldn't eat only one. I ate five more, trying to understand what the hell Jake was saying.

"You're making no sense," I said.

He frowned, his thick, dark eyebrows drawing together. I remembered one day I had offered to pluck a few of the stray hairs to make their shape perfect. He batted my hand away and told me they already were. He was right about that.

"I'm making no sense?" he echoed. "How is that?"

"Over a year ago you didn't give a shit. Why should you care now?" As soon as the words were out of my mouth, I clamped my lips together. I had promised myself to leave well enough alone, but damn it if I didn't have a bone to pick with this man.

As always, he clammed up and looked as if he were biting his tongue not to give me a piece of his mind. I needed to stop harping on this. Jake hadn't loved me—at least not the way he'd led me to believe. Or maybe I've been the fool who'd blown things out of proportion and scared him away.

He took a deep breath and met my gaze. "Whatever you may think of me, Toni, get this in your head. I *do* care. I'm not a cold-hearted bastard. I don't want anything to happen to you or your friend."

"I see." I took a huge bite out of my sandwich. A piece of lettuce slid out from between the bread slices and flopped onto my face. Chin accessory. *Great look!* I picked it off, put it on the plate, and struggled to chew the doughy mess I'd stuffed inside my mouth. I sneaked in a bit of milk to help me along.

Jake raised an eyebrow, stole one of my potato chips, and ate it.

I swallowed audibly and had to drink more milk to clear the lump in my throat. I was so sick of dancing around this issue. If I could learn anything from this, it should be to speak honestly and without shame because trying to guess what the hell was on in this man's mind was harder than learning sign language.

"Tell me something, Jake, and please be honest."

"I'm always honest." He spread both hands out and puffed his chest as if saying "look at all my honesty."

I narrowed my eyes at him, afraid he was mocking me. "Are you ever going to tell me why you left?"

He released a heavy sigh and stood, the chair scraping against the floor behind him. "No," he said plainly, then turned and walked back to the sofa.

I was on my feet, my impulses getting the best of me again. "You're an asshole."

He kept walking as if I hadn't spoken, but I needed a reaction from him. Something. Anything. So I said the first thing that came to mind.

"I lied to you, Jake. There are so many things I never told you because I never trusted you all the way."

He stopped, his silhouette freezing in the middle of the dark living room.

Satisfaction washed over me. *Yeah, that's right. I hope that hurts. I hope it makes you doubt everything we ever shared.*

Without turning to look at me, he said, "I deserve all the resentment you feel toward me."

I thought he would say more, but he just lay down on the sofa, becoming nothing but a big shadowy lump as he curled up to sleep.

Cursing under my breath, I took my food and went back to my room.

"Bastard!"

Tomorrow, he could go find someone else to "protect." Rosalina and I didn't need him. Now that I had tried and failed to find Stephen, those stupid kidnappers didn't have to worry about me spoiling their fun anymore, and everything could go back to normal.

CHAPTER 25

When Rosalina and I woke up the next morning, Jake was gone. He had jotted a note and left it on the kitchen table.

Thank you, both.

A phone number followed.

"Very eloquent," I said.

Rosalina looked sheepish. "Um, he insisted on staying the night."

"I know. I got up to get something to eat and saw him. Thanks for the sandwich, by the way. It hit the spot." I rubbed my stomach. "Also it means breakfast's on me."

While I cooked omelets and squeezed fresh orange juice, I told her about my conversation with Jake.

"Wuh, that's intense," she said, buttering a piece of toast. "Do you really think he'll leave you alone now?"

"He'd better."

"Well, one way or another, we need to get back to business, Triple T."

"Triple T?"

"Yeah, Toni the Tiger or Toni the Tracker, either one works."

I chuckled and drank some juice as Rosalina started ticking a list on her fingers.

"You need to find Celina's mate 'cause he won't find himself. I need to get in touch with the insurance company to see what our claim status is on our laptops and damage. You need to take another trip to Pharowyn for potion ingredients. Also, I need to get a few potential customers back on the schedule. Do you think it's safe going back to the office?"

"Since I'm a complete failure and can't find Stephen, yes, I think so."

"You're not a failure. Maybe when it comes to men, but not tracking."

"Gee, thanks for your support."

"You're welcome. What you do is not easy, nor is the price you pay for using your skill."

I put my fork down and chewed slowly, thoughtfully.

Rosalina frowned at me. "What's going through your mind?"

"I don't know... just thinking about how weird it was... all the things I picked up during the trance. It was as if the people holding Stephen were expecting someone like me. I mean, every tracker's different. Some are guided to the place, others come up with town names or street names, others use maps to figure out a general area. I'm sure there's a thousand ways, some that wouldn't make sense to anyone but the trackers themselves. Few know how my skill works, but whoever's keeping Stephen, they're covering all their bases. I saw nothing but darkness, Rosalina. There even was a smell that overpowered everything."

"What about your hearing?"

I shook my head. "Just the constant hum of an engine. Like he was in a car or something."

Rosalina's perfect eyebrows rose. "That actually makes sense."

"What do you mean?"

"The kidnappers know that Erickson's gonna try to use trackers to find his son, so what if they're not keeping him in one place? What if they drive him to different locations?"

I nodded, my thoughts quickly catching up with hers. "Better yet, what if they're keeping him on the move all the time?"

"Yes, yes, YES! We're geniuses!" Rosalina exclaimed.

"Not really. Should have figured it out right away. Duh!"

Rosalina waved a hand in my direction. "Whatever."

I fiddled with my hair, readjusting my ponytail. "We're never gonna find him like that."

"I don't guess it's any of our business anymore. Just tell Jake and Ulfen about it, and let's get back to business."

"You're right."

I tried to call Jake at the number he'd left on his note, but the call immediately went to voicemail. I left a message: "Jake, call me back when you get a chance."

After that, I found Ulfen Erickson's business card and dialed him. He answered on the first ring.

I cleared my throat. "Mr. Erickson, it's Toni Sunder."

There was a lot of noise on the other side, people arguing.

"Everybody shut the fuck up!" Ulfen yelled. As if he were God, and he'd just said "let there be silence," there was. "I'm sorry, Ms. Sunder. Please, tell me, did you find Stephen?"

Ulfen's voice was high-pitched and urgent. I could tell he was trying to rein in his stress, but it bled through the speaker all the same. Wherever he was, he seemed to be dealing with a lot, and maybe he was hoping my call would temper the chaos. Too bad I didn't have good news.

"No, I didn't."

"Fuck!" he shouted in a booming voice that seemed to explode out of my telephone.

I shuddered on my end of the line. His anger was almost palpable as if he were standing next to me.

"Everything all right?" Rosalina mouthed.

I grimaced and gave a shrug.

"I'm sorry," Ulfen apologized again. "It's just… you were my last hope."

I could understand his desperation. Stephen only had two more days to live.

"I'm not sure if this will help," I said, "but I don't think they're keeping Stephen in one place. I think… they might be keeping him mobile, like in a vehicle of some kind."

There was silence for a moment. "That… that kind of makes sense. That would explain why the two trackers I hired couldn't pinpoint a location. Any idea what kind of vehicle?"

"I'm sorry, no." Stephen was on his own, and I felt responsible. I had failed him.

"Anything else you can tell me that could help me find my son? Anything at all."

"I'm afraid not. That's all I've got. I'm sorry I couldn't be of more help."

"Thank you for trying."

I never thought I would feel sorry for Ulfen Erickson, but there it was. No one deserved what he was going through—not even a major asshole like him.

❧⬧☙

While I got ready to go back to the office, a dark cloud seemed to hang over me. I kept seeing Stephen, his handsome face and open smile, his self-assured demeanor and straight-forward way, his severed finger. He didn't deserve this. I should have tried harder. What if I'd missed something?

When we got on our way, I felt glad to have work that would keep my mind from whirring like a clock on steroids. I drove my Camaro, and we made it to the office in fifteen minutes. We approached cautiously, peeking through the glass window. Everything appeared to be just as we'd left it the last time we'd been here.

"What do you think? Will you feel safe by yourself?" I asked Rosalina.

"Yeah." She nodded, glancing around, hands on her hips. "It's daytime. There are people around."

She gestured down the sidewalk at a couple walking arm in arm. A chocolate lab bounded in front of them, stretching its leash. It was a beautiful spring day, and there would be lots of people out and about, getting coffee, ice cream, and pizza.

"Okay, I'll head out to the Basilica to scout for Celina's mate. I feel pretty confident I'll find him."

"That's the attitude."

I walked back to the car. The beautiful day had put a much-needed spring in my step. The air was crisp, the sun was shining, and I had someone to make happy today. Celina wouldn't have to worry about that *buttwipe* who broke her heart anymore. Once I found Mr. Morelli, and he melted into a puddle at her feet, her checkbook would *cha-ching* Rosalina and me straight into tracking stardom—not to mention I would have enough money for my condo's down payment.

The day called for driving with the top down. It felt amazing and reminded me of how much I missed driving, especially this car. My hair flew about, and the sun sparkled on the hood and bounced off my sunglasses. I even splurged on a Venti caramel frappuccino at a drive-through, and by the time I parked and walked toward the Basilica, I felt almost back to normal. And the best part... I was doing great keeping both Jake and Stephen out of my mind, and ignoring the heavy weight of guilt on my back.

Slurping my drink, I walked down Lindell Blvd, assessing the area. Cathedral Basilica of St. Louis lay to my right. The church was a beautiful structure of symmetrical design with a cupola in the middle and towers on either side. Two sets of wide steps led up to its elaborate stone, three-arch entrance.

The boulevard was pretty, with an ample, tree-lined sidewalk. Several tall apartment buildings, a high school, and a few office buildings surrounded the church. Celina's mate could be in any of those places. He might live in one of the units. He might be a teacher at the high school. Or maybe he was a lawyer or accountant at one of the office buildings. The possibilities were endless.

I enjoyed this part of tracking. It was easy, and I got to use all my senses. It could be time-consuming, but it relaxed me. Plus I liked people watching. If it ever became an Olympic sport, I would win a gold medal... or two.

Spotting a cement bench, I sat and prepared for my stakeout. I had snacks in my shoulder pack, a book in case I got bored, a few games on my phone, and a pad to jot down notes if needed.

I'd been sitting there ten minutes when the church bells started to toll. I counted and inhaled deeply, taking in all the scents that surrounded me. Mostly it was flowers, mulch, and pine straw. The area had fantastic curb appeal.

The sidewalks were fairly busy for the time of day. People walked up and down, going in and out of different buildings. Every time someone walked in front of me, my nose twitched as I took in their scent. A few of them gave me distrustful glances, probably thinking I had an overactive nose syndrome or something, but I was used to it.

In high school, a guy I refused to kiss because he always had cantaloupe breath—I hate melons in general—nicknamed me Slutty Bunny. He told everyone I was a lousy kisser, who wouldn't stop twitching her nose while ramming my tongue down his throat. Gratefully, the nickname didn't stick for more than a few weeks.

Five guys in suits, two of them quite good-looking, passed by, carrying briefcases and walking at a clipped pace. None of them had the scent I'd locked on during the trance. A group of kids in plaid uniforms sauntered down the sidewalk. I caught the scent of an array of perfumes from the girls, and weed and BO from the boys. Seriously, if they could afford a fancy high school, they could afford deodorant. Ew.

A strange, but pleasant scent hit me next. My eyes snapped toward its source. A Fae male dressed in supple leather pants, boots, and no shirt strolled by with the grace of a dancer. I blinked up at his matching yellow hair and eyes. His features were delicate and extremely beautiful. His ears were pointed, sticking through strands of straight hair. A rare sight to say the least. Fae preferred to stick to Elf-hame and were rarely seen in our neck of the woods. Maybe he needed an accountant to keep track of his gold. I snickered.

An hour later, I'd started to get restless, thinking about Rosalina, alone at the office, Stephen, Jake, and Tom, who was still at the hospital.

With a sigh, I dialed the agency. Rosalina answered right away and reassured me everything was okay. After that, I called the hospital to ask about Tom's condition, but they wouldn't give me any information because of stupid privacy regulations. I would have to go and find out personally.

I cursed under my breath, trying to refocus on my job. Normally, I could sit watching people for hours, but my mind kept wandering off. To help me pay better attention, I started playing a game I enjoyed: guessing strangers' names, what they did, and where they worked.

For instance, the guy a few yards down the sidewalk… the one sweeping the church steps with his back to me. He wore all black—slacks and shirt—and had a cloud of dust around him that made my nose triple twitch. I pinched it to avoid sneezing and kept watching him. I got the feeling, judging by his clothes, that sweeping wasn't his job, and maybe he had taken to the task as an excuse to be outside on this beautiful day. Unless I was way off, and he was some sort of emo janitor who went by the name of Thorn and wore heavy eyeliner.

The guy stamped his broom against the ground, set it aside, and walked away from the little pile of debris he'd gathered. Placing his hands on his hips, he faced the church and glanced up at its emerald-green cupola. He wore a proud smile on his face. He was about thirty-five, handsome, tall, and clean-shaven with perfectly trimmed hair. And he was wearing a clerical collar.

Ah, so not an emo janitor, but a priest who was very proud of his place of worship.

As the cloud of dust around him dissipated, and the wind blew in my direction from the church, the scent I'd been searching for suddenly hit me.

Shit!

No, it couldn't be. Why did my luck have to suck balls?! Celina's mate was a priest. Now what?

CHAPTER 26

N ot good. Not good at all. I picked up the phone and dialed Rosalina.

"He's a priest," I said, a bit hysterically. What were the odds?

"Huh? Who's a priest?"

"Celina's mate."

Rosalina gasped. "Shit!"

"Exactly."

"Um, what do we do?" she asked.

"I don't know. That's why I'm calling. I can't pull a man away from his calling to serve the Lord. I just can't. It's all kinds of screwed up."

"But... they're mates. Once he meets her, he'll be too busy slobbering all over his hot lady to remember his calling. Right?"

I stood and started pacing in front of the bench. "Maybe."

"Okay, so you find another one."

"I'm not sure there's another in St. Louis, and I don't want to ask her for more tears. It was hard the first time around. Plus, it'll look unprofessional. Gah! I guess I will have to tell her we couldn't find anyone."

Rosalina groaned.

"What?"

"I called her this morning and told her that you had."

I collapsed back on the bench. "Then, I'll have to tell her I made a mistake or something."

"That'll look unprofessional too and won't be good for the reputation we're trying to build. She'll tell everyone in her circles that we're useless."

I pulled at my hair, my frustration mounting. We couldn't let that happen. Moving into a tier of more exclusive customers was crucial to our business plan. I could only serve a few clients a month, and it would be impossible to stay afloat for long any other way. Our little savings wouldn't last and my new place... I would have to give it up. I stomped my foot and pulled at my hair again.

"It's your decision, Toni," Rosalina said. "I'll be okay with whatever you choose to do."

I couldn't fail Rosalina. She'd put all her trust in me. Maybe the guy was miserable being a priest. Celibacy sucked. I could attest to that. Maybe if I—

"Are you all right?" a melodious voice asked from my left.

I glanced up to find Celina's priest standing next to the bench. He wore a concerned expression and seemed ready to offer help and save me from whatever evils plagued my life, and his face was so kind and wise-looking that I had no doubt he could rescue me from the very claws of deadly sin.

"Toni?" Rosalina said on the other end of the line.

"Let me call you back." I pressed the "end" button and turned to the priest. "Um, hi."

He smiled, his hands clasped in front of him. He had gentle brown eyes that immediately inspired trust. "I couldn't help but notice your… distress, and I thought, perhaps, I could be of assistance. May I?" He inclined his head toward the bench.

I scooted over a bit to give him more room. "Sure."

He sat and took a big deep breath, looking content. "Gorgeous spring day, isn't it?"

"Mm-hmm." I didn't know what to say. I'd never talked to a priest before. I wasn't a religious person. Regardless, I sensed this man was made out of something wholesome.

Damn, I'm done for.

I would have to give Celina's money back. I couldn't sow doubt in this man's heart. Because that was exactly what would happen. If he met Celina, he would immediately be torn between his current life of service and the possibility of a different kind of happiness.

He glanced toward me. "I noticed you've been sitting here a while. What's your name?"

"Toni."

"My name is Vincent. I'm a priest at the Basilica."

"I figured that much."

He sheepishly touched his collar and smiled with such gentleness I felt my heart melt into a puddle of toffee, which would take hours to scrape off the bottom of my chest. *Sheesh*, the man held the power of a thousand cute puppies packed into one set of brown eyes. One look at this man and Celina would turn into a priest-eating, god-defying lunatic. She probably wouldn't stop until she'd torn the tunics off his back and ravaged him on the spot.

"What brings you here?" he asked. "I haven't seen you before. Do you live in one of the apartments? A new tenant perhaps?" He glanced toward the tall building across from the Cathedral.

"No, I was here looking for someone, part of my job."

166

"I see."

"It's not going well though."

He nodded. "Is there anything I can do to help?"

If he only knew. I pondered whether to tell him, warring with my feelings for selfish self-preservation and the desire to do the right thing for someone else.

"Not really," I said at last.

He frowned. "I sense you're not being honest."

Okay, that had to be like some sort of superpower shit. Maybe he was a Skew of some kind, though I wasn't getting a special scent from him. He smelled totally human. Maybe he was just wise beyond his years.

"Well, it's hard," I said. "See, there is a choice I have to make, and I'm struggling with it because… it could change someone's life drastically."

He made a contemplative sound in the back of his throat, then said, "I guess you should ask yourself, would it change their life for the better?"

"There's really no way of telling. It might. It might not. I think it would make them happy in a way, but it also might leave them with doubts and regrets for the rest of their life."

He rubbed his chin. "Interesting dilemma you have."

"Now you see why I'm so frustrated."

"I do," he paused. "Well, as a priest, I sometimes have to face these types of situations. There are things people tell me during confession that require stern advice and warnings. Sometimes the things I hear are a burden on me, but I have to trust in God and his plan. So I listen, advise the best I can, and leave the rest in God's hands."

Dammit, he's not making this easier.

He shifted to face me. "It sort of feels this choice is a burden on you as well. Why is that?"

I decided to put all the cards on the table, so he could lay it on me a bit thicker. "Because I stand to gain something from it."

"Ahhh, a moral dilemma, truly."

"You got that right."

"Well, child," he gave me those gentle puppy eyes again, making me feel terrible, "this speaks to the strength of your character. Most people wouldn't hesitate to put themselves first."

Oh, hell. I sighed, my mind made up. I couldn't do this to him. I just couldn't. For some stupid reason, tears pooled in my eyes. I swallowed hard and blinked rapidly.

"It'll be okay." He patted my hand, which rested on the bench.

"I know." I sniffled, feeling proud of myself for holding back the tears. "Thanks for your help."

"But I didn't do anything."

"You did." I picked up my bag from the ground, stood, and slung it over my shoulder. "It was great meeting you, father."

"You can call me Vincent." He stood and put out a hand.

I shook it, feeling better as the decision settled and I accepted it. Rosalina and I would find another way to keep the agency afloat without wrecking anyone's life, especially this man's. I turned to leave, then stopped, a thought striking me.

"Um, are you busy right now?"

He hooked a thumb toward the church steps. "I was sweeping." He gave me a charming smile that would make any woman wish he would give up God and go rogue.

"There's a friend of mine. He's in the hospital. I know it would mean a great deal to him if you came to see him and... talk to him." My voice broke. Tom was Catholic, and maybe Vincent could give him the strength to power toward recovery. Surely they

168

had priests at the hospital, but none as special as Vincent. I was sure.

Damn, if the tears weren't making a comeback. Too much was going on, and my emotions were a complete wreck. I had to give myself credit, though. At least, I wasn't hiding under my bed counting dust bunnies.

"It would be my honor to visit your friend," Vincent said. "Were you going there now?"

I nodded.

"Then let's go."

CHAPTER 27

y the time Vincent and I left the hospital, it was past
lunchtime. They hadn't let me go in to see the detective,
but they'd allowed Vincent since he had credentials for
such things. I sat in the waiting area, fiddling with my bag strap
until he came out. He reassured me that, even though Tom was in
critical condition, he had seemed like the kind of man who didn't
give up, and he had a feeling the detective would be all right.

I thanked him for taking the time out of his day to visit my
friend.

"It was nothing. I'll make sure to visit him every day," Vincent
had said as I dropped him off by the Basilica.

After that, I drove around for a bit to clear my head and find a
place for lunch. My stomach was queasy, but I knew if I didn't eat,
I would get a major headache and wouldn't feel like going back to
the office to deal with the fallout of my oh-so-selfless decision.

I was feeling down in the dumps, so I decided to treat myself to
Pizza-A-Go-Go, a great place that had been in business since the
60s and served New York-style pizza, cash only.

Their tiny parking lot was packed, so I parked a block down and started walking toward the restaurant. I'd almost gotten there when a black car with tinted windows pulled up next to me. It caught my attention because, as it appeared in my peripheral vision, the damn thing kept going and going and going until it stopped. A limousine.

Damn, that thing is long.

I wondered if the occupant needed to compensate for something. Snickering, I continued on my way, trying to decide whether I wanted pepperoni or sausage.

The driver got out of the limousine. He wore a black suit and looked as thick as a bouncer from an exclusive nightclub. He had dark brown eyes, pale skin, a shaved head, and a well-trimmed goatee. I thought he would open the door to let the limousine passengers out, but instead, he walked up to me, making eye contact. Reflexively, I came to an abrupt stop and glanced all around, feeling threatened.

He stopped a few paces away and respectfully inclined his head. "Good afternoon, Ms. Sunder. My name is Bertram, and my mistress would like to talk to you." He had a deep voice with a vague German accent.

"Your *mistress?*"

"Yes, Bernadetta Fiore, I'm sure you've heard of her."

Oh, shit.

Now, my eyeballs really started shifting all around, searching for an escape. My palms began to sweat, and my heart climbed into my throat. She had sent two people to kidnap me, and they'd failed. Had she decided to take matters into her own hands?

"I… I'm afraid I have nothing to discuss with your mistress." I sidestepped, trying to walk around the driver. He sidestepped, too, blocking my path.

"She insists." Bertram gave me a cold smile that made it clear he and his mistress wouldn't take *no* for an answer.

I opened my mouth maybe to scream, I wasn't sure, but the limousine's back window slid open with a hiss and a pair of slightly glowing red eyes peered at me from the dark interior, and all I could do was stare.

"Ms. Sunder," a deep feminine voice said from inside, "I would come out and introduce myself, but the sun makes it impossible. Would you mind stepping in to talk to me for a moment? I promise it won't take long."

The voice sounded refined and calm. It enunciated every word, pronouncing the syllables with care. Something in the timbre made me think of an older person, someone who had first learned to speak when words carried weight. I knew the Dark Donna had been a vampire for hundreds of years, but that wasn't the only reason for her arresting voice. Something else made it hard to ignore, an allure that probably had everything to do with her vampire skills and not her ancient ass. I wondered when she'd been bitten and created, if she'd be willing or a victim. Some Stales thought werewolves were created the same way, but that was ridiculous. Werewolves were born, not bitten.

Against my will, I found my feet shuffling toward the car. Bertram opened the door, and before I knew it, I was sitting across from the most stunning creature I'd ever seen in my life. The limousine door slammed shut and the tinted window automatically went up.

Bernadetta Fiore appeared in the newspapers enough, so any self-respecting St. Louis resident had seen her likeness gracing the social column. I'd known of her beauty, but what I'd seen in photographs paled in comparison to real life.

She had jet black hair and skin as smooth as marble. I expected her to be pale, but she had an olive complexion much like mine. Inside the car, her eyes didn't glow red but appeared perfectly black. Her full mouth sported nude lipstick, and her long lashes fluttered like tranquil butterflies. She wore black leather pants stuffed into boots with four-inch heels, a midnight blue top with a low square neckline, and an honest-to-god cloak pinned together at her throat by an elaborate silver broach encrusted with rubies. She appeared slight and short, maybe five-foot-one, another thing I'd misjudged from the papers. Still, her small body oozed control, calculated judgment, and latent strength.

My heart skipped around like a jackrabbit. I pressed a hand to my chest, feeling as if I could somehow keep it from punching a hole through my ribs and skidding into the limousine's carpeted floor like a yummy treat for the vampiress. My skin started to itch like crazy, but I refrained from scratching. *Damn*, I seriously needed to go see a dermatologist, but who has money for that?

I glanced around the limousine's interior to distract myself. Four massive, cream leather bucket seats—two facing each other—occupied most of the space. Chestnut-colored wood, polished to a shine, accentuated a minibar and a mounted monitor displaying a company logo that read "Fiore Enterprises."

"I am so sorry to inconvenience you in this manner," Bernadetta said, inclining her head.

"It's okay. No problem. I was just going in to get me some pepperoni pizza. Or maybe sausage. I can't decide. Anyway, I have nothing pressing on my calendar and I…"

Oh, shut up already, Toni.

If the vamp didn't already have thoughts of slashing my throat and draining me dry, all my rambling would surely give her the idea.

"Good," she said, illustrating what a verbal wreck I was with her succinctness. A slow smile spread over her Kylie-Jenner lips.

I resisted the urge to say anything else and waited for the Dark Donna to initiate conversation. She'd been the one to seek me out, after all.

"It has come to my attention that you are working with Ulfen Erickson, and I assume it has something to do with his son's disappearance."

I hugged my shoulder bag tightly to my stomach. "Um... I... well, you see, I..."

I clenched my lips together, aware of the fact that my verbal wreck had turned into a pileup, one of those that happen on bad snow days. She had kidnapped Ulfen's son and wanted to know if I'd found out where she was keeping him.

Nope, no ma'am. I didn't find anything out. You hid him well. That's what I should've said, except for that last part, of course.

I took a deep breath, trying to calm myself. A strangely familiar sweet, warm scent combined with the metallic sharpness of blood filled my head. I'd been so busy trying not to pee my pants that I hadn't noticed the stomach-churning odor. My poor bladder almost let go as I remembered where I'd sensed something similar.

Oh, crap! My eyes darted toward the door handle. Would I be able to move fast enough to jump out of the car before Bernadetta pinned me to the seat and ate me for lunch? I doubted it. Vampires could move at preternatural speeds. I had never seen one do it, but it was common knowledge.

Bernadetta gave me a raised eyebrow. "I take that as a *yes*."

"Yes," I squeaked. "B-but I didn't find him." The last few words rushed out of my mouth like bullets.

INGRID SEYMOUR

The vamp narrowed her eyes. They pierced through me like needles, making me feel bare and unhinged as if my joints had turned to rubber.

"You tell the truth," she said, not a question but a statement.

"Always, I always tell the truth. It's like a compulsion, like I can't help myself. People ask me stuff, and I just tell them everything. Sometimes I think there's something wrong with me and I—"

Bernadetta's teeth snapped together once as if saying "enough." I shut my mouth.

Holy witchlights! What was wrong with me? I'd just told her a big, fat lie as I tried to convince her that I spoke nothing but the truth. Man, could today get any worse?

"Not that it matters what you think," she said, looking me up and down as if I wasn't worth the air I breathed, "but I did not kidnap Stephen Erickson. Somebody wants to start a war and it's not me. I like the way things are."

Yeah, right. Who was the liar, now? The limousine reeked of that same overpowering scent I'd spotted during my trance.

"Ulfen needs to look elsewhere," she added, "and he needs to find better trackers."

Excuse me? That got my hackles up. I'm a damn good tracker. Stephen was the only known mark I'd been unable to find, and only because an evil vamp was involved.

She leaned forward in her seat, making the huge car shrink with her closeness. "Tell him to leave me alone or there *will* be war."

"Tell him yourself," I snapped, surprising myself.

I *was* scared, but I'd had it. I was done with being intimidated by her. Or anyone else, for that matter. I already had enough to worry about to add a deranged vamp to the list.

175

"I don't work for him," I added. "I was trying to do him a favor because I know his son. That is all. So leave me out of it."

She reassessed me, leaning back and letting her gaze travel the length of my body. After a moment, she said, "Then let me give you some advice, be careful who you do favors for. It will do you no good to get involved in things you don't understand. You might... get yourself killed."

"Is that a threat?"

Bernadetta chuckled, deep in her throat. "I don't do threats, Ms. Sunder. When something bothers me, I simply take care of it. Have a good day."

As she said the words, Bertram opened the door and sunlight cut through the door. The vamp pushed back in her seat. I let out a pent-up breath and would have hugged the particles of light if I'd been able to.

I'm alive. I'm alive.

Apparently, the Dark Donna didn't stoop to personally killing little peons like me. She preferred others to get their hands dirty, thank goodness. I jumped out, and without a glance back, hurried back toward my car.

I had completely lost my appetite.

CHAPTER
28

I drove back to the office on autopilot. I parked a few spaces down from the front door, shut the engine off, and went limp in my seat. Maybe packing and moving to where nobody knew me was the real answer to everything. I could FaceTime with Rosalina and my family. They might hate me for being a coward, but at least I would be alive and safe from all St. Louis's Skew badasses. I could get a job as a barista, my biggest worry tracking the hazelnut creamer on the shelves. It would certainly be a lot easier than this mess.

I'd almost convinced myself this was the worst idea in the world when Jake walked up to the car. He knocked on the glass twice, even though I saw him coming. I heaved a sigh. *China here I come.*

He wore his customary tight jeans, a black T-shirt that didn't seem to have enough fabric around the biceps, and a pair of very expensive-looking boots. I stared at his left pec for a second, which seemed on the verge of talking to me as it flexed.

Flipping my hair, I forced my gaze upward and found purple circles under his tired eyes. As a werewolf, Jake could go without sleep for days before it started to affect him. From the looks of it, he'd probably gone without it for weeks, which meant he hadn't really slept on Rosalina's couch last night. His hair was tousled as if he'd been running his fingers through it, trying to pull it out. I bit my lower lip at the disheveled look as it reminded me of mornings when we woke up together. I shook the errant thought away.

"Any news about Stephen?" I asked.

He shook his head. "I got your message. I was busy and couldn't call back. What is it?"

"Oh, yeah." With everything that had been going on, I'd forgotten about it. "Um," I glanced around, worried this might not be the best place to discuss dark things like kidnappings and vampire threats. "We shouldn't talk here. Have you eaten lunch? I haven't, and I'm starving."

"I'm starving, too."

"How about pizza?" I gestured across the street.

"Perfect."

"Let me check on Rosalina first, I'll meet you there."

He walked away, and I tried to resist the urge to glance over my shoulder and check out his ass. I failed. The jeans fit him perfectly. They were well-worn with faded lines in the shape of his wallet in one of the pockets. He walked with, not quite a swagger, but something that spoke of his infinite confidence.

I tore my eyes away from him and went into the office. Rosalina was on her cell phone, scribbling notes furiously on a yellow pad. She held up one finger, and I waited for her to hang up. After a minute, she disconnected the call, set her pen down, and reclined on her chair with an expression of relief.

"That was the insurance company," she said. "The adjuster was here earlier, and he has just approved payment for our laptops, damaged ingredients, and other repairs." She picked up a credit card from the top of the desk and shook it with delight. "Now I can go to the store and load this baby up with some new macs. We'll be back in business in no time."

I put on a smile that probably looked more like a cringe.

"Oh, no." Rosalina stood and walked toward me. She put her hands on my shoulders. "You decided to condemn the man to a life of celibacy, didn't you?"

I didn't have to explain myself. She knew me too well not to guess what I'd done. "I talked to him. He's happy doing what he does, and not only that, he's good at it. I get the feeling he's the kind of man who makes a difference wherever he goes."

"Want *me* to do it? I have no qualms about it. He'll be happy either way."

"No. It might be bad karma."

Her mouth twisted to one side. "I hate to see you lose your condo, and things are getting a bit tight around here."

I searched her face, feeling wretched.

"You know what. You're right." She waved her hand around. "You have to live by your principles. Otherwise, the job will make you unhappy, and that's not worth it."

Tears pricked the back of my eyes. "Thank you for understanding."

"It'll be okay. I have two customers lined up. One is coming later this afternoon at 3:30. He's not as high profile, but we need customers. Jim Morris referred him."

Jim Morris was the neighborhood bachelor I'd set up soon after we opened the agency.

"That's great." I gave her a one-hundred-percent genuine smile.

She walked back to the desk and grabbed her purse. "I guess I'll run to the mall."

I let her go without telling her about my impending lunch with Jake. For some reason, the thought of sitting with him, just the two of us, made me nervous. So far, we'd mostly talked about Stephen and his kidnapping. Would other things, personal ones, come up while we ate? I was torn between running there or calling to tell him something had come up.

In the end, my urge to be close to him won, and I locked the office and walked across the street.

Jake sat in a booth at the corner. From the looks of it, he'd already ordered our drinks and an appetizer. I approached hesitantly. He was staring at his clasped hands, which rested on top of the table. I knew the intense expression well. His deep concentration told me he might be trying to figure something out.

He glanced up when I slid into the booth.

"I ordered you an orange soda and garlic knots," he said.

A lump rose in my throat. He still remembered my favorites. Few people knew so many things about me. Jake's leaving had taught me not to open up to people, and I'd forgotten how good it felt to have someone who cared about the little things that made me happy.

"Thank you." I took a sip of the soda. It was cold, tangy, and sparkly, just the way I liked it. The garlic knots were crunchy and buttery on the outside and gooey on the inside. *Yum.*

I ordered lasagna because pizza reminded me of Bernadetta, and Jake got a meat lovers pie. We sat in awkward silence after the waiter left, looking at everything, except each other.

"So… what did you want to tell me?" His voice sounded both hopeful and scared at the same time, which made me wonder what he was expecting to hear. Something of a personal nature, perhaps?

Oh, get a grip, Toni! He only cares about Stephen.

He'd made it very clear last night that he had no intention of talking about *us* at all.

"I don't know if this will help," I started, "but as I thought about how things felt while I tracked Stephen, it occurred to me that maybe they're not keeping him at a fixed location. I got the impression that maybe they're constantly moving him."

"You mean they aren't keeping him in one place for long?"

I shook my head. "No, I mean it feels like he's constantly on the move. I think maybe they're keeping him in a moving vehicle."

"Shit," Jake said under his breath. "No wonder no one can find him." He ran his fingers through his already messy hair, managing to flatten a lock that had been standing at an odd angle. "I have been all over the city, trying to catch Stephen's scent at locations that belong to Ulfen's worst enemies. I've spent hours researching real estate records and driving all over town, it was all a waste of time."

He clenched his teeth and a muscle jumped in his jaw. He took a deep breath and let it out slowly, making a monumental effort to control his frustration and anger.

"Don't be so hard on yourself," I said. "You're doing your best. There's no way you could have known."

Jake shook himself, forcing away all emotion. "Did you tell Ulfen?"

"I did."

"Hopefully, this will give him some ideas. I'm afraid I'm fresh out of them."

I hesitated, wondering if I should tell him about the Dark Donna. She was a dangerous creature, and I didn't want Jake to get in trouble with her and her people, but I reminded myself that it wasn't my job to take care of him. He was a big boy and had already been prying in all the wrong places. Giving him accurate information might do some good.

"There's something else," I said.

He straightened. "What?"

"I'm pretty sure Bernadetta Fiore is involved. I mean... she's the prime suspect already, but I think I have proof. Sort of."

"Go on," he said.

"I... had a very unpleasant meeting with her today."

Jake did a slow blink and spoke with forced calm. "Please explain."

"She pretty much mini kidnapped me into her bigass limousine."

"What?!"

Jake's body trembled on the spot, and I feared he might shift right on top of his garlic knots. I stared wide-eyed, my heartbeat kicking up a notch. Clearly, he was on edge, literally teetering at the brink of going postal. He seriously needed a nap. He regained his control by taking a deep breath and closing his eyes for a few seconds.

"Are you all right? Did she hurt you?" he asked, opening his eyes.

"No, she didn't hurt me. In fact," I frowned, "she was mostly polite. She tried to deny having anything to do with Stephen's disappearance, but she was lying."

"What makes you say that?"

I shrugged. "My skill."

Anytime Jake asked these types of questions, I gave him the same answer. I never offered any specifics about how I knew things after tracking someone. He had no idea it involved my senses, so I couldn't tell him about the scent in Bernadetta's limousine.

He made a disgusted sound in the back of his throat.

When we'd worked together, I hadn't felt comfortable with my skills and its consequences—not enough to trust anyone with the truth, especially those closest to me. The first time I tracked someone, the side effects scared the crap out of me, which made me cagey, defensive, and afraid my family and Jake would forbid me to use them. I had begged Nonna not to tell anyone and assured her I wouldn't track anyone without help. Since she lived in New York City, it had been easy to lie.

Now, it was different. I never came out of a trance or suffered through my lack of senses alone. Rosalina always kept me company and figured out a way to make things bearable, even coming up with the idea of learning sign language together. There was no one else in the world I could trust or feel comfortable with while in that vulnerable state—not to mention I didn't want to be a burden on anyone for any length of time, no matter how brief.

Like before, Jake wasn't pleased with my evasive answer. He pursed his lips and leaned back on the booth.

The waiter came with our food. Steam and a delicious scent rose from it. I practically inhaled half of my serving while Jake poked at his pie with disinterest.

"You should eat," I said. "You look like shit."

He chuckled, taking no offense, and started eating.

I told him about Tom and the priest. He seemed relieved when I mentioned Tom showed good signs of recovering. Then we went silent again.

Feeling the pressure of our awkwardness, I let curiosity get the best of me and asked, "Where did you go, Jake?" I thought he might brush away the question, but he didn't.

"New Orleans. Remember Kaden Smith? He lives there."

Kaden had been my brother and Jake's classmate through high school. They'd been inseparable. All three popular Skews, who played varsity and had gaggles of girls chasing after them.

"I've never been to New Orleans," I said. "I need to visit."

It was one of those cities on my list of places to scout for new scents, sounds, and insights. It would certainly expand my options and the likelihood of finding mates. Every new place I managed to visit had a great impact on my success rate.

"It's a great place," Jake said. "Awesome food, incredible nightlife. Very unique."

"Did something there prompt you to start your PI business?"

He pushed a piece of toasty sausage to the edge of his plate, reminding me what a picky eater he could be. "Nah, I got that idea here, after we found Emily Garner. Returning her to her family felt… amazing."

"Yes, it did."

I still remembered her parents' faces when we walked into the police station, Jake cradling Emily in his arms. It had been as if we'd not only rescued the little girl but her entire family as well. That day, we gave them back more than just a child. We gave them back hope and the desire to keep going.

And we'd done that together, combining our skills and smarts to accomplish it.

"I've helped other people, and it's felt just as good every time." He set his fork down. "Then I heard about Stephen. He spent some time in New Orleans with Kaden and me. He was trying to get away from his father and… get over a certain relationship."

I never thought Stephen would have to get over *me*. I wasn't happy about the way our relationship ended, but I couldn't say he had affected me much. I liked Stephen, and maybe, if we'd been allowed to keep seeing each other, I would have eventually developed feelings for him, but that hadn't been the case.

Everyone loves at different rates, I suppose.

"I wish he hadn't returned to St. Louis," Jake continued. "Then this wouldn't have happened. But Ulfen called him back, told him he needed him here, that it was time he took up his heir responsibilities."

Ironically, if Stephen hadn't come back, I wouldn't have been sitting there with Jake, aching to ask him all the questions he didn't want to answer.

"What about you?" Jake asked. "How long since you opened the agency?"

"Almost a year ago."

"Do you like what you do?"

I felt the judgment in his voice. Finding somebody's mate compared to returning a child to her parents didn't score high in his book. And yeah, I had to admit that on a scale of Mother Teresa to Hitler, my new job leaned a little right from the middle. Still, that didn't make me a bad person. I was still helping others find their happiness while I kept mine.

"I do like it," I said. "I've also helped people, and it felt good. Best of all, I'm doing what's best for me. If you think that makes me selfish, then I guess I am."

Jake reached across the table and grabbed my hand, surprising me. The touch sent a thrill up my arm that made me catch my breath. I froze, unable to pull away as his thumb went back and forth over my knuckles.

"I've been unfair to you," he said, his voice a low whisper that reminded me of many intimate moments. "I'm sorry about that. It's not my place to judge you. Your life is yours to live and I…" He swallowed, making it evident that this was hard for him. "I have

185

no business sticking my nose in it. You should be safe now, I trust. No one should bother you anymore. I'm glad you were clear about Ulfen with that damn vamp. She had no business trying to intimidate you like that. I'll call him and tell him about your run-in with the Dark Donna. Try to get back to normal. If my presence next door bothers you, I'll leave, find another place. Though I am in St. Louis to stay." He pulled his hand away, and I had to slide mine under the table to stop from reaching back.

His touch opened a door that I'd slammed shut many months ago, and everything I'd crammed in there came spilling out like junk from an overstuffed closet. All it had taken was the electrifying brush of his skin against mine to shatter the lies I'd been telling myself all along.

I was not over Jacob Knight. Not by a long shot.

In that moment of realization, I wanted to tell him to get the hell away from me, to go and find another place in the nether regions of St. Louis—somewhere the sun didn't shine—so I would never have to see him again and be reminded of what a weak, pathetic, self-defeating woman I was.

But if I did that, he would realize he still had power over me, and dammit, if I wasn't too proud to let him see that. So I put on a smile and lied through my teeth.

"It's fine, Jake. It doesn't bother me. Not really." My tone was cold and detached, and I waved my hand around carelessly. "I doubt we'll be seeing much of each other anyway since we are in such different lines of business."

Jake's eyes tightened, and he watched me closely as I spoke. When I was done, a smile stretched slowly over his chiseled lips, and a know-it-all expression shaped his face.

"What's so funny?" I asked.

He turned his mouth upside down and shook his head. "Nothing, it's just that's exactly what I was thinking."

I mimicked his sarcastic smile.

This seemed to be the way *frienemies* got along, spewing blatant lies at each other while pretending to believe them. Despite everything, I felt I would be able to handle his closeness, and if I turned out to be wrong, St. Louis was a big city. *I* could find another place to operate. I had plans to move up the social scale anyway, so other areas of the city would be more appropriate for the clientele that would soon overfill my agenda.

That evening I went to kickboxing class and imagined Jake's face stamped on the punching bag. I had a hell of a workout and got all my aggression out. I'd done what I could to try to help. Now, I could go back to normal.

CHAPTER 29

t the end of the day, as soon as we got to Rosalina's place, I fed Cupid his pellets and crawled into bed without eating dinner, feeling emotionally exhausted. Too much had happened in the expanse of a few days, and even though Rosalina suggested take-out, my only thoughts were of fluffy pillows and cozy blankets.

I closed my eyes as the events of the day played in my head like a movie in an infinite loop. I kept feeling Jake's finger caressing my knuckles while his intense silver eyes peered into my soul. I grew hot all over, remembering the first time we had sex.

It had been perfect. He had made sure of it.

"I want you to always remember today as the most special day of your life," he'd whispered in my ear as we sat on a luscious bed at the Four Seasons Hotel, a backdrop of The Gateway Arch in our window.

More than once before that night, I'd asked him to take me in the back of his pickup truck as we made out. We'd come close, but he'd been a lot stronger than me and made good on his promise to make my first time memorable.

For a while now, I hadn't tortured myself with memories of that night and others that followed, but since his simple touch had opened that door, I found myself in that luxurious room again. The sheets were white, soft cotton. I wore a strappy black dress and high heel shoes, the same outfit I'd worn to prom. Jake wore a dark gray suit and looked breathtaking.

He seduced me carefully and perfectly, starting from the moment he picked me up at home to the instant our bodies became one. All night, his hands lingered on me. On my waist, my hips, the nape of my neck. He dispensed kisses that were sensual and sweet all at the same time. And by the time we were alone, my desire had reached its peak and his touch was like hot flames on my skin.

That night was, indeed, the most special of my life, and I both loved and hated Jake for giving it to me. He had ruined me. That night and all he meant to me was the reason I'd been incapable of getting close to anyone. No one could measure up to that, especially because I'd been so madly in love with him.

"*You loved that man like in the books and the movies,*" Mom had said to me once. "*It wasn't healthy. Good riddance.*" I would have given my life for him. I would have borne his babies, a whole litter of half werewolves. Instead, he'd torn my heart out.

I tossed and turned in bed, struggling to get him out of my mind and calm down my overactive hormones, until I finally went to sleep.

"Toni."

The hum of an engine filled my ears, loud and incessant. My sense of hearing felt overwhelmed, and it seemed to be the only one functioning properly. I couldn't smell anything. I couldn't see anything either.

Was this a trance? I didn't remember taking a potion.

"Toni."

Tires against pavement. Rattling of metal. Squeak of brakes. Blaring of horns. Maddening, like being right in the middle of an interstate at the very top of rush hour.

Weaving through the nonstop cacophony, a voice fought to rise above.

"Toni."

I could barely perceive it, but it seemed the voice was calling my name. I tried to hone in on it. The voice was familiar. I'd heard it before, but I couldn't place it.

"Toni, is that you?"

My breath caught.

Stephen!

"Yes, it's me." My arms flailed in the darkness, trying to find him. "Where are you?"

My heart hammered. He was close by.

"Please, help me," he begged.

I had to be in a trance. Had to be. It was the only explanation, and somehow, Stephen knew I'd come looking for him.

"I'm trying to find you," I said. "Where are you?"

"I'm here," he screamed.

I whirled, following the raw sound of his voice. I stumbled forward, hands in front of me. *That* scent suddenly saturated the air: sweet and warm, coating my throat. My hands got hold of something. I felt around. A person.

"Stephen?"

He said nothing.

I kept feeling with my hands, moving them upward. They reached what felt like a collarbone, a neck, a face. It was wet and sticky. I pulled back, wishing I could see in this blackness. As the wish materialized so did my sight. It came back gradually. I blinked, held my hands closer to my face. Darkness still surrounded me, but I could make out shapes. I wiggled my fingers. Something dark was smeared on them, then I saw color.

Red.

Red, sticky blood.

Shaking all over, I lowered my hands. A figure etched in darkness stood in front of me. My heart hammered.

"Stephen?" I murmured, lips trembling.

The figure stepped forward, and his face became visible. I pressed a wet, sticky hand to my mouth to hold back a scream.

It *was* Stephen.

I could tell even though his face was a bloody mess. A cut ran across his eyebrow, dripping blood onto a swollen-shut eye. His lower lip was busted and streaks of red ran down his chin.

"Help me." He took a step closer. "Help me." Another step. "Help me." He stopped a foot away from me and held up his hands. "Look at what they've done to me. Why won't you help me?!"

All of his fingers were missing, and only bloody, bloated stumps remained.

Oh, God.

Vomit burned in my throat.

"Lusiola," Stephen said, then he reached for my throat with his mutilated hands.

I screamed and screamed and screamed.

In the next instant, everything went dark and silent.

Someone grabbed my shoulders. I screamed again and flung my arms out, knocking the hands away. I lost my balance and fell with a *thud*. Desperately, I crawled away on my hands and knees until I reached a barrier.

My head and my heart pounded out of control.

I felt around, fingers fumbling, trying to find an exit, but I'd ran into a wall. I felt along its length until I reached the corner.

There was no escape.

I pressed my back against the corner and huddled there, hugging my legs, burying my face in my knees. I waited for Stephen, or whoever, to yank me to my feet and... and what? I didn't know.

I sobbed into my legs, my body trembling with tension as I anticipated the worst.

Minutes ticked by. Nothing happened. I still couldn't hear or see anything.

I don't know how long I spent in that position, but when the gentle sound of bird song reached my ears, I opened my eyes to find I was cowering in the corner of my room with Rosalina sitting on the bed, watching me closely.

"Toni," she said my name carefully as if afraid I would break.

Tears of relief spilled down my cheeks. She approached carefully, making no sudden movements as if I were a skittish cat. When she reached me, she wrapped me tightly in her arms and rocked me back and forth until my tears ran out.

CHAPTER 30

"I heard you screaming," Rosalina said.

We sat on the sofa, nursing identical cups of tea. I had calmed down and taken a hot shower that had succeeded in making me feel half-human again.

"So I ran into your room. You were sitting up in bed, wailing. I tried talking to you, but I think you couldn't hear me. When I touched you, you jumped off the bed and crawled to the corner. You couldn't see me. Your eyes were blank, just like when you come out of a trance."

Her words made me shake as I remembered the panic.

Rosalina laid her hand on mine. "Are you okay? We don't have to talk about this if you're not ready."

"No, it's fine. I want to understand what happened."

"It was more than a nightmare. I can tell you that. You were blind and deaf, Toni."

I nodded, feeling the truth of her words.

"What if, somehow, you put yourself in a trance during your sleep?"

I set my teacup on the coffee table. "Maybe."

"But that's never happened before."

"No, but Skew powers are known to change with time." The possibility of not being able to control the trance scared the crap out of me. I might never sleep again.

Rosalina half winced. "I'm afraid to ask, but… what did you see?"

Pushing through my fear, I told her everything, sparing no details. When I finished and glanced up at her face, she was pale—or her version of pale, anyway. Her beautiful tan skin looked as if someone had turned off its golden glow.

"That had to be a nightmare. You weren't really there, right?" she asked, doubtfully.

"I don't know. It felt so real. All the sounds and that smell. What do you think that word he said means?"

Rosalina shook her head. "I have no idea. Maybe we should Google it." She went for her phone, which rested on the arm of the sofa. "How do you think it's spelled?"

I shrugged. "L-U-S-I-O-L-A."

Quickly, she typed the letters into the search box, then glanced up. "Apparently, it's a city in Kenya. Shit, do you think that's where Stephen is?"

"No." For some reason, I had the feeling he was near. "Maybe it's spelled differently. What if you try L-U-C-I-O-L-A?"

She used Google again. "A genus of flashing fireflies," she read. "That helps me as much as saying a 'constellation of neutron stars.'" Rosalina gave me worried eyes and confused me with her analogy. She was too smart for me. "Maybe you just had a nightmare, after all, a very lucid one."

"The more I think about it, the more I'm convinced it wasn't. Maybe this word will mean something to Jake."

Rosalina sighed. "Do you feel up to working today?"

"Yeah, I think so. I need something to take my mind off things."

"All right, let's get ready and go. Oh, by the way, your mom called several times. She wants you to call her back. She sounded pretty insistent."

"Yeah, she's been pestering me about coming to eat lunch. She's making me tortellini. I'll call her back."

On our way to the office, we grabbed breakfast at a drive-through. I got a double espresso and two oversized blueberry muffins, while Rosalina went the healthy route and got tea and an egg on a wheat toast.

"At this rate, all those curves are gonna go flat," I teased, gesturing toward her boobs.

"Pfft, they aren't going anywhere. They're a family curse. Abuela Esperanza has them, my mama has them, my sister has them, and if I had a brother, he'd have them, too."

"A curse?" I rolled my eyes as I turned the Camaro onto our street. "Men love that shit."

She nodded reluctantly. "True, but they should be removable or something. Some days I just can't stand them. You don't get it because…" She trailed off.

I raised my eyebrows at her and gave her a look. "Don't you dare offend my pair. They may be humble, but they're all I've got."

We got out of the car laughing. I felt a little lighter, even if the one blueberry muffin I'd eaten had been nearly five pounds. Rosalina had that effect on me. I loved seeing her smile, and our banter always got her going, so it motivated me to tease her.

She keyed the lock, and we walked inside. It seemed every time I came in, I held my breath expecting the place to be a wreck, but everything looked fine. I wondered how long it would take me to shake the feeling off. I didn't know, though one thing was for sure, I was never spending another night up in the loft.

After my 3:30 PM client from yesterday, I had started a potion. The ingredients Rosalina reordered had arrived quickly, though not cheaply. With everything that was going on, I couldn't pick them up myself, so we'd had to pay a courier to cross into Elf-hame plus a rushed delivery fee. It had been worth it though, even if expensive. We'd lost a few precious days in the fray and had to play catch-up to make rent and bill money. And of course, our salaries, which always took a hit when shit like this happened.

I had another appointment scheduled for 9:00 AM, which gave me an hour to do a few things such as call Celina Morelli to give her the bad news. I really didn't want to do that. I'd given the woman false hopes, and I was afraid my call would only break her heart a little more—not to mention hurt the agency.

Chickening out of the task for the moment, I decided to face my other problem.

"Hey, I'm going next door to see if Jake's there." I had called him, but again, he hadn't answered.

Rosalina, already at her desk, glanced up with worry in her eyes. "Okay, I hope he can help."

"Me, too."

Jake's door was locked this time. I knocked and waited. Nothing. Apparently, he wasn't in. I tried his phone again. No answer. I sighed, went back to the office, and set about my day, starting with the dreaded call to Celina Morelli.

"I've been expecting your call," she said.

Did I detect a little hope in her voice? *Well, shit!* "Ms. Morelli, I'm sorry to call with bad news." I expected her to say she wasn't surprised or something biting like that, but she remained silent. "I was unable to locate a mate. I apologize. This is a rare occurrence. My mate tracker rate is very good, but not perfect and—"

"But your partner said you did," she interrupted.

"I know, and I apologize for the miscommunication. I thought I'd found someone, but I was wrong."

"You sounded so confident about finding someone. What happened?"

"I can't give you specific details," I said. "If you remember, our agency's contract has a clause about the secrecy of our methods. All I can say is that my skills didn't reveal anyone."

"How is that possible? Is there… something wrong with me?"

"Oh, no," I assured her. "Of course not."

"Then what?"

"I'm sorry. This is all I can say. My partner will issue a refund for your deposit."

"This is unacceptable."

"I'm sorry."

Celina went on a rant about false promises and shams, and I took it all patiently. I almost broke and told her about Vincent but kept my cool and my dignity. Hopefully, the latter wouldn't cost me my livelihood.

Throughout the rest of the morning and afternoon, I kept glancing at my phone, hoping for a call, but it seemed Jake had better things to do. Maybe he was following a true lead while my "Luciola" nightmare was just that.

Lunch and my 3:45 PM appointment came and went. I reclined on my chair, absentmindedly eating my second giant blueberry muffin. It hit the spot, the sugar waking me up from my afternoon lethargy. Feeling energized, I walked out of the office.

"Hey, I'll go see if Jake is back," I told Rosalina, who was staring at a budgeting spreadsheet making sure we could make ends meet this month.

This time, Jake's door was open when I pulled on it.

Like the last time, there was no sign of him inside. I called out a couple of times, but he didn't answer, so I went in through the next door. Protective plastic covered the floor as well as cans of paint, fresh rollers and brushes, and rolls of blue tape. No sign of Jake there either. I climbed the steps to the loft. The layout of the place was identical to mine, so the bare walls struck me as odd since I expected to find black-and-white photographs hanging there.

I found Jake upstairs, sacked out on a mattress directly on the floor. He lay face down, wearing nothing but a pair of tight, black boxer briefs. My eyes raked the length of his long frame. His wide back tapered gently toward a narrow waist with two dimples at its base. In the time he'd been away, he'd grown more muscular and acquired yet another tattoo down his left flank. I took a step closer for a better look. The body art consisted of words inked in a pretty scroll. I tried to read them, but they were not in English.

His left arm hung off the mattress, and his hand rested flat on the floor. His feet were also off the mattress. He was simply too big for it. I held my breath as I admired him, trying to keep his delicious scent at bay. He was hot as hell, a sight to behold, especially to someone who'd gone celibate for a while—not to mention, someone whose last sex partner had been *him*.

Yet, it wasn't his amazing body that stunned me the most. Instead, it was how vulnerable he seemed. No one got the drop on Jacob Knight and his werewolf senses. That was what he'd told me once, and yet, there he lay while I watched him sleep.

His brow was furrowed, making him look stressed, even in his sleep. He must've really developed a close relationship with

Stephen for his disappearance to affect him this badly. I fought the urge to kneel by his side and smooth his hair back. I wanted to tell him that it would be all right, that he would find Stephen, but I had no idea if it was true.

Clothes lay strewn on the floor in two piles. I imagined them labeled as "dirty pile" and "it doesn't stink that much pile."

"Are you done looking at my ass yet?" he asked without opening his eyes.

Dammit! Jake wasn't even asleep, and here I'd thought he looked vulnerable.

He rolled over onto his back, stretching his arms over his head, and giving me a good morning greeting with a tall flag right in his middle. I turned to face the stairs, my cheeks growing hot.

Sweet buttered toast, my memories weren't at all exaggerated. The man was really that... impressive.

He groaned and yawned, then said, "Didn't take you for a peeping Toni."

"Ha ha, clever."

Inhaling deeply, I faced him again, unwilling to let him embarrass me. He had sat up and reclined against the wall, one knee up and his arm resting on it while a satisfied smile stretched his lips.

"That's not what I was doing," I said. "I didn't want to wake you. You looked... peaceful and tired, but I was torn because, well, something happened last night that may have given me a clue about Stephen."

Jake immediately jumped to his feet, found a pair of frayed jeans in one of the clothes piles, and put them on. He rubbed the sleep from his eyes and slapped his cheeks.

"What clue?" he asked.

199

"I had… a nightmare." I didn't want to go into details about exactly what had happened, and a nightmare felt like the easiest explanation. "It featured Stephen. He was hurt and asking for help, but right before I woke up, he said something odd. Just one word, but it stuck with me."

"What was it?"

"Luciola."

He frowned and repeated the word under his breath. "Luciola."

"Do you know what it means?"

Rubbing his forehead, he started pacing the room. "It sounds familiar, but I can't remember why." He stopped and suddenly whirled in my direction. "Let's go downstairs." He ran past me, his back muscles rippling as he lithely took the steps two at a time.

Downstairs, he glanced around his messy work area.

"Where is it?" he mumbled to himself. "There!"

He knelt next to a canvas tarp, pulled a pile of manila folders from under it, then riffled through them. He ran his finger down several pieces of paper, his eyes quickly scanning the words. I waited with my heart in my throat, praying he would find something that would help us find Stephen.

Wait, Us?!

Since when had it become us?

"Here!" He jumped to his feet and walked over to me, holding one sheet of paper. "Luciola." He pointed at a spot at the bottom of the page.

The word was spelled L-U-C-C-I-O-L-A with two "Cs," and it seemed to be a physical location, not just some abstract term because the sheet listed an address.

"It's one of Bernadetta's properties," Jake said. He stood frozen for a moment, his gaze darting from side to side, then he ran back upstairs, leaving me standing next to a five-gallon bucket of paint.

Adrenaline buzzed through my body, making me fidget on the spot. My mind whirled with questions. Was this a coincidence? Had I really come up with a clue? If I had, what did that say about my skills? What exactly had happened last night? And why?

Jake came down a few moments later. He was fully dressed, wearing a T-shirt, a brown leather jacket, and matching boots. Without stopping, he snatched his bike helmet from the worktable and pressed it into my hands.

"C'mon, let's go." He grabbed me by the elbow and pulled me along.

I probably should have protested, should have told him I had things to do, but instead, I went along, a feeling of determination and certainty growing inside me. Stephen's life had been hanging on the balance for days, and maybe today, we would find him. We would take him home, and he would be all right.

"Give me a sec," I said and ran into the office to retrieve my purse and tell Rosalina I was off for the day. I went in and out quickly. Jake was already straddling his bike.

He started the engine. "Put on the helmet."

"What about you?" I asked as I climbed on behind him.

"I have a thick skull, remember?"

I snorted a laugh. He did have a thick skull, both figuratively and literally. He keyed the address into his cell phone, snapped the device in a holder mounted on the dashboard, and we rolled off the sidewalk heading north.

CHAPTER 31

We got to the Delmar Loop fifteen minutes later. Jake parked his bike a block away from the address in his file, and we walked the rest of the way. The area buzzed with the usual pedestrians going in and out of the shops and restaurants that lined the boulevard, so we had no trouble blending in.

We approached from the north side, walking casually.

"Huh? Lucciola is a candle shop?" I said, confused, when I laid eyes on the quaint shop. It had a black awning over its door and window display, golden accents on the trim.

"She has lots of businesses all over the city," Jake said. "All kinds of them."

I felt self-conscious and started to wonder if I should be there at all. I didn't think Bernadetta would like seeing me nosing around one of her properties. I let my hair hang forward, covering my face. Jake gestured toward a coffee shop across the street from *Lucciola - Fine Candle Shop.*

"Let's go in. I'll get us some coffee. Why don't you snatch us a table?"

We went into the coffee shop, and I sat at one of the window tables with a good view of the candle shop. I set my purse down. It thudded with the heavy gun. *Oops!*

My cell phone buzzed, the caller ID flashing "Mom." I dismissed the call and typed "Lucciola" into the search bar and found a New York City restaurant by that name. I also learned the word had a Latin origin that meant "I shine," and that in Italian the word meant firefly. I figured since the Dark Donna was originally from Italy, she was going for Firefly Candle Shop. Not a bad name. I put my phone away and surreptitiously glanced across the street. Not much activity there.

Jake returned with two cups of coffee and two croissant sandwiches and set them on the table. He pushed one of the coffees in my direction. "Cream and three sugars."

Damn, he also remembered how I liked my coffee. I slow blinked and took a sip. Delicious. The croissant was tempting, but I had to keep my girlish figure.

I gestured toward the food. "If you're hungry enough, eat both sandwiches. I had a giant blueberry muffin earlier."

"Oh, I'm hungry." Jake seemed to always be hungry. It was a werewolf thing. His metabolism ran hot and fast like a space rocket.

We sipped our coffees silently while we watched the candle shop. People passed in front of our window. As I scrutinized them closely, it reminded me of scouting for a mark. The difference... I had no idea what we were waiting for here. We already knew they were keeping Stephen mobile. He wouldn't be in the candle shop.

God, we needed to find him. We had less than twenty-four hours before it was too late.

Trying not to sound impertinent, I asked, "So... what exactly are we doing?"

Jake's silver eyes wandered away from the shop to meet mine. He shrugged one shoulder. "Gathering clues. PI work can seem frustrating and irrational sometimes, but the smallest details can make a huge difference in solving a case."

"What do you think we'll see here?"

"I've no idea. Maybe I'll walk over there and buy you a candle." His mouth tipped into one of his wicked smiles. "Lavender, citrus, vanilla? Which would you prefer?"

I gasped.

"What?"

I shook my head. I was so stupid. Why hadn't I made this connection as soon as I saw that Lucciola was a candle shop?

Jake frowned, waiting for an answer.

Dammit, how could I explain what I'd just realized without divulging the way my skills worked? I struggled with what to do, feeling like a piece of smelly trash as I did so. Stephen's life was on the line, and here I sat, worried about myself and my *baggaged* relationship with Jake.

"Toni, whatever it is, you have to tell me."

"I know." I lowered my head and took a deep breath. "Okay, but you have to keep this to yourself. You can't tell anyone."

"You can trust me. You know that."

"Do I?"

Okay, maybe the question was a bit unfair since my professional secrets had nothing to do with our relationship. I waved a hand to dismiss my own comment and lowered my voice as I explained. "When I go into a trance, I use my senses to find my mark."

Jake's brow furrowed, but he didn't interrupt.

"You know how strong my sense of smell is," I said, remembering how he'd constantly remarked about it in the past. He used to say that it rivaled his own sense of smell, and werewolves were well known for that trait. "Well," I continued, "when I was trying to track Stephen I smelled cinnamon, vanilla, and lavender."

I let that sink in. Jake's gaze sparked as he made the connection. He glanced toward the candle shop. "Maybe they're keeping him there." He squeezed the edge of the table so hard that the wood groaned.

I shook my head. "No, I told you he's on the move."

He regarded me with narrowed eyes. "And your... senses helped you figure that out, too?"

"Yes. I could hear a car's engine, tires rolling on asphalt, traffic sounds."

"And what did you *see*?"

"Nothing. It was dark—not a pinprick of light."

Jake lowered his head, appearing deep in thought. As he ran fingers through his golden-brown hair, I caught movement out of the corner of my eye. In front of the candle shop, a white delivery van rolled to a stop. It had a logo on the side painted with black and golden letters that read Lucciola Candle Shop.

Before I knew what I was doing, I rose to my feet and rushed out of the coffee shop. I crossed the street in a few strides and found myself standing behind the van's rear double doors. The back windows were tinted. I took a step forward, my hand reaching for the handle.

"May I help you?" A man, clearly a Stale, came around the side of the van. He wore black slacks and a gray shirt with the company's logo on its breast pocket. A beer gut stuck out, barely held in place by a worn belt.

"Open this door," I demanded.

The man furrowed thin eyebrows and glanced from me to the candle shop behind him.

"Um, I—" his mouth slammed shut when Jake appeared behind me. Beer Gut took a step back, looking ready to bolt.

"Do as the lady asked," Jake growled in his alpha tone, a blood-curdling sound that carried the command of a thousand pissed-off dads.

Beer Gut shuddered visibly, his face going slack with fear. I wouldn't have been surprised if he'd peed his pants. I could see the moment he decided it wasn't worth arguing. He put both hands up and slowly approached the van. Trembling, he reached for the handle and pulled the door open.

Light spilled into the van's interior, revealing metal shelves running along the sides, creating an empty middle aisle. Cardboard boxes filled the shelves and a hand truck was secured against the back wall.

A wave of scents flowed out through the doors, hitting me with its pungent quality and making me take a step back. My knees weakened as flashes of severed fingers ran through my mind. My stomach flipped. This was exactly the jumble of olfactory stimuli I'd experienced during my trance.

Jake sniffled, wrinkling his nose, taking in the scents. His head snapped in my direction. "Is this it? Is this what you smelled?"

I nodded, fighting the tears that filled my eyes.

Jake turned to Beer Gut. "How many vans like this one are there?"

The man held his hands up again and started backing away toward the shop's entrance. "Look, man, I don't know. I just drive the stupid thing and deliver the candles. That's all."

In the blink of an eye, Jake jumped on Beer Gut, holding him by the collar and pushing him against Lucciola's glass-paneled door. A woman who was approaching down the sidewalk gave a yelp, turned on her heel, and ran back the way she'd come.

I approached Jake carefully. His temper could be so volatile at the wrong times. For the most part, he controlled his wolf well, but anger sometimes got the better of him, causing him to shift involuntarily. Maybe in the last year and a half, his mastery had improved, but I didn't know for sure. He didn't need a Shifting Under Duress charge. No shifter wanted that on their record, just like no one wanted a DUI.

"Jake," I stood next to him, so he could see me. "Don't hurt him. He may be telling the truth."

His silver eyes flicked toward me, then back to the man. Jake's jaw unclenched, and his hands around Beer Gut started to relax. I exhaled in relief, but then the shop's door opened, and both men went tumbling inside.

A towering vampiress, well over six-foot tall, gracefully stepped aside as Jake and Beer Gut thudded to the floor.

"What is going on here?" she demanded, wrinkling her nose at the spectacle before her. She wore a black, gossamer sheath that fell to the floor and could have made a nice curtain. Blond curls spilled over her shoulders, the kind of luscious locks that took hours to get just right. Her skin was smooth and pale like porcelain, and flawless makeup accentuated her large blue eyes. She would have been beautiful if not for her resting bitch face. I swear it would scare the cockroaches from any filthy kitchen.

She took a step back, reached toward a table display piled with candles in a pyramid shape, and came up with a phone, probably getting ready to dial 911.

"Jake," I snapped, "I think she's gonna call the cops."

"Damn right, I am." She started to dial, but before she could finish, Jake leaped to his feet and snatched the phone from her hand.

"How dare you?!" She wrinkled her nose and gave Jake a disgusted glare. "Your type of werewolf isn't welcome here."

Finding himself free, Beer Gut lurched to his feet and stumbled out of the store.

Jake had lost interest in him and was now scanning the vamp up and down, returning her glare. "My type of werewolf?"

"Yes, violent and foul." She sniffed. "When was the last time you took a shower?"

He hadn't taken a shower today. I knew that for a fact, but to me, his scent was intoxicating, not repellent. Vampires and werewolves didn't get along, though. Everybody knew that. But how she could smell anything over the cloying sweetness that filled the store, I didn't know.

"What that hell is that sweet smell?" I said out loud, without realizing it.

"That is just the best organic beeswax around," the vamp said.

Beeswax? Of course!

Outside, Beer Gut's van screeched out of the parking spot.

"When was the last time you saw Stephen Erickson?" Jake demanded.

The vamp's expression changed. The disgust disappeared and calculated deliberation replaced it. "I don't get involved in... *skirmishes* of that nature," she said at last. "That goes well beyond my pay grade. I will kindly ask you to leave this establishment. We sell candles, if you're not here to purchase one, you can take your stink elsewhere."

"I don't stink," Jake complained irrationally. The vamp was really getting on his nerves with that one.

Time for a different approach.

"I apologize for this… outburst," I said, putting on my friendliest smile. "You see, my… partner and I are private investigators, and a clue in our search of Stephen Erickson led us here."

The blonde retreated, shaking her hands at us and staying away from a shaft of sunlight seeping through the display window. "Nah-ah, I told you already, this goes beyond my pay grade. I sell candles, nothing else."

I glanced toward a door in the back of the store. "Would you mind if we search the premises?"

"No way. Unless you have some kind of legal *paper thingy* the only place you're going is out of here."

She meant a warrant, I guessed, but nope, we didn't have one of those—we weren't even cops—but asking had been worth a try.

"Then maybe you can answer a question for us." I gave her another smile, but it might as well have been a growl because she rushed behind the counter, putting distance between us.

"I'm not answering any questions." She reached under the register to do something.

Press an alarm button? That would be bad. Instead, she came up with a telephone receiver, one with a spiraling cord connected to it, and pressed it to her ear. She waited for a connection, her clear blue eyes shifting from Jake to me and back again.

My thoughts raced, trying to figure out how to get any type of useful information from this person. I knew Stephen wasn't here. Bernadetta wasn't stupid. She was keeping him on the move. Of that, I was certain, but what could I ask next?

Jake thought of something first. "Five drivers, five delivery vans," he said. "Where are the rest?"

"You've got your facts wrong, stink pile. We only have two drivers, and Garrett has been out sick," she finished saying just as a voice piped through the receiver. "Yes, hello, this is Chrissa at The Loop location. We have a situation."

Jake leaned closer and whispered in my ear. "Time to go."

I didn't wait to be told twice and took the lead out of the shop. We didn't stop our clipped pace until we reached Jake's bike. We tore out of there, my body pressed tightly to his, my arms wrapped around his waist.

Only two drivers and the other one had been sick for a while. I was willing to bet his sick time amounted to the same number of days Stephen had been missing. And he was either driving the van, or he'd been told to sit on the sidelines while they used his ride for other purposes.

My mind whirled with possibilities. How could we find out more? Was there a way to get a hold of Lucciola's employee ledgers to find out the driver's address? Or maybe we just needed the other van's license plate, then the cops could put an ATL out for it. I wished I could ring Tom to ask him. Or maybe Jake had his own connections. I really hoped so.

My heart pounded against my chest, and I wondered if Jake could feel it as I reclined against him. *Damn*, my blood hadn't pumped this fast in a long time, and I didn't like how alive it made me feel.

CHAPTER
32

J ake took a turn in the opposite direction of The Hill.

"Hey, where are we going?" I yelled over the sounds of traffic.

"Going to see someone who might be able to help us," he yelled back. "You can call your friend when we get there."

Part of me wanted to protest, but the other part, the one that seemed to be an adrenaline junkie, was okay with it, especially when Jake twisted the throttle, and we sped down the street going faster than allowed. The wind blew cool and pierced through my blue jeans, sending a shiver up my spine.

Fifteen minutes later, we found ourselves in the Central West End area, specifically in the historic district on Westmoreland Place, a private community with grand homes built as far back as the 1800s. Who did Jake know around here who could help us? My confusion grew when he pulled up to one of the biggest mansions on the street and parked in the front.

We got off of the bike, and I blinked up at the house from the sidewalk. The place was simply beautiful. It had an elegant architecture for which I had no name, though it certainly seemed European with its castle-like towers, ornate stone, and arches. A red brick path lined with manicured hedges led to the front door, which sported a big, ornate letter "K" on top of it.

Could that possibly stand for *Knight*?

Was this Jake's house?! No, it couldn't be. His parents had left him money, but not this much, right? Besides, I'd found him sleeping on a mattress on the floor of his would-be office. Why would he sleep there if he owned a place like this?

As we walked up the path, I peered up at the warmly lit windows, and the twilight sky framing the structure. The place almost looked like it belonged in a fairytale.

From the right corner, a man came around attacking a row of hedges with big clippers. He paused for a moment to wave. "Hello, Mr. Knight."

"Hi, Clyde."

Jake bounded up the steps and, without knocking, strolled into the house.

My confusion-meter kicked up to red.

A giant schnauzer came bounding into the foyer. Jake knelt in front of the animal and allowed it to lick his face.

"Hey, buddy." He grabbed the dog by the scruff and gave him a shake.

I'd seen schnauzers before but none this big. This guy had to be on steroids—or more likely just a separate breed. His coat shone black, and he was groomed to perfection, including his beard and bushy eyebrows.

Without even bothering to wipe his face, Jake stood and legit introduced the dog to me. "Toni meet Bones. Bones, this is Toni."

I blinked at the animal, wondering if I should shake his paw. Instead, I went for a little wave. "Hi there, Bones."

I swear the dog gave me a dirty look. Wait a minute, was he a shifter?

"She's all right… most of the time. Be nice to her, Bones." Jake patted the dog's head and started walking toward a door at the back of the foyer. "C'mon, at this hour, he's probably in the kitchen."

"Who's probably in the kitchen?" I asked, following him and giving Bones a wary glance as he padded next to me as if making sure I wouldn't steal any of the many vases and gilded portraits hanging from the walls. The place was Fancy with a capital "F." Polished wooden staircase. Marble tables with fresh, aromatic flowers in porcelain vases. High ceilings. Lush rugs and a color scheme clearly envisioned by a professional interior decorator.

We traversed a mile-long hall lined with black-and-white photographs of wolves in wooded landscapes. I wanted to pause and look at them closer, but Jake's strides were long, so I barely had time to drink everything in. At the end of the hall, my phone buzzed. I checked it quickly, screening another call from Mom. I put the cell away as we entered an ample kitchen flooded with the mouthwatering smells of cooking.

Bones rushed ahead and curled up on top of a huge fluffy pillow. The kitchen was the size of Rosalina's entire apartment. An eight-foot island sat in the middle, lined with stools. Cherry cabinets ran up to the tall ceilings and stainless steel appliances shone like mirrors.

A man with gray hair stood in front of a massive gas stove, cooking what looked like ribeye steaks on an indoor grill.

"Hey, Grandpa," Jake greeted the man.

I skidded to a stop. Grandpa?! Why had he never talked about him? The man turned to face us with a smile as bright as a 100 Watt bulb.

"I just dropped another rib eye on the grill," he said. "You should've let me know we would have company."

Jake leaned close and gave him a man-hug, thumping him hard on the back. They were both the same height and build, and I swear, the old man's profile looked as if someone had traced it to make a mold for Jake's. The resemblance was uncanny.

"So this is the famous Toni," the old man said, setting a large pronged fork next to the stove and walking in my direction with open arms. "It's good to finally meet you." He gave me a warm and welcoming hug.

His friendliness and words took me aback. From the sounds of it, Jake had told him a lot about me. I glanced at Jake over the man's shoulder, but he wasn't making eye contact. Instead, he busied himself with picking a cherry tomato from a salad bowl and popping it in his mouth.

"Um, it's good to meet you too, Mr.... " I didn't know what to call him.

"My name is Walter, Walter Knight." He continued smiling warmly and held me at arms' length.

His eyes were deep brown and stared down into mine with an intense quality that seemed quite opposed to his gentle smile. He held me there for a long moment, his gaze drilling into mine. My eyelids fluttered as a strange thrill went through me. Something in my chest felt disarmed and analyzed by his stare as if my soul had been rendered naked for him to peruse, as if he could decipher my deepest secrets as easily as if I were a large-print, open book—no reading glasses needed. After a long moment, he finally pulled away, patting my shoulder and letting me go. I lurched forward and caught myself on the island.

What the hell was that? I wanted to demand, except I wasn't so sure anything had happened, and the sense of disorientation was quickly dissolving.

I glanced up as Walter walked away, his back to me. Jake had a questioning look on his face and was pointedly staring at his grandfather. The old man shook his head slightly and a wave of disappointment seemed to wash over Jake's face and body. His gaze lowered to the floor, and his shoulders fell as if he'd received a wealth of bad news.

Still dizzy, I filled my lungs with a deep inhale. My eyes roved around the kitchen searching for something, but I didn't know what. *What had just happened?* We walked in... Jake's grandfather introduced himself and then... he'd gone back to the stove. So why did I feel so weird? I tried hard to put a finger on the strange sensation, but it quickly dissipated, leaving me questioning my sanity.

Walter picked up the large fork and flipped the steaks. "Why don't you two set the table outside? It's a beautiful evening."

"Actually, I need your help," Jake said.

"Oh?" The old man gave his grandson a raised bushy eyebrow.

"Yeah, we need you to help us locate a vehicle. Can you put your people to the task?"

"Does this have anything to do with Stephen Erickson?"

Jake nodded.

"Good," Walter said, causing a regiment of questions to march into my head.

Why was that good? As if he'd heard my question out loud, Walter elaborated.

"I don't like to owe Ulfen any favors. If we find his son, that'll wipe the slate clean, don't you think?" he asked, sounding amused.

Jake smiled crookedly. "I'd say so."

What favors? God, my head was going to explode with questions.

"Write down the details," Walter pointed the fork toward a desk area that held a few notepads and pens in a wooden holder. "Then fetch me the phone and set the table as I asked, will ya?"

I was flabbergasted, to say the least. Jake had a rich grandfather that he'd never told me about, and apparently, the man had *people* who could potentially find kidnapped, rich heirs.

Jake jotted down the information on a notepad and set a cordless phone, which he'd retrieved from the wall, on top of it. Then, he walked to a cupboard and started pulling out plates and wine glasses. From a drawer, he withdrew cloth napkins and silverware. I helped him with the latter and walked through a set of French doors and onto a covered patio.

A huge, manicured yard extended past the patio. A bottom-lit, kidney-shaped pool sat in the middle of the backyard. Up-lit trees and bushes created a boundary that extended about forty feet in every direction. Flowerbeds overflowed with seasonal blooms, leaving me no doubt that Clyde spent many hours landscaping to keep things looking tiptop.

Out on the covered patio, Jake and I set an intricately designed, wrought iron table with fancy dinnerware. Jake moved so fast, I didn't have a chance to even form any questions before he was headed back to the kitchen.

"Why don't you let Toni pick a bottle of wine to go with dinner?" Walter said.

"Sure. C'mon." Jake gestured for me to follow.

A moment later, we walked through a heavy oak door and descended a wide stone staircase into a semi-dark wine cellar. The temperature dropped several degrees as we reached the bottom of the stairs. The room's dim lighting brought a calm to all of my senses.

I frowned at the rows and rows of wooden shelving, replete with bottles of wine. There had to be a fortune stored here. More than Rosalina and I had made during our entire lives.

"Um, Jake, I don't know anything about wine and what goes with what. Can you pick?"

"Of course." He walked down the line of shelves then took a right and disappeared.

I followed him, walking leisurely as I admired the abundance. I found Jake frowning at a dusty bottle and reading the label.

"You don't know what you're doing either, do you?" I asked, amused.

"Not really." He glanced over at me. "Google it. See what goes with red meat?"

I pulled out my phone and typed in a search.

"So it says here that a Petite Sirah or Cabernet Sauvignon would go well with a rich cut of beef."

I glanced up from the phone to find Jake's attention immersed in my features. A thrill went down to my lower belly, tightening my muscles. It was like an electric jolt, something that no one else but Jake had made me feel.

"God, you're beautiful," he said in a heady voice that made me slow-blink and go all tingly in places.

Shit, Toni. Really?

Without taking his eyes off me, he slid the wine bottle back into the rack and slowly turned to face me. A current of palpable energy flowed between us. He took a step closer until we were about an inch apart, the tips of his boots touching mine, the back of his hand brushing my hip.

A voice in the back of my head was screaming for me to run upstairs and jump inside the fridge until my ovaries turned into popsicles. Sadly, the voice was weak, and it didn't compare to the stronger one that told me to stay put, and overpowered every rational thought in my being. Because when it came to Jacob Knight, logic didn't seem to count.

Only instincts.

His darkened gaze fell to my lips. He inhaled sharply, leaning closer. He had told me before that my scent drove him crazy, that it did things to him that he'd never experienced before. Did it still work the same way? I really hoped it did because otherwise, it wouldn't be fair—not when his intoxicating smell could send my thoughts into the gutter from zero to sixty in under a nanosecond.

He let out a trembling breath through parted lips. His large hand snaked around my waist and pulled me against him. My breasts nestled perfectly under his pecs. He hissed in a breath as our bodies fit together. I slid my fingers up his side, enjoying his solidity.

I was dying to kiss him, but this slow way was delicious, like savoring a favorite dessert to make it last to the last bite. His other hand cupped my face.

"Toni, why can't I resist you?" he said, his sweet breath brushing my lips and sending a spark of heat to my core.

"You're asking me?" My voice sounded husky, deep, and it seemed to undo whatever shred of willpower he was holding onto.

His lips crashed into mine. The world exploded with sensations I hadn't experienced in a very long time. My entire body tingled and became alive with desire. His tongue slipped into my mouth, hungry to taste me. Memories washed over me, his naked body on top of mine, the rocking of his hips against my own, expert fingers caressing secret places.

He slipped his hands around my ass, picked me up, and walked me to the wall. He pinned me there, a barrier of hard muscle and sinew conquering me. I felt his erection against me, and I let out an involuntary moan. His chest rumbled, and his mouth left mine to explore my neck. His tongue traced a pattern over my jugular.

I whispered in his ear. "Jake, I've missed you so much."

Damn! Where did that come from? That wasn't something I wanted to admit. I needed to stop this. I needed to push him away and let him know this was unplanned and meant nothing. I didn't forgive him for leaving me. I wasn't opening the door to invite him in again, even if my legs were wrapped tightly around him as inviting as ever.

And why was he doing this anyway? If he wanted me this badly, why had he left me in the first place?

Gah, the hell with all the questions.

His stubbled jaw scratched against mine as his lips returned to my mouth. There, his tongue ran the length of my lower lip, tasting me. I knew his kiss well and loved the fullness of his lower lip. It gave me something to bite, to suck, to delight in.

He tugged at my blouse, pulling it from my waistband. His hand slid over my stomach, and suddenly I wished the entire world would disappear, leaving only the two of us, wrapped together in heat. His finger traced a path toward my breasts. I raked my own fingers into his hair and arched my back.

"You'd better stop that and bring the wine up," Walter called from upstairs.

Jake jumped away from me, panting, his eyes wide, his lower lip swollen. I felt bereft and cold without his body pressed against mine.

I shook my head, feeling angry at myself. "Shit, what are we doing? We shouldn't have…"

"I'm sorry, Toni. You're right. We shouldn't." He raised a hand through his light brown hair and turned his back on me.

I hastily stuffed my blouse back into my pants and smoothed the front, stretching the wrinkles out. I patted my hair down and wiped a hand over my lips, trying to ignore the lingering feeling of Jake's weight against my body.

He walked down one of the wine aisles and quickly selected a bottle. "Cabernet Sauvignon. All right, this should do."

Turning, he walked past me without a glance. "Take your time."

He started climbing the stairs, leaving me standing there, still bereft and confused.

After this, he couldn't refuse to talk to me and tell me why he'd left. If the same attraction still existed between us, if I still had this effect on him, he owed me an explanation that made sense. All this time, I'd imagined he'd grown tired of me. I told myself that he'd gone to find someone new because I'd bored him. But maybe, there was another reason, one I couldn't begin to fathom or understand.

A moment later, I stepped into the kitchen. It was empty. I found Jake and his grandfather sitting outside, impatiently waiting for me so they could dig into their steaks. Feeling self-conscious, I joined them. Gratefully, Walter acted normal, ignoring what he knew well had happened in his cellar.

I barely touched my food, even though it tasted delicious. The steak melted in my mouth and was cooked to medium-rare perfection. The steamed broccoli was bright green and crunchy, and the homemade vinaigrette went wonderfully over the lettuce, cucumber, and tomatoes.

A few times I met Jake's gaze. He seemed preoccupied, though he had no trouble devouring his steak and later polishing off two slices of apple pie.

Walter made pleasant conversation about the wonderful spring weather and the bats that flitted over the yard as they came out of their hiding places when the evening settled. He was talking about what to cook for lunch tomorrow when the phone in the kitchen rang. He excused himself and left for a few minutes. When he came back, he had a notebook in his hand.

"I got someone who spotted a van that fits the description." He tossed the notepad in front of Jake. "They're tailing it as we speak. That's the latest location and the number where you can contact my guy."

Jake grabbed the notebook and rushed into the house.

"Jake, wait!" I caught up with him as he exited the kitchen.

He glanced over his shoulder.

"I'm coming with you."

"No. Too dangerous."

I rushed after him, jogging along the corridor that led to the front door, Bones trailing behind us. Jake left the front door ajar and when I got there, he was already on his bike, cranking the engine.

"You can't leave me here!" I yelled over the revving motorcycle.

Jake released the brake and tore off in a squeal of rubber and acrid smoke.

I watched him leave, fists clenched at my sides.

Walter appeared next to me, huffing and shaking his head. "Always acts now and asks questions later."

That was Jake all right.

"Where is he going?" I demanded, turning to face the old man.

Walter offered me a folded piece of paper. "I just received another call. It seems the van may be in need of a little maintenance."

I unfolded the note and read it.

"Stan's Auto & Truck Repair" the paper read. I glanced up and met Walter's eyes.

"Why?" The question came out before I could stop it.

"You wanted to go with him, didn't you?"

I did, but why would Walter go against his grandson's wishes to protect me? Or men's general need to keep women safe and on a leash?

"I'm not your mommy or his... for that matter." Walter turned on his heel and walked back inside.

I pondered what to do for a long moment, then ordered an Uber.

Damn if I was going to let Jake take all the credit for finding Stephen. In the end, this high-profile case might turn out good for my tracking business. At least that was what I told myself as I climbed in and gave the driver the address to the repair shop.

CHAPTER 33

I fidgeted in the back of the Uber, my thoughts going back and forth about whether my decision to follow Jake was brilliant or down-right stupid.

The fact that I'd created a justification for my actions didn't escape me. The agency focused on mate tracking, not *kidnappee* tracking for Pete's sake. So what was I doing? True, finding Stephen would put us in the news spotlight, but that sort of attention didn't fit what Rosalina and I were looking for. In fact, we wanted to stay away from that.

More than once, I leaned forward and started to tell the driver to turn around and take me home, but every time I would recline back and chew on my bottom lip while the driver gave me a pinched glare in the rearview mirror. I did call Ulfen and left a voicemail when he didn't answer. I told him we might have a lead on Stephen's location and spelled out the address. If there was trouble, maybe he and his pack would get there in time to help.

I realized that I'd rationalized my decision to come, but in truth, I needed to admit that logic had nothing to do with what I was doing. A strange resolve and—if I was being honest—a craving for danger were driving me onward, making my body sing with anticipation. My skin itched more furiously as I thought about helping Jake rescue Stephen right from the jaws of his kidnappers.

"Are you sure you're getting off here?" the driver asked when we reached the corner of Warne and Lee Avenue. I glanced around, hugging my purse closely. This area of town was certainly not the safest, and at this time, there were no signs of life.

A big full moon shone in the sky, for which I was grateful since all the lampposts appeared broken. It illuminated the scraggly trees, cracked pavement, and weedy empty lot across the street.

Go home, Toni. Stay alive. The voice of reason in my head made itself heard, but when it came to Jake, reason took a back seat.

"Yep, this is it," I told the driver, putting on a chipper smile.

When I got out of the car at the corner and the driver disappeared, leaving me standing there all alone, I seriously reevaluated my decision.

Gah, what's wrong with me?! I'm losing my sanity.

Never mind the iffy neighborhood, vampires and werewolves stood at the brink of war. If things got hairy, I might get eaten alive. I tried to draw comfort from the gun in my purse, but it might as well have been a banana.

My worry for Jake immediately doubled as I imagined a horde of vampires tearing him to pieces. He was strong, yes, but not indestructible, and his tendency to act irrationally landed him into trouble more often than not.

No, I couldn't leave. I didn't have to rush in to rescue Stephen, but I could approach carefully, gauge the situation, and call the police if needed.

My heart pounded as I turned the corner and cautiously walked toward the repair shop, the yellowish moonlight illuminating my way.

The repair shop was on the next corner from where I'd been dropped off. I crossed the street and walked close to the buildings, trying to stay in the shadows. When the shop finally came into view, I drew back into a narrow alley, though not before sending a wary glance past a dumpster and a tall stack of discarded wooden crates. The pungent smell of garbage rode the air, rotten fruit with a hint of dead rat. I wrinkled my nose.

Very smart, Toni, hiding in a dark, stinky alley. Just the way to avoid ever becoming a grandma.

The alley appeared empty though, so I huddled against the wall and peered across the street. The repair shop consisted of an uncovered garage with a massive metal door, razor wire atop each brick wall, and a small office space to the right. Eyes roving around, I tried to spot signs of life but saw nothing, not even Jake and his motorcycle. Had Walter sent me on a wild goose chase? I got the sensation that he hadn't liked me very much, so maybe this was an attempt to get me mugged and murdered and out of his grandson's life.

I shook my head at the irrational thought. Really?! Where had that come from? I barely knew the man, and I'd already tagged him as a *creepo*? He had been nothing but nice.

I was considering whether or not to casually approach the repair shop when a heavy hand wrapped around my mouth, and I was yanked deep into the alley. I kicked and squirmed, trying to get free, but whoever had me was too strong.

"What do we have here?" A deep, accented voice asked close to my ear.

I shuddered, trying to place the voice, but it was the warm, sweet scent that triggered my memories first. Beeswax with a metallic tang of blood, the same scent I'd caught in Bernadetta's limousine.

The voice belonged to Bertram. The vamp's driver. Oh, God, if he was here, it meant Stephen's location had truly been compromised, and his captors knew it. This couldn't be good.

The vampire flipped me and pressed my back against the wall, his dark eyes piercing mine with a powerful compulsion that ordered me not to scream.

I tried to cry out for help, but the words crowded in my throat.

"Ms. Sunder," he said in his vaguely German accent. "This is no place for the likes of you. I advise you to leave."

To my surprise, he released me, and before I knew it, he disappeared in a blur of movement that rustled my hair. I stayed against the wall, my heart thundering like an approaching storm. A loud crash reverberated down the street. I didn't move for a full minute. When I finally felt confident that I wasn't going to wet my panties, I peered toward the repair shop again. The door to the office was busted, and Bertram nowhere to be seen.

Not that I was complaining, but why had he let me off with a simple warning? This didn't make any sense. Still, the relief that washed over me seemed like a second chance at life. For a moment there, I'd thought I was done for.

Suddenly assaulted by a fit of sensibility, I decided to leave the premises. I started to walk from the alley, when, across the street, I spotted Jake slinking along the pitch of the roof. *Oh, no!* Heart drumming, I pressed a hand to my mouth to resist the urge to call out a warning that would give away his location. Crouching, he drew closer, peered down into the open garage area, then leaped inside, disappearing out of sight.

Holy crap! Bertram was in the shop. Jake was in the shop. This was bad!

I couldn't leave now. I reached inside my purse, feeling for the gun. My hand squeezed around the handle.

You're trained to use it. You're not defenseless.

Regular bullets wouldn't stop a vampire, but I could buy Jake some time if he got in a bind and needed to escape.

Nope. Nope. Don't be stupid. Get the hell out of here, a sensible voice called inside my head. But that sensible voice mattered very little when it came to Jake. That sensible voice could go take a hike down Shit Street. No way I could *not* help Jake. Being honest, even after all that had happened, I would give my life for him. Yep, that was the kind of loyal idiot I tended to be. So...

Screw it. Here goes nothing.

I pulled the gun out, hid my purse behind the dumpster, and crossed the street.

CHAPTER 34

Slinking like a thief, I crept to the repair shop and pressed my back to the wall next to the busted door. My heart and my senses kicked into hyper-mode, overwhelming me with an intensity I'd never experienced. The scent of grease and gasoline were pungent enough to mask everything else, dizzying me. Over the pounding of my heart, I thought I heard someone's breathing and soft padding steps, but that was impossible. No one was in sight, and my ears weren't that sensitive. It had to be my imagination. That or the adrenaline coursing through my body was the best I'd ever produced, and it could probably auction for millions on the black market.

Focus. Quit messing around, Toni.

I squeezed my eyes shut, doing my best to push aside the sensory overload. Slowly, I took a knee on the sidewalk and peered inside the office. Darkness greeted me. As my eyes adapted, I made out the silhouettes of furniture: a desk, a file cabinet, shelves on the walls. I squinted, trying to spot movement. I didn't notice any.

In the back of the room, another busted door lay on the floor.

Damn! Bertram was like a steamroller.

Staying low, I walked into the room, gun at the ready. I crept in with the moonlight behind me. A bead of sweat trailed down my back as I slid along the wall, inching toward the other door. A long corridor stretched from there, flanked by shelves on the right and windows on the left. Moonlight bathed the shelves, revealing boxes of automotive parts. The smell of gasoline and grease grew thicker.

I exited the office and stepped into the corridor. The windows were waist-high, so I squatted then peeked over the edge at the outdoor garage area. The space looked as big as a basketball court, and a variety of vehicles waited for repairs.

One of them was the Lucciola Candle Shop van.

My breath hitched and my heart sped up to near-death speed.

Stephen.

Was he inside the van? I inhaled sharply as if, among all the intense scents, I would be able to detect his familiar one coming from the van. For all I knew, they'd transferred him to another vehicle. It would make sense if this one needed repairs.

I scanned the garage for movement and hiding spots. Jake had jumped in there, but where was he? And what about Bertram? Was he the van's driver? Probably not. He seemed too high in the pecking order for such a job. He'd been driving Fiore herself.

I felt stuck. Should I go check the van for Stephen, possibly exposing myself?

No. Jake was already out there, and I had a clear view of everything. From here, I could take good aim and let loose a few shots if it came to it.

Movement caught my attention. Holding my breath, I stared down the sights at the figure sneaking around the car parked in front of the van.

Jake.

He was still in human form but might as well have been walking on all fours, stalking like a predator toward the white van. I wanted to yell in warning and tell him a vampire was around, but that would only give away his presence... and mine.

I bit my lower lip and tried to calm my breathing. My body tingled and itched all over again, feeling like it didn't belong to me, like my skin had shrunk.

Suddenly, the vampire flew out of nowhere and landed on top of the van with a crunch of metal, his face twisted in a mask of savagery, fangs elongated, eyes pools of black ink, hands tipped with two-inch claws.

Without thinking, I stretched to my full height and aimed the gun at Bertram. Vision tunneling, I pulled the trigger and hit him square in the chest. He barely staggered backward and glanced down at the hole in his shirt with annoyance. He shook his head and sent me a withering glare that should have frozen me on the spot, but instead, I pulled the trigger again and again until I emptied the gun. Each explosion reverberated loudly, like hammer blows pounding straight against my brain.

The shots hit their mark with incredible accuracy. The practice sessions with Tom at the shooting range had paid off. Bertram twitched with each hit, distracting him long enough for Jake to shift.

A beautiful dark gray wolf leaped onto the van's hood. He was massive and filled me with awe. I had seen his animal only twice before. The first time after I begged him to show me, and the second time the night we rescued Emily Garner while he used his extraordinary senses to spot her exact location.

But now, he looked bigger.

Even on all fours, he stood nearly five-foot tall from his massive paws to the top of his head. His shoulders were wide, and he was made of pure, taut sinew. His paws were the size of softballs and tipped with dark claws as sharp as surgical scalpels.

His chest rumbled deeply in an unequivocal threat to the vampire. Leaping over the van's windshield in one fluid motion, he landed on the roof, then bounded again, claws screeching against metal. Like a wrecking ball, he slammed against the vampire, knocking him off.

Bertram hit the ground with a *thud* and tried to scramble to his feet, but Jake landed on top of him, claws ripping his chest open. The vampire growled in pain as Jake raked his claws down and angled his jaw toward his neck. But this creature was no easy prey, and he wrapped his hands around the wolf's neck, raking with his own claws, making Jake yelp.

No!

I didn't have any more bullets, and even if I did, what good were they?

As Jake and Bertram scrambled on the ground, snarling and tearing each other to pieces, a figure suddenly moved inside the Lucciola van.

What the…?

I squinted through the dim light as the person opened the door, gingerly stepped out, and slunk away from the van and the snarling creatures. As the figure moved away to hide behind another vehicle, I gasped. It was a female with a short, tufted tail and small fawn horns.

A Fae!

Was she the one who'd been driving Stephen around and maybe he was still in the van? Did this mean the Fae were responsible for kidnapping him? Had they done it to start a war between vampires and werewolves as I'd imagined? They would certainly benefit from it, strengthening their foothold in the human realm as that of the others weakened. Or did this Fae work for the Dark Donna? It was uncommon for Fae to trust others but not unheard of.

Crouching low, she ran toward the garage door. Skillfully, she leaped, climbed over the sidewall, avoiding the razor wire with ease, and disappeared on the other side.

Shit! I couldn't let her escape. I had to stop her, so we could find out the truth. Whirling, I dashed back outside, running at a full pelt. On the sidewalk, I skidded to a stop, my eyes immediately homing in on her moving shape. She was fast like a gazelle, her short tail bouncing behind her as she ran.

Damn, there's no way I can catch her. Despite my certainty, something inside me snapped, an instinct that urged me to give chase.

"Hey, stop right there!" I yelled, the cry echoing down the deserted street.

The Fae glanced over her shoulder, then ran faster.

Every one of her steps seemed to be three of mine. I would never match her speed. Anger and frustration built inside me as my legs and arms pumped to their max, yet the distance between us grew.

Suddenly, I caught her scent in the wind, a combination of earth and wood, like a spring day after rain. The scent and the chase unleashed something wild inside of me, restless energy and that hunger which had been inside of me all along, and I hadn't known how to satiate. Its intensity scared me, almost bringing me to a halt. But I couldn't stop, not now that my limbs had come alive with power, and the Fae seemed within reach. I blinked in surprise, realizing how close I'd gotten in a matter of seconds.

Before I knew what I was doing, I lunged in her direction and tackled her to the ground. We fell in a heap of arms and legs and rolled around on the pavement. I ended up on top of her, straddling her. She stared at me with terrified eyes, her vertical pupils wide. Her thin, black mouth opened and a trembling voice came out.

"Don't hurt me, beast," she begged in her lilting accent.

Beast?

I tried to speak and a growl came out instead. I froze, my hands pinning the Fae's shoulders down. She let out a whimper as my thumbs dug into her, ripping her skin. Warm, sticky blood oozed out of her supple skin. I yanked my hands back and stared at clawed fingertips. I began to shake at the monstrous sight. What was happening? What kind of trick was this?

A glamour from the Fae. That had to be it. There was no other explanation.

"Stop!" I ordered her, and my voice was a growl again, the word barely recognizable.

"Please, please, I was just the driver today. That's all," the Fae said.

I was hyperventilating, and her voice had become but a buzz, barely able to break through the thunderous roaring in my ears. Words of denial echoed inside my head.

Not real. Not real.

"Quit, you bitch!" I grabbed her by the throat and forced her to her feet. She stood on tiptoes as I wrapped my hands around her neck. "Stop the glamour!"

She shook her head an infinitesimal amount. "I'm not..." She croaked, looking confused.

I forced her back toward the repair shop, pushing her along and causing her to stumble. She didn't try to run again, which added to my confusion. Fae were good at fighting, but she seemed truly intimidated by me. I examined my hands as I shoved her down the length of one entire block. No more glamour. The claws had disappeared. Good.

We approached the garage. Loud clangs and growls came from behind the metal door.

Jake.

My chest tightened with worry. Judging by the racket, they were still fighting, but was he winning?

I pushed the Fae against the shop's outer wall. "Is Stephen Erickson in the van?" This time, my voice sounded more like my own. The Fae had finally realized her cheap glamours wouldn't work on me.

She nodded, her slitted eyes taking me in, analyzing my face with fear.

"Is he... is he alive?"

"Yes," she said.

A jumble of emotions came undone inside of me. Stephen was alive, and none of this had been in vain.

I was trying to decide what to do next when the Fae's expression changed and a satisfied smile stretched her black lips. The fear that had twisted her features slowly disappeared and glee replaced it. Her gaze lingered on something behind me. A shiver ran down my spine as the sound of steps reached me.

Slowly, I let go of the Fae and moved away, angling my body sideways. I glanced back and found four dark figures standing across the street, untouched by the moonlight as if they weren't really there.

"Let's see what your little claws can do against my friends," the Fae said with amusement.

One of the figures pulled away from the group. I held my breath as moonlight bathed the handsome features of none other than Prince Kalyll Adanorin. The female next to me let out a

234

whimper, and her smugness died a quick death and putrefied into horror. Not who she'd been expecting, it seemed.

She lowered her head and fell to one knee, looking contrite.

"At last, I find you, Gonira, and entangled in unsavory trade, no less." Kalyll's voice dripped with cold anger and disappointment. "Your punishment shall be... deliberate." He lifted a hand and waved two fingers. Two figures peeled from the dark and came forward. They were dressed in their black tunics with the embroidered shield in the chest. They each took one of Gonira's arms and walked her away.

"We meet again, Antonietta Sunder," Prince Kalyll said.

Wow, the Seelie Prince remembers my name! I was star-struck to say the least.

"You should leave this place," he said.

"I can't... my friend..." I crooked a finger toward the shop. Inside, something banged against the garage door, making a loud clanking noise. I jumped, my heart knocking against my ribs.

Moonlight shone on Kalyll's midnight-blue hair as he made a regretful face. "I would stay and help you, but I cannot get involved in human matters, especially not this one. It's bad enough Gonira has been making friends with the wrong people."

From the sounds of it, this Gonira had been acting on her own. So did that mean the Fae had nothing to do with this mess? It seemed that way.

Growls and more bangs came from inside.

"Are you sure you wish to stay?" The Prince lifted a perfect eyebrow as if evaluating my intelligence and finding it lacking

I nodded, that same resolve that had driven me here coursing through my veins.

"Well met, then." Kalyll said as he realized I wouldn't be dissuaded. He pressed a fist to his chest, inclined his head, and was gone.

The shapes retreated into the darkness and disappeared. I was about to run inside to check on Jake, when something moved in the shadows. It seemed the Prince has decided to stay after all, except the shapes that reappeared didn't belong to Kalyll and his guards. They varied in shapes and sizes. Two of them were massive men while the others had the proportion and stances of large shifters.

What the hell?! I had a feeling these were the friends *Gonira had referred to earlier!*

I squinted for a better look, and as I watched, the figures tore in my direction, growling and snarling. Adrenaline ignited my blood, and I whirled and ran.

CHAPTER 35

I hurried into the repair shop through the torn door. Without stopping, I dashed through the back door. The shelves and windows whizzed by in a blur. Pressure built up in my fingertips, and I felt my skin tearing as claws materialized again.

What the hell? Why this glamour again?

One of the shifters followed, tearing into the office, hot on my tail. I could sense him, hear his panting, smell his foul sweat. He was *that* close. I didn't dare glance back.

I skidded to a stop and took a sharp left. A crash sounded behind me. I kept running and reached a landing with a set of steps that led up and another that led down. A door stood to my left. I tried it, but it didn't budge. I froze for a beat, unsure of which way to go.

A horrible snarl rent the tight space, and I whirled to face a huge creature the size and shape of a gorilla. It stood on two legs and pounded his chest with boulder-sized fists. A shifter unlike any I'd ever seen before. My hyper-sensitive ears reverberated with its growl. My nose wrinkled as the stench of animal musk hit me. And my eyes... everything looked different, sharper somehow, especially the creature's claws and pointed teeth.

The next thing I knew, I was snarling back at the beast, crouching low, one hand on the floor.

Um, what the hell?

Was a glamour capable of scrambling your brains this badly and making you believe you were Queen of the Jungle? I didn't think so. At least, I'd never heard of anything like that, but the world held many secrets, so, who knew.

A small voice inside an even smaller corner of my brain tried to make itself heard.

This isn't a glamour, you idiot.

Then what the hell is it?

Whatever the answer, it didn't matter—not with King Kong advancing in my direction.

I pounced.

Really? What in the dreadful world of Planet of the Apes had gotten into me?!

I soared through the air like some acrobat, and a second later, I slammed into the beast's chest. My claws slashed and teeth gnashed, snapping shut on something. King Kong's ear?

Gah, nasty!

I bounced away, flipping in midair, then landed on all fours and spat. King Kong roared, a leathery hand pressed to the side of his head. With a shake, he leaned forward and dropped on his knuckles, bearing his throat in a furious growl.

"Ew, ever heard of mouthwash? Or mints?"

Another stinky growl.

Shit! I'd really pissed him off.

He charged. I held still for a heartbeat, then jumped out of the way. The beast went flying down the staircase, bouncing on the steps, crashing through the railing, and rolling to a stop at the bottom landing.

I whirled and kicked at the locked door. I stared open-mouthed as it swung open with the sound of splintering wood. What had Walter cooked into that ribeye? I rushed through the door and found myself in a covered garage with a couple of cars up on racks, and a few empty spaces for more. It was dark, and I shouldn't have been able to see, but my eyes seemed to be doing some Superman shit.

The smell of gasoline and grease was worse here, nauseating. Huge, closed metal doors lined the left side, the kind that roll up on a chain. Outside the doors, I could hear the sounds of a battle raging. How many was Jake fighting now?

God, please, let him be okay.

My eyes roved around looking for an exit, but I'd reached a dead end. King Kong roared behind me, his massive feet thundering. He was coming. Frantically, I searched the wall for a button that would open the garage doors. Nothing. I ran to the other end and searched there. Still nothing.

King Kong burst into the room, stomping like a giant. His savage glare homed in on me right away. He could see me as clearly as I saw him.

I dropped to all fours—what was the deal with that?—and hid behind a wide rolling toolbox, the kind with a bunch of little drawers. The beast came at me, feet thudding against the concrete floor. My eyes darted left and right, looking for an escape. There was none.

The beast came around, and without thinking, I jumped inside the closest inspection pit, dropping to the bottom in a crouch. I glanced back up from its depths. King Kong's head appeared above, a massive noggin the size of a car tire.

He's too big to fit. He's too big to fit.

The beast's shoulders were as wide as a wardrobe, and this space was only big enough for one human, preferably a mechanic. This reasoning was all well and good, but it didn't change the fact that I was freaking trapped in a hole that could easily become my greasy grave. I wrinkled my nose at the tarry smell and wiped sleek hands on my pants. The stuff had smeared all over me and I reeked.

Without taking my eyes off the beast, I moved toward the metal rungs that led out of the pit. King Kong bounded in their direction and blocked the exit with its massive body. Placing one hand to either side of the slit, he roared into the tight space. I clasped my hands over my ears, my eardrums threatening to burst. He reached one arm in, his enormous hand grasping, trying to reach me. I crouched low, heart in my throat.

My panic mounted. Tingling energy coursed through my body, growing, pounding. My heart hammered in my ears, speeding up like a locomotive. My anxiety surged like lava inside a volcano, looking for release. My body convulsed.

Oh, crap! Panic attack.

Breathe, Toni, breathe.

My heart was bursting. I was having a seizure.

King Kong roared again. The sound drove me over the edge, and I blacked out.

CHAPTER 36

A wave of *change* rippled through my body.

It was release and closure, both at the same time. Part of me reveled in the moment while the other fought to make it stop. But the former had been denied for so long, it wouldn't back down.

The time had come.

At last.

My every limb flailed out of control, rippling from within, finding a new shape that it had craved since the beginning of time. Bones elongated and thickened, twisting in different directions. Sinew knitted itself thicker, growing in bulk. My clothes ripped and fell away in tatters.

Pain racked me. It was exquisite, and I welcomed it. I'd yearned for it, craved it, and it was finally here. No one could stop it now.

I've been caged, repressed, and forbidden, but no more!

Fur and claws and a tail… They all sprang into place, exactly where they should have always have been. My senses, which I had always thought sharp and keen, revealed their true power. What I could hear, see, and smell now put my past to shame. Even the many years of grease accumulated in the dark corners of the pit revealed themselves.

Joy rippled through me, and I howled, lifting my head, flattening my ears, reveling in the knowledge of what I was: a werewolf.

My head snapped toward my enemy still blocking the exit. It had stopped roaring and stared at me curiously, his reaching arm frozen.

Without fear, without inhibitions of any kind, I attacked.

I leaped and snapped my jaw around the beast's forearm. He pulled back, but I didn't let go. This enemy was strong, but I wasn't afraid of him. I could hold my own. I was strong, too. He swung his arm, and I still held on, bitter blood filling my mouth.

As he prepared to slam me against the floor, I released him, soared through the air, and landed on all fours. Teeth bared, I circled the beast. My thoughts had turned to liquid, incensed by the taste of blood. Instincts took control, letting me know exactly what I needed to do.

I feigned toward the pit, and when the beast leaned that way to block me, I jumped toward the wall in the opposite direction, bounced against it, then toward the beast's heavy body. I slammed against his shoulder, setting him off balance, then landed a few feet away. My enemy teetered for a couple of beats then, with a final push of my haunches against his leg, King Kong fell sideways and got wedged inside the pit. For good measure, I pounced on him, then hopped back onto firm concrete.

His visible arm and leg flailed as he struggled to pull himself out, but he only managed to embed himself further. I snapped my teeth in triumph, then turned my attention toward the sounds of battle outside.

I trotted out of the garage in leaps and bounds, going the way I'd come. When I reached the window-lined hall, I sprang toward the glass panels without a pause. I crashed through them, shards raining all around me, and landed in the outer garage.

My keen eyes scanned the area. I'd landed next to a dark SUV, sandwiching myself between it and the wall. With another push of my hind legs, I jumped on top of the car, bounding from its hood to the roof. From there, the battle took shape, igniting a wild yearning to join and brawl. But against whom?

Chaos reigned, and I had no idea who was friend or foe. Cars were smashed. The metal door that led to the street was thrown open, twisted. Claw marks raked one side. A couple of bodies lay bleeding on the grease-stained ground—about a dozen others still fought. Where had they come from?

Claws, fangs, tusks, horns flashed. I saw vampires, werebears, werecoyotes, but where was the wolf? He was my friend. I had to help *him*.

A panicked feeling built in my chest. I couldn't spot him. Then I heard a snarl that spiked my awareness. I whirled to find a dark gray wolf pushed against the corner, two vampires looming over him. He was bleeding from a gash by his snout and another by his side.

Bounding over two cars, I reached him and pounced on one of his attackers. Caught by surprise, the female vamp let out a piercing cry. My jaw clamped around her neck, and I bit with all my strength. As we toppled over, the vampire reached back and dug her claws in my throat.

We landed with a thud. I was large, so much larger than her. I pressed my full weight on the vampire, sinking my own sharp claws into her. I jerked my head, tearing half of her neck off. She screamed in agony. I spit and bit again. My large muzzle encompassed what was left of her neck, and as I snapped my jaw closed, her head broke off. I snarled, shaking myself. The vampire's head rolled off to the side, its oily black eyes unblinking, its tongue lolling.

Something inside me twitched at the sight of the severed head.

What are you doing?!

I shook my great head—pushing the small, bothersome voice aside—and turned toward the second vampire and the wolf. He was deeply injured, favoring his right side, limping, but he still held his own against his enemy. I joined his side and snarled at the vampire, a tall male with a thick neck and shoulder-length hair.

The gray wolf gave me a sideways glance, his nose twitching, inhaling my scent. Distrust filled his eyes. My fur reeked in a cloying way with that dark stuff from the pit. I could smell it myself. He didn't like it any more than I did. I figured he couldn't recognize me, but that didn't matter. I knew him, and I knew I had to protect him.

He was pack.

The thought seemed both right and wrong, but at the moment, only the battle mattered.

In unison, we attacked. I aimed high while the gray wolf aimed low. The vampire moved fast, his arms striking in a blur of movement that slammed against the side of my head. I flew sideways and crashed against a car. Dazzled, I stood and blinked.

The gray wolf had his jaws clenched around the vampire's ankle. The vampire leaned down to grab him, but I lunged forward and smashed into him. He lost his balance and fell. The gray wolf and I went for the neck. He got there first, and with one powerful snap, took the vampire's head off.

The gray wolf spat blood, his long pink tongue flicking to one side in disgust. His eyes met mine. They shone with mesmerizing silver light. He lowered his head in thanks. I bowed slightly, watching him closely, relieved that he was all right, his wounds already healing.

The fight went on around us. A small coyote soared overhead and crashed through the windows and into the building.

Suddenly, the sound of sirens filled the air. They wailed, piercing the night, getting louder by the second. My ears perked up and so did the gray wolf's.

Help is coming, a part of me said, though I couldn't quite fathom why. The only help I knew were my fangs and claws, and my own strength.

The battle slowly came to a halt. Then, everyone scrambled, running out of the twisted metal door, jumping on top of cars and leaping to the roof, escaping.

Whirling toward a white van, the gray wolf rushed in its direction. I followed him, intent on staying by his side to make sure he remained safe. He circled the van to the back doors. There he shifted, his magnificent furred body elongating and becoming slick—foreign and familiar at the same time.

I angled my head, regarding him curiously. He attacked the van, breaking one of its back windows with his elbow, then reaching inside to pull on something, and finally yanked the doors open. He seemed to hold his breath as he peered inside the dark interior.

I moved closer for a better look.

A sweet, warm scent pierced through my nose, making me want to sneeze. I blew air out, shaking my head. A man sat inside the van, strapped to a bolted chair, and swathed in many scents.

"Stephen!" The one who had been the gray wolf exclaimed. He darted into the van and went to the odd-smelling man.

Stretching up, I put my front paws on the back of the van and peered in. I blinked at the humans, a strange sensation of calm descending over me. I didn't want to fight anymore. It was all going to be all right.

Jake pressed his fingers to Stephen's neck.

I shook my head.

Jake? Stephen?

Yes. Those were their names, weren't they?

A whimper escaped me as more and more confusing thoughts popped into my head.

"Thank God!" Jake exclaimed. "You're going to be all right, buddy."

I pulled away from the van, front paws landing on cold concrete. Jake glanced in my direction, frowning at me.

"Thank you," he said, lowering his head. "What's your name?"

I shuddered. My name? What *was* my name?!

The sirens had reached us. Car doors slammed shut outside. Voices. Rushing steps. Panic filled my chest. They couldn't find me. I wasn't supposed to be here. I turned tail and ran.

"Wait!" Jake called behind me. "Tell me who you are."

I ignored him and jumped through the hole I'd made in the windows. I landed inside, skidded to a stop, then ran toward the steps where I had first fought King Kong. I hurtled up the stairs, ignoring the beast's angry growls echoing from inside the garage. It seemed he was still stuck in the pit.

With four giant leaps, I climbed to the third floor where, without stopping, I rammed against a flimsy door and burst onto a flat roof. Without pausing, I dashed in the direction of the shining moon, bounding from roof to roof until I lost myself in the sounds, sights, and the smells of the city.

CHAPTER
37

I awoke by degrees, becoming painfully aware of something prickly against my skin. My entire left side felt irritated. Also, I was cold, very cold. I blinked my eyes open to a purplish sky painted with yellow and orange at the edges. A few birds sang in the distance.

What the hell?!

I sprang to a sitting position to find the only thing I was wearing was nail polish. And it was pretty chipped. With a gasp, I draped my right arm over my breasts and placed my left hand over my crotch. My gaze danced frantically, and my lungs worked double-duty.

Where in the world am I? And how in the witchlights did I get here?

I set to answering the first question. From the looks of it, I sat atop a roof, sitting on a bit of gravel next to an air-conditioning unit.

Now, to that second question... The last thing I remembered was...

Wait, no!

The last thing I remembered must be part of a dream because there was no freaking way I sprang up claws and caught up to a gazelle-fast Fae. I also remembered four figures appearing out of nowhere and then... And then what?

I had no idea. And what about Jake? Was he all right?

Trembling, I rose to my feet, and still covering my important bits, walked to the edge of the roof. Across the street, Cup o' Java stood with its blinds closed.

Crap!

I was on top of my office building, but how? Maybe I'd passed out and Jake had brought me here. I shook my head. No, that made no sense at all. He wouldn't leave me naked on a roof. Maybe I'd been abducted by aliens, and now I was pregnant with a buggy-eyed green baby. I shuddered.

And what about Stephen? Had Jake found him?

The questions kept multiplying inside my head like rabbits on hormone therapy, and no matter how creative I got with my answers, none of them made any sense. As important as figuring out what had happened was, I had a more pressing issue... I needed to get down from here before people started filling the street below. It was probably close to 6 AM, so it wouldn't be long.

I ran to the back of the building, tiptoeing and cringing as gravel poked the soles of my feet. There wasn't a fire escape, so an ivy-infested old trellis might be my best bet. When I got there, I sighed, relieved to find that the trellis reached to the top of the building.

After making sure no one was around, I swung a leg over the ledge and lowered my bare ass onto the trellis, my feet and hands searching for purchase through the dense vines. A chili wind blasted my butt cheeks, making me shiver. Adding insult to injury, goosebumps rose all over my skin and my breasts perked up. A blush rushed into my cheeks as I imagined some perv watching me climb down. But I refused to check again and reassured myself that no one roamed the alley at this early hour.

The trellis creaked, making me fear it would give under my weight, but it held, and I made it to the ground. When I scanned the area, I confirmed that the alley was, indeed, empty, and no one had ogled my behind. Or my spleen.

The smell of garbage wafting from the nearby dumpster reminded me I'd left my purse back by the repair shop. *Damn*, would anyone notice it? I had to get back there to retrieve it. But that was a problem for later since I was still working on the "naked" one.

Scanning the alley in both directions, I found my path still free of Peeping Toms, ran out of the alley and around the building. If someone saw me, I would surely be booked for indecent exposure, and I would get kicked out of the building. No doubt my contract included a clause dealing with streaker females.

At the corner, I halted and checked the street. No one. I was about to run toward my office but stopped when I heard a car. I waited, heart in my throat, pressing my backside tightly to the wall. The car eased by and disappeared.

Exhaling, I dashed out, passing in front of Jake's place. When I reached my door, I pulled on the handle, but of course, it was locked. Cursing, I started heading back toward Jake's but froze when I realized someone was watching me from across the street.

For a moment, I acted as if not moving would make me invisible. Then I swallowed and glanced toward the coffee shop. Willow McNeel, Cup 'o Java's owner was staring, her jaw hanging open. I grinned and almost wiggled my fingers in greeting, except my hands were otherwise occupied. She gave no sign of acknowledgment and continued to stare in astonishment.

This is it. This is how I lose my agency.

"Sidewalk," I said under my breath, "open up and swallow me, please."

The sidewalk didn't oblige, so I tore my mortified gaze from Willow, and walking in a dignified fashion, I reached Jake's door. I said a little prayer under my breath. Almost every time I'd come here, his door had been open. It would be open this time, too. I reached for the handle, twisted it and pulled.

"Dammit, dammit, dammit!" I cursed as tears filled my eyes.

What now? What NOW?!

"*Psst, psst.*"

I glanced over my shoulder. Willow hooked a finger and moved it in a come-here motion. Well, she had already seen all my attributes from afar. Time for her to see them up close. After checking for traffic, I ran across the street, my bare feet slapping the blacktop.

Dexterously, Willow slipped a key in the lock, opened the coffee shop's door, and stood out of the way as I ran inside and didn't stop until I reached the bathroom and locked myself inside, shivering from the cold. The mirror over the sink showed me a bleary-eyed woman with a tumbleweed of pink-tipped hair and grease-stained perky breasts.

What the hell did I get into?!

I reeked of burnt motor oil. Grimacing, I ran my fingers over the stuff, then proceeded to attack myself with soap and paper towels until my skin was clean and bright red from scrubbing.

A few moments later, a knock came at the door. "Are you all right, honey?"

"Um, yes?" I stuffed the black-smeared towels as far as they would go into the garbage can. I'd almost used the entire roll.

"I have something for you to wear," Willow said. "Also, you can borrow my cell phone to call Rosalina or whoever you need."

Swallowing my pride, which went down my throat like an oversized grapefruit, I opened the door a crack. Willow gave me a gentle smile and passed me her phone along with what looked like one of the green aprons her staff wore.

"There are two aprons," Willow said. "I figured you could wear one over the front and one over the back."

"Thank you."

My face felt as if it were cracking from shame. I checked in the mirror to make sure it wasn't about to fall off. No, it was still holding on, though maybe not for long.

I did as she suggested and hung one apron over my neck the right way and tied it at the back. I hung the second one backward, tied a knot at the front, and sighed with relief. The aprons didn't meet at my sides and left two long gaps, but they were better than nothing.

Holding my head high, I shuffled out of the bathroom to face Willow. She stood behind the counter, filling the machines with ground coffee, preparing them for rush hour.

"Thank you," I said again. "I don't know what I would have done if…"

"No worries, sweetheart. It happens to the best of us." She gave me a complicit smile that made me wonder what she got into when she was young. She was in her late sixties with wiry gray hair that normally fell in a mass of curls all around her, though at the moment, a blue bow held it back in place. She had piercing brown eyes and plenty of laugh lines around them. Today, she'd gone to town on the blue eyeshadow and red lipstick, looking in desperate need of Rosalina's advice.

"To be honest, I don't know what happened," I said.

Willow dusted her hands and faced me. Her apron draped over a flower-print dress that made me think of tropical jungles. "That tends to happen when one drinks too much, young girl." She shook a finger at me. "You have to know your limits."

I opened my mouth to protest, then decided that drunkenness was the perfect excuse for this debacle. "I… shall endeavor to learn what they are."

"You do that." She shuffled around the shop, replenishing napkins, stirrers, and sugar packets with practiced efficiency while I dialed Rosalina's number.

"Hello?" she answered and I could practically hear her frown at the strange number on her caller ID.

"Rosalina, it's me."

"Toni! Where the hell are you? I've been worried to death. I called you like a thousand times and sent you a million text messages."

"Wow, I'll have a time sifting through those."

"Don't mess with me, Antonietta Luna Sunder. I had to call your mother, and I don't know what the deal is, but she's frantic. You need to call her back. Right now."

Crap! Sometimes, it sucked when people cared about you. Why did Rosalina have to call Mom? She would drill me about this. She knew Rosalina didn't freak out easily. Plus, I'd been ignoring Mom's calls for a couple of days.

"Okay, I'll call her, but… do you think you could pick me up and… bring me some clothes?"

A pause. "Where are you?"

"Willow's coffee shop."

"And why do you need clothes?"

"Umm, it's complicated. I can explain later."

"Did something happen with Jake? Did he hurt you? Because if he did, I swear—Oh, God! Tell me you didn't sleep with him."

"No, nothing like that, but hey, do you remember his telephone number?"

"I don't. You took the card."

And it was in my purse. With my phone. "Never mind. Just come get me."

I heaved a sigh as I disconnected the call. I considered calling Mom, but I didn't want to deal with her at this moment. Who I really wanted to talk to was Jake. I desperately needed to find out what happened.

I turned to Willow. "Thanks for letting me borrow your phone."

"Any time." She barely glanced at me as she slipped the cell into the front pocket of her apron, then moved around from table to table, using disinfectant wipes on their already-clean surfaces.

I opened my mouth to ask for a cup of coffee and a muffin when a loud engine rumbled outside, and Jake pulled up in front of his office.

With a yelp, I dashed out the door and ran across the street. A gust of wind blew up my backside, lifting the apron. I smacked it down, and shuffling awkwardly, made it to the other side.

"Jake!"

Startled, he turned to face me. He looked terrible. His hair was in disarray and a bruise with a gash in the middle spread over his jaw. Huge circles ran under his eyes, which drooped with exhaustion.

"Toni." He scanned me up and down. "What in the world are you wearing? Where are your shoes?" He stared at my toes, and I wiggled them uncomfortably.

"Uh, wild party, but never mind that. Stephen, did you find him?"

A slow smile spread across his face. "I did. He's in the hospital. I just came from there. He's gonna be all right."

"Oh, thank God!"

"It was a hell of a fight. There were vampires and shifters working together. But Ulfen's pack showed up, and I had some unlikely help." He frowned, his eyes getting distant for a moment. He snapped out of it and went on. "When the police showed up, everyone ran, though. No one was arrested."

"That sucks!" Ulfen had gotten my message, then. Good.

He nodded, and despite his exhaustion, I could tell a huge weight had been lifted off his shoulders. He had accomplished what he'd set out to do. He'd found his friend. Alive.

"I couldn't have done it without you," he said.

I batted the comment away and considered telling him I'd followed him to the repair shop after his grandfather had told me where to find him, but something about that entire situation wasn't sitting right with me—not to mention the fact that I didn't remember half the night. So instead, I chose recrimination.

"That wasn't cool, you leaving me at your grandfather's," I said.

He cocked his head to one side. "I thought you wanted nothing to do with this... PI business."

"That's not fair, and you know it. By then, I was... vested."

He made a sound in the back of his throat as if considering, then his eyes found the gaps the aprons left at my sides. Heat traveled up my neck, lighting up my cheeks.

"I think I like this outfit," he said. "It's sort of *barista chic*. You might start a fashion trend."

I refused to be embarrassed by him, so I put my hands around my waist and jutted my hip out. "That, I might."

"You should try different colors. Red looks the best on you."

"I'll make sure to have male versions, too."

"Ooh, kinky." He pursed his lips as if he liked the idea.

My imagination ran with it, and I had to glance away before he could figure out I was picturing him in a loincloth.

"Toni." He took a step closer and grabbed my hand.

My gaze snapped back to his.

"I want to thank you. Like I said, without your help… Stephen's life would still be in danger or worse." His words were low and deep and did something strange to my chest. I let out a hot breath, not knowing what to say. In the beginning, I hadn't wanted to help. I had been selfish. I didn't deserve any credit.

As if reading my mind, he said, "I had no right to drag you into this and turn your life on its head. I wouldn't have done it if I hadn't exhausted every other avenue. I'm sorry for not being the easiest person to deal with."

"That's an understatement."

He chuckled and started tracing small circles on the back of my hand.

"I'm sorry I was… selfish," I managed.

Jake shook his head. "You weren't. You were doing what was right by you, and I admire that." He took a tiny step closer, his silver eyes falling to my lips.

Giant butterflies flapped inside my stomach as I remembered I was wearing nothing under my aprons.

He leaned closer, reminding me of that moment in his grandfather's wine cellar.

I cleared my throat. "Jake, why did you kiss me last night?"

That seemed to make him realize he was about to kiss me again, and he took a step back and let go of my hand.

I huffed. "So that's how it's gonna be?" I lifted my chin and swallowed the lump that climbed into my throat. I opened my mouth to say something else, something I would've regretted, but luckily, Rosalina pulled up in her box car, salsa music playing on the radio totally at odds with my mood. I glanced back at my friend, who narrowed her eyes at my state.

Resentment heavy on my heart, I backed away from Jake. "My ride's here."

He leaned forward and seemed on the verge of saying something, but in the end, he bit down on his lower lip and gave me a small wave.

Whirling, I climbed into the car and glanced over at Rosalina. "Let's go."

She pressed her lips into a tight line as she assessed my outfit. To her credit, she said nothing about it and simply drove us home.

CHAPTER
38

The next day was an awesome spring day, sunny, and a perfect seventy-two degrees. I strolled into Barnes-Jewish Hospital, holding two large bouquets—one for Tom and one for Stephen. Both men were doing well, close to being released, which was a relief.

Yesterday, after my naked debacle, I'd been busy retrieving my purse from behind that dumpster. Fun, fun. At least it had still been there, and only one roach had crawled inside. The repair shop across the street had looked like a nuclear disaster zone in the daylight, but I didn't linger. I was in and out through the back of the alley before anyone noticed me. Also, I'd spent no small amount of time explaining to Rosalina that I didn't know how I'd ended up in my birthday suit on top of our office, and now she was as worried as me about that lovely piece of mystery.

I held my chin high, trying to draw optimism from the beautiful day and my friends' wellbeing. I had two appointments with two potential clients later today, and I needed all the confidence I could get. None of the people I'd talked to after Celina Morelli's debacle had panned out, and I had started to get worried. First thing this morning, I'd gone over our budget, trying to figure out how long we had before we defaulted on our loan. We had a couple of months max if we tightened our belts. In fact, after this visit, I would have to call my realtor to tell her the Compton Heights condo was a no go. Shit, it felt like my life was crumbling to pieces.

Clearing my thoughts, I took the elevator to the second floor and got a smile from an old lady riding with me.

"Beautiful flowers," she said.

"Aren't they?"

The elevator *dinged*, and the doors slid open. I decided I should see Stephen first. I always liked getting the hardest tasks done first. It would be awkward seeing him again, but it had to be done. Besides, Jake had said Stephen wanted to see me and thank me for my help in his rescue.

"Can I set these flowers here while I visit my first patient?" I asked a gray-headed nurse at the front station.

"Sure, honey."

"Thank you."

I left one bouquet behind, then walked to room 2366 and knocked on the door.

"Come in," a familiar voice called from within.

I pushed the door open and was taken aback when Ulfen Erickson greeted me with a tight smile. My surprise was stupid since it was only natural for a father to visit his son after an awful ordeal like the one Stephen had been through—no matter how estranged they had been.

"Oh, I can come back later." My eyes met Stephen's across the length of the room.

He seemed surprised for a moment, then a smile spread across his lips, erasing the somber expression he'd been wearing.

"Toni!" he exclaimed from his bed, pushing to his elbow. "Please, come in."

I glanced toward Ulfen, unsure.

"Come on in, Ms. Sunder." Ulfen waved a hand. "I was about to leave."

"Are you sure?"

"Yes." Ulfen nodded, graciously inclining his head. He wore a gray suit with a silver tie, his red hair and beard perfectly trimmed. Towering over the bed, all six feet of him, he shook his son's hand in goodbye. I frowned, bothered by the businesslike quality in his demeanor. "I'll be by tomorrow to pick you up," he said, turning toward the door.

I stepped aside to let him through, standing awkwardly with my flowers and peering over the dense petals. They smelled wonderful, and I had been enjoying their sweet scent ever since I picked them up at the florist. Now, I was enjoying the way they defended me from the mean werewolf.

Ulfen stopped at the threshold and glanced sideways at me. "I've been told you were instrumental in finding my son."

"Oh, I wouldn't say that."

He ignored my weak protest and added, "I would like to thank you." His blue eyes were serious, unkind despite his words of thanks, like he hated owing me something.

I inclined my head slightly and smiled. I hadn't done it for him. In fact, I hadn't even done it for Stephen. If Ulfen wanted to thank someone, it should be Jake. I wondered if he had or if he'd been his usual arrogant self.

With that out of the way, he left the room, his expensive leather shoes tapping firmly. I turned to Stephen, who heaved a sigh of relief and turned his full attention to me.

"I brought you flowers." I walked over and set the bouquet by his bedside.

"You didn't have to."

He peered up at me, his blue eyes so much like his father's, and yet so different. Genuine kindness filled them, and faint laugh lines sprang from their corners. The resemblance also went beyond the eyes. He had the same red hair and broad shoulders, except at the moment, he was thin and pale.

I scanned him over with concern. A yellowish bruise stained his left cheek, spreading to his eye, which was slightly swollen. Bandages covered his left hand, and I had to glance away as I remembered his severed finger.

Noticing my reaction, he held his hand up. "Won't be able to properly sport a wedding band. They took the ring finger," he said with a deprecating laugh.

"I'm so sorry, Stephen."

"Oh, don't be. It could've been worse. Poor Blake didn't fare so well." He lowered his head, sadness descending on him. He had grown up with that bodyguard. They'd been the best of friends. Stephen glanced toward the end table on the other side of the bed. Something familiar sat on top of it, which reminded me I had more than just the flowers to give him.

I reached inside my jeans pocket and pulled out the silver cufflink I'd used to track him, the one Ulfen had given me at his club. Stretching my hand, palm up, I offered it to him. "Here."

He snatched it from my hand in surprise. "Where did you get this?"

"You're father gave it to me to help me track you."

His frown deepened as he grabbed the other cufflink from the end table and laid it on his hand next to the other one, two crescent moons.

"Blake gave me these as a birthday present last year," Stephen said in a whisper.

A lump formed in my throat.

He rubbed his chin, his eyes narrowing as he seemed to think hard on something. "H-how did my father get it?" he asked no one in particular. "I thought... I remember..." He trailed off.

I leaned forward. "What?"

Stephen shook his head and chuckled in a self-deprecating manner. "Nothing. I thought I had both cufflinks with me in the van, but my memory has been foggy on all kinds of things. They hit me over the head a few times."

My breath hitched as I caught up with his train of thought. If he'd had both cufflinks with him in the van, it would mean that Ulfen got his from the kidnappers. Suddenly, a million questions sent my mind reeling. Was it possible? Could Ulfen have kidnapped his own son to incite a war? Had he sent those men to get me? And if so, why? So I couldn't spoil his plans? I glanced down at Stephen's bandaged hand. Was Ulfen responsible for the mutilated finger?

"Hey," Stephen pulled me back into the moment. He wore a reassuring smile. "Chill, I know what you're thinking, but he would never do anything like that."

I gave him a weak smile. I thought Ulfen was capable of many things, but I didn't know him well enough to suppose he would hurt his son this way.

Stephen huffed. "He cares too much about his fucking legacy to endanger his only *heir*." He pronounced the last word with mockery.

I nodded. That was true enough. "Then who did it?" I asked. "Any clues on who's responsible?"

He shook his head. "No. The van was reported stolen a month ago, and so far they've found no evidence of wrongdoing against Bernadetta and her people. She insists she had nothing to do with it."

Damn, this was so confusing. I had seen Bernadetta's driver there, and here I was wondering if Ulfen had done it. And what about the Fae female and the Prince? God, I needed to tell someone what I knew. I'd been so busy worrying about my naked episode that I didn't realize I might be the only one holding information that would lead to the culprits. I had to talk to Tom. He would know exactly what to do.

"Everything all right?" Stephen asked, reaching for my hand with his good one.

His warm touch took me by surprise as his large hand engulfed mine.

"Yes, of course." There was no use burdening Stephen with what I knew—not unless it led to his kidnappers.

"Jake told me what you did. Thank you, Toni."

"You don't have to thank me." Heat climbed up my neck as I remembered how selfish I'd been in the beginning. "The one you should thank is Jake."

Stephen nodded thoughtfully. "I know that. He stayed with me until my family got here last night. He's a great friend."

"He told me how you met in New Orleans."

"Imagine our surprise when we figured out you were a... mutual acquaintance."

"Acquaintance" was one way of putting it, but I was glad he didn't say "girlfriend," instead.

"I must admit I was jealous," Stephen said, his blue eyes burning into mine with the same intensity they always had.

I licked my lips, feeling self-conscious. If I was reading this correctly, he still felt attracted to me, and honestly, so did I. He was handsome and thoughtful, what was there *not* to like?

"I'm getting out tomorrow," he said, his fingers squeezing mine. "I would like to thank you properly. Let me take you out to lunch. You pick the place."

Was he asking me out on a date? It felt like he was.

"Um... your father..."

"Never mind my father. He should have never gotten his nose between us, and I shouldn't have let him. I always regretted it. I've changed a lot during this past year, Toni, and I've learned not to let him control me. Please, go out with me. I would love to catch up."

"But shouldn't you rest?"

He shook his head adamantly. "That's the last thing I want. I thought I was gonna die. You don't know how damn good it feels to be alive. I can't wait to be outside. I was trapped inside that van for eleven days and fifteen hours. I need some fresh air."

I totally understood how he felt, but going out with him didn't seem like a good idea. Yet, how could I say no after what he'd been through?

"Sure, I'd love to catch up." One lunch. That would be all.

He smiled from ear to ear, his eyes twinkling up at me. Then, they shifted toward the door, and I turned to see what had gotten his attention. My heart dropped into my stomach. Jake stood there, his expression neutral, but his hands balled into tight fists.

"Hey, Jake!" Stephen exclaimed, oblivious to the fact that Jake seemed about to blow a gasket. "We were just talking about you, saying what a great friend you are."

Jake's left eye twitched at the word *friend*. The way he glared at me seemed to indicate he didn't appreciate me using that word, except I hadn't been the one to use it. It had been Stephen. For my part, Jake wasn't even on my friend list. I kept his name all by itself in a separate catalog, one titled with the word "douchebag." Not that he was the only douchebag I'd ever met, but certainly the only one worth keeping track of, mainly because of my weakness for him.

Damn my dumb attraction to Jake Knight!

He smoothly strolled into the room, his hands relaxing, a careless expression reshaping his features. He was trying to act oh-so-cool, but I'd noticed the jealousy. And lousy person that I was, I wished that turning green from envy was actually a thing.

"I should go," I said.

Stephen held me in place. "No, stay."

Jake's cool eyes lowered to our clasped hands. A muscle jumped in his jaw.

I gently extricated my hand from Stephen's. "I have someone else to visit, and later I have appointments with a few customers, but I'll see you later."

"Okay." He dug out a cell phone from under the sheets and handed it to me. "Leave me your number so I can call you."

I punched my number into his phone and gave it back with a huge smile. "I look forward to seeing you."

"Me, too."

"Later Jake." I gave him a light wave and left the room. I paused outside and exhaled—unsure of how I felt about what'd just happened.

"You don't mind me asking her out, do you?" Stephen's voice drifted from the room and straight into my ears. I perked up.

No answer from Jake.

"I mean, last time we talked, you said you were done with her."

"That was months ago," Jake said, his voice low.

"Oh, you mean you want to…"

Jake laughed. "No, dude. Just giving you a hard time. Go ahead. I don't care."

This time, my heart sank straight to my feet, and *dammit*, my eyes prickled with tears. I marched away, picking up Tom's bouquet from the nurses' station.

"Thanks for keeping it for me," I said, swallowing the lump in my throat.

"Sure thing, babe," the nurse said, without looking up from her computer screen.

I tried, as I went, to push my anger away, but I couldn't. I hated myself for letting Jake affect me this way. I shouldn't care that he didn't care. I should hate him, or better yet, I should feel nothing at all, as if he didn't exist.

I'd been doing just fine before he showed up, and now...

Stopping outside of room 2221, I took a deep calming breath, determined to put Jake out of my mind. If he could so easily dismiss me despite our undeniable attraction, I could do the same. Yes, the chemistry between us had always been out of control, but that wasn't the same thing as love. It seemed I'd mixed those two things together before, and I refused to do the same again.

Squaring my shoulders and composing my expression into the upbeat and friendly Toni that Detective Tom Freeman deserved, I knocked on his door and slipped inside.

CHAPTER 39

"Toni!" Tom greeted me warmly with a matching smile. He'd been watching television and pressed the off button on his remote control. His salt-and-pepper goatee was missing, and he looked strange without it. "I was wondering when you were going to come see me."

I set his flowers on the night table and planted a kiss on his forehead. "It's so good to see you."

"It's good to see you too, kiddo." He mock-punched my chin.

"You look great!"

"Don't I?" He ran his hands over his hospital gown as if to demonstrate how great he looked.

"I was here to see you several times, but they wouldn't let me 'cause I'm not family."

He huffed. "Fools! You're more family than any of the damn people that claim to be. Maybe there's something we can do about it. For future, you know."

"Um, sure, but I hope you don't plan to be back anytime soon." I waggled my finger at him.

"No, siree. I sure don't. A couple more days and I should be out of here. The healers are making sure my foot is gonna stay put. It was a wonder they were able to reattach it. The explosion blew it right off, but the paramedics picked it up, which was a good thing."

I winced, remembering how awful it had been. The chaos, the smoke, the screams. Whoever had planted that bomb needed to be put behind bars, and maybe I could help make that happen.

"I can tell there's something on your mind." He pointed at a chair in the corner. "Why don't you sit down?"

I pulled the chair closer and settled into it. "I'm sure you heard we found Stephen."

"Indeed, I did." He narrowed his dark eyes. "And I heard you played a big part in it. Thought you didn't want to get involved in that sort of stuff again."

"I didn't, but Jake was… persistent, and it was the right thing to do. I'm glad I could help."

"Then why you look so worried?"

"Well, I haven't told anyone, but I was there when Jake found him, and I got a good look at two of the people there, including one of Bernadetta Fiore's men."

Tom cocked his head to one side, and without saying a word, listened to my story. It wasn't the entire thing. I had to leave out my blackout and the fact that I woke up naked on my agency's rooftop. I didn't want him to worry about me, or start asking questions I couldn't answer, so I thought it best to leave all the inexplicable bits out. Basically, my story amounted to how Bertram cornered me in the alley and how Prince Kalyll showed up to remove the female Fae from the premises. Of course, I didn't mention how I'd manhandled her as if she were a child—especially since I still hadn't decided whether or not I'd gone temporarily insane and had imagined the whole thing.

When I finished, Tom considered quietly for a long moment. I wondered if he'd spotted my lies, but I really couldn't tell.

Finally, he said, "I'll make a few phone calls. You need to go in and make a statement, then we can bring Bernadetta's driver up for questioning. Also, we'll get a sketch artist to make a likeness of this Gonira character in case she shows up here again."

"Sounds good. I hope something comes out of it."

"Me too. Me too." He nodded thoughtfully. "We need a break. They found the body of the woman who planted the bomb, so that led nowhere. Whoever sent her took care to silence her."

I couldn't help but feel that she deserved it.

A knock came at the door, and to my surprise, Father Vincent walked in dressed in casual clothing, jeans, oxfords, and a dress shirt rolled up to the elbows. He looked different without his clerical collar and dark clothes. Relaxed and more handsome.

"I was starting to worry you wouldn't show," Tom said.

Father Vincent checked his wristwatch. "Um, I'm two minutes late."

"Exactly."

The priest chuckled, shook his head, and turned his attention to me. "Toni, it's good to see you." His cheeks colored as if he were embarrassed for some reason.

"Me, too." I gave him a warm smile, sensing, by their banter, that the two had become friends.

"You... look different." I gestured toward his clothes.

"Yeah, about that..." He held a finger up, opened the door, and stuck his head out. "Hey, come on in."

I frowned and exchanged a glance with Tom, giving him a "what is going on?" expression. He shrugged. A moment later, I almost fell out of my chair when Celina Morelli walked into the room. My mouth opened and closed as a squeak of shock got stuck in my throat.

"Celina, look who's here." Father Vincent inclined his head in my direction.

"Oh, hello, Toni." She gave me a wide smile. Her brown eyes sparkled as if stars had gotten stuck inside them. In fact, an angelic glow seemed to surround her entire face.

"How... did you two...?"

"Your partner," Celina said.

"What?!" I couldn't believe it. Rosalina had gone against my decision? She had betrayed me?

Celina took a step closer. "Oh, please, don't be mad at her. It's not her fault. After our telephone conversation, I was angry, so I went by your office to reclaim my deposit and get the truth about your supposed failure. As you can see, I got it out of her."

"Got it out of her? How?" And why in the hell hadn't Rosalina told me anything about this?

"I might have... threatened to sue your agency."

"You what?!"

"I wouldn't have, of course."

Somehow, I didn't believe her. My eyes drifted to Father Vincent. Should I even call him that anymore? He stood with his hand stuffed in his pockets, rocking on his heels. Tom, for his part, sat quietly on the bed, observing the situation with rabid interest, as if he were watching a soap opera.

Celina locked arms with... Vincent. "After your partner told me, I went and found him and explained everything. It's just as you promised. We're perfect for each other."

"But... what about his job?" I felt mortified. This was all my fault. He had abandoned his calling, and all those people he could have helped now had one less angel on their side. "Oh, God, I feel horrible."

"Please, don't," Vincent said, glancing shyly at Celina. "I must confess... nothing has ever felt this right in my entire life. Besides, there is more than one way to be happy and serve the Lord."

The what?! He must be really having a religious experience, a truly *ecstatic* one, to change his tune so drastically.

Damn, Toni, get your mind out of the gutter.

"Am I correct to assume that you've quit the church?" Tom asked, folding his arms over his chest.

"I have," Vincent confirmed.

"All for some skirt?"

I winced. Tom wasn't always tactful with his choice of words.

"Mm-hmm." Vincent looked like he was holding back a smile, like he and Tom were sharing an inside joke. "Yes."

"Well, hot damn, congratulations!" Tom exclaimed.

I did a double-take. Tom was supposed to be a devout Catholic, and he approved of this? What was going on here? And why did I suddenly feel like the oldest person in the room when I was the youngest?

Tom and Vincent shook hands, the latter smiling like an idiot.

"Sunder's Mate Tracker Agency," Tom said in a jovial tone, "bringing happiness to lost souls everywhere. Maybe I'll have to take you up on your offer to find me someone." He shook a finger at me, smiling, happy to be alive—like Stephen.

"Well," I stood, "it seems my work is done here."

Unexpectedly, Celina wrapped me tightly in her arms. "Thank you. You're amazing." She pulled away and held me at arms' length. "I was skeptical, to say the least, but you have made a believer out of me. I paid your partner, and a few of my friends are eager to talk to you."

"Really?" I blinked repeatedly, the dreams of keeping the agency and securing my new place quickly retaking shape before my eyes.

I left the hospital with a big smile on my face. My life wasn't crumbling to pieces, after all.

୫୦ଓଃ

My smile faded when I approached my car in the parking lot and found Jake leaning on it. He wore reflective glasses and had his arms crossed over his chest. When he noticed me, he pulled away from the Camaro, took off the glasses, and hung them from the collar of his gray Henley.

"Hey." His silver eyes scanned me from head to toe.

I marked the changes I'd barely noticed when I first saw him inside. He looked freshly showered, and he'd trimmed his beard closely and shaved it to make pristine lines at the edges. There were no circles under his eyes, and his wild scent of pine and rain intermingled with a dash of sandalwood soap. Even though I felt like melting into a puddle, I hardened my expression and barely offered him a nod.

"Um, Stephen looks good, doesn't he?" he said.

"Yes."

"I was finally able to get some good sleep, knowing that he was all right."

"Good for you."

He heaved a sigh. "Okay, I guess I'd better get to the point. I'm here because I want to thank you for—"

"No need to do that again." I walked around him and opened the driver's side door.

"Toni, wait."

I glanced back with raised eyebrows.

He swallowed. "I owe you an explanation, one I should've given you before I left to go to New Orleans."

I turned away from the car and gave him my undivided attention, my heart suddenly racing. Was this it? Was he finally going to tell me why he left me?

"I realize that a *thank you* isn't enough for what you did to help me find Stephen," he continued, "and even though I think that sharing my reasons for leaving you will only make things worse, maybe it's a better way to express my gratitude since it's what you want."

I wasn't sure this would serve as thanks, but I needed to know, needed to understand, so I could finally be done with him just as he was done with me.

He moved a step closer, his gaze locked with mine. "I wish I hadn't been such a coward and had told you face-to-face why I had to leave. But I was afraid that if I talked to you, I... I wouldn't be able to end things."

I slow blinked. What was he saying?

"Toni, I didn't leave because I didn't care for you. I left because... I cared too much."

Confusion washed over me. "That doesn't make any sense."

"We should've never moved in together. I should've never let it get that far knowing that a long-term relationship between you and me was impossible."

I shook my head. "Impossible? Why?"

"Because I have a duty to fulfill. You see, after my brother went missing and my dad finally gave up the search, he asked me to keep our bloodline alive. With Neil gone, I'm the last one in what once was a powerful werewolf dynasty."

I took a step backward, my thoughts and emotions whirling out of control, slowly wrapping around his meaning.

"I didn't want to leave, Toni, but I had to. I made a promise. I owe it to my father, my grandfather, and Neil to pass on our legacy, and with you... that would be impossible." His voice grew quiet at that last bit.

Tears slid down my face as the extent of what he was saying hit me. He didn't leave me because he'd stopped caring. He'd left me because I wasn't a werewolf, and as such, I would never be able to give him children to continue the Knight bloodline. But, more accurately, he'd left because he'd made a promise to his father.

Oh, God, this was the reason he didn't like to make promises.

He reached over and touched my cheek, wiping away a tear with his thumb. His silver gaze wavered with emotion and regret. "There hasn't been a day since I felt that I haven't thought about you, and when I saw you again I realized that all that time apart did nothing to change the way I feel about you."

"Jake," his name came out in a sob as my heart lurched in my chest.

He pressed on, his large hand cupping my face. "I took you to see my grandfather because I hoped he might be able to detect in you what I couldn't. Sometimes, non-werewolf women can bear our children. It's rare, but it happens. But he didn't find that potential in you. You and I, we would never be able to—"

"Oh, God, please stop." I pulled away from him, tears falling freely now. He'd been right. This was worse than not knowing. Understanding that he cared for me but had to choose someone else who could give him the children I couldn't was torture.

He lowered his head, the fringe of his dark lashes hiding his eyes. "Forgive me."

273

Jake took a step back as if to leave. I gripped his hand. It took him a moment, but he met my gaze, revealing a deep sadness that mirrored mine.

"I understand." I nodded, fighting back my tears. "I don't know if I can forgive you for leaving without telling me the truth or for the pain I've lived with all this time, but I understand."

"Toni." He pulled on my hand and wrapped me in his arms, squeezing me against his hard chest and burying his nose in my hair. I bit my tongue and shut my eyes.

We held each other for a long time without saying a word. What was there to say? The pain I thought I'd left behind blossomed freshly, tearing at my heart and delivering a sense of finality greater than the one I'd felt the day he left me. I couldn't be the reason he broke the promise he'd made to his father, nor the reason his bloodline came to an end.

Of course, I understood.

Slowly, I pulled away and put some distance between us. "Thanks for telling me. I know it wasn't easy, but I think it's for the best. I don't have to hold it against you anymore." I smiled. "Good luck finding someone. If you want, I could help."

"Please don't joke."

"Sorry."

He chuckled sadly. "You never change."

"Well," I hooked my thumb toward the car, "I'd better go. Mom's waiting for me."

"I'll see you around then, and like I promised, I'll leave you alone."

I got in the car and tore out of the parking lot, the many tears I'd held back flowing freely down my face as my heart shattered to pieces for the second time in my life.

CHAPTER
40

I drove in circles around The Hill until I got my emotions under control and managed to push Jake out of my head long enough for my eyes to dry. To help compartmentalize those feelings, I focused on my mother, who had been hounding me about coming to see her for days.

I had pacified her over the phone earlier today, but only after promising that I would come home for lunch. She assured me that if I didn't show up on time, she would come to find me and bind me in a protection spell so tight that it would make a chastity belt jealous. Not that her threat scared me. I didn't need a chastity belt the way my sex life was going—or not going. But she'd never threatened me so colorfully before, so I figured that whatever she wanted must be important. Besides, she had promised to make me creamy tortellini for lunch.

As I parked my Camaro by Mom's curb, I considered calling Rosalina to talk about Celina Morelli. But I would wait to see her since I wanted to kiss her for saving our asses and ignoring my attempts to be noble.

Screw doing the right *thing. Who needs that?*

Chuckling to myself, I walked up the pathway. Mom pulled open the door before I even climbed the steps to the porch. Her brown eyes opened wide as she assessed me from top to bottom.

"Are you all right, honey?" She grabbed me by the shoulders as I stepped into the foyer and turned me this way and that, meticulously scanning me.

"I'm fine, Mom." I swatted her hands away and set my purse on the console table. I lifted my nose, trying to get a whiff of the tortellini, but I smelled no garlic or Parmesan cheese in the air. Frowning, I headed toward the kitchen, determined to find my food.

When I entered the breakfast nook, I froze. A slender man wearing a black cloak and a silken top hat stood in the middle of the kitchen. He had short white hair, a pointy chin, and wore round, black glasses that hid his eyes.

Mom came up behind me and put a hand on my shoulder. I glanced back, questioningly.

"Um, you didn't mention you would have company," I said.

"This is Damien Ward. He's a friend."

"Oh?"

Wait?! Was Mom dating a mage? From what I knew, only mages went around dressed in cloaks and ridiculous top hats. Was this the reason she'd been so desperate to get me here? She probably didn't want my sisters spilling the beans before she had a chance to tell me herself. He didn't look like Mom's type but to each their own.

"We went to college together." Mom's voice trembled.

She was nervous. Funny. I repressed a smile. I gave the guy a once over. He'd interlaced his manicured hands in front of him and stood rigidly, giving off a vibe I didn't like. I frowned. If Mom had known him since college, how come I'd never heard of him before?

My heart sped up uncomfortably. "Uh, what's going on Mom? Where's the tortellini?"

Maybe I'd read this all wrong, and this man was here to… claim payment for some old debt or wrongdoing? My mind reeled with different scenarios as some basic instinct raised an alarm inside me, telling me this situation was off.

"Nothing is going on, honey." She smiled, but it didn't reach her eyes. "He's just paying me a visit. Why don't you sit? And I'll reheat you some tortellini." She walked to the refrigerator.

Reheat? Now I knew something was terribly wrong. Mom would never serve reheated anything. She always cooked exact portions. She had a thing against leftovers. She said half of them always ended up in the garbage, and she hated wasting food.

I remained standing, my fight or flight reflex too riled up for anything else.

Damien removed his dark glasses to reveal a set of copper-colored eyes. A shiver ran across my shoulders, and my senses went into overdrive like the night before. I sniffed the air and glanced around like a caged animal. A Copper Mage stood in my mother's house. How? Why? They were the most powerful mages, aside from Black Mages. He had no business in our home.

Without a word, the mage lifted a hand in my direction. I jumped back, heart hammering out of control, energy tingling over my skin.

"Mom, he's doing something!" Panic bled through my voice.

But Mom didn't even glance back. In fact, she stood facing the fridge, her back to me, a hand on the handle. A strange smell filled the air, a combination of something sour and sweet. The scent was immediately familiar.

Magic.

277

I had encountered it in trick parlors, where weak mages worked entertaining patrons with cheap performances.

"Mom, let's get out of here." I tried to reach for her, to pull her away with me, but I found myself unable to move.

The mage came closer, still holding his hand up and wearing a sneer. He frowned, watching me with curiosity. His pupils weren't round but instead looked like ink blotches. I'd never seen such eyes before. They seemed to reach inside of me, probing, searching for something. I tried to look away, but his gaze held me. Out of the corner of my eye, I noticed Mom finally turning to face us.

The mage placed his index finger on my forehead and started tracing an intricate pattern. Heat built up inside my cranium, making me feel feverish all over. Disjointed images flashed before my eyes. Somehow, I knew they were memories, even if I couldn't quite remember when they'd happened. Snarling, running toward the moon, power, and ferocity sizzling in my veins.

Oh, God, what is this? And why wasn't Mom doing anything to stop this madman?

I started shaking. Pain cut through my body as I tried to break free, fighting against the fierce magic that had made its way into my mind trying to… trying to…

I growled and shook myself, finally able to move. Claws sprang at my fingertips. Mom gave out a strangled cry, tears spilling down her face. The mage hissed, rubbing his hand and grimacing in pain.

"Oh, no." Mom covered her mouth with a trembling hand.

"It's too late, Amalia," the mage said. "She's already shifted. Renewing the spell is impossible."

ACKNOWLEDGMENTS

Creating and writing the Sunderverse has been incredibly fun, and I'm excited to finally be able to share the first book with everyone. The research work has been fulfilling, a part of storytelling I enjoy very much. I have visited St. Louis but don't know the city as a local would. I do hope I've done that vibrant community justice.

As always, I need to thank Michael, Ella, Isabella and Alexander. Your support and encouragement keep me going every day and fuel my creative brain. I couldn't do this without you.

Infinite thanks go to my beta reader and editor Bret Williams for always being willing to read and discuss projects with me, and to Billie to whom this book is dedicated. Our friendship is a constant source of happiness. You shine!

Last, but most importantly, to Olena Makovey and Tutsie, Kay for beta reading, and to my readers. When you visit my wild worlds and enjoy them, it makes all the hard work worth it.

WWW.INGRIDSEYMOUR.COM

Made in the USA
Columbia, SC
23 June 2021